Women, in his experience, were timid creatures who fainted at any sign of violence, who obeyed when told to keep out of it. They sat at their sewing, drank tea and gossiped about fashion and the latest *on dit*, and left the men to govern and keep order among the people for whom they were responsible. Helen Wayland was not a bit like that.

She plunged in where others feared to go and spoke her mind when she would have done better to remain silent. How could you tame a woman like that? Why, in heaven's name, did he want to tame her? She was not his wife. She was not even eligible to be his wife.

Why, then, did he enjoy their meetings so much? Why did he savour the cut and thrust of her debate, even welcome her fiery temper? He remembered his mother looking sideways at him and asking him if he had developed a *tendre* for her and his sharp denial. Now, if she asked him again, he would not know how to answer. Miss Helen Wayland had him in thrall—so much so that he had been fool enough to ask her to dance with him. He had not danced since he had been wounded and did not know if he could. And what would she make of it if he found he could not? Why, in heaven's name, had he said he would go?

Born in Singapore, **Mary Nichols** came to England when she was three, and has spent most of her life in different parts of East Anglia. She has been a radiographer, school secretary, information officer and industrial editor, as well as a writer. She has three grown-up children, and four grandchildren.

Previous novels by the same author:

RAGS-TO-RICHES BRIDE
THE EARL AND THE HOYDEN
CLAIMING THE ASHBROOKE HEIR
   (part of *The Secret Baby Bargain*)
HONOURABLE DOCTOR, IMPROPER
   ARRANGEMENT
THE CAPTAIN'S MYSTERIOUS LADY*
THE VISCOUNT'S UNCONVENTIONAL BRIDE*
LORD PORTMAN'S TROUBLESOME WIFE*
SIR ASHLEY'S METTLESOME MATCH*

*The Piccadilly Gentlemen's Club mini-series

And available through
Mills & Boon® Historical eBooks:

WITH VICTORIA'S BLESSING
   (part of *Royal Weddings Through the Ages*)

Did you know that some of these novels
are also available as eBooks?
Visit www.millsandboon.co.uk

WINNING THE WAR HERO'S HEART

Mary Nichols

MILLS
BOON®

TM

All the characters in this book have no existence outside the imagination
of the author, and have no relation whatsoever to anyone bearing the
same name or names. They are not even distantly inspired by any
individual known or unknown to the author, and all the incidents are
pure invention.

First published in Great Britain 2011
by Mills & Boon, an imprint of Harlequin (UK) Limited.
Large Print edition 2012
Harlequin (UK) Limited, Eton House, 18-24 Paradise Road,
Richmond, Surrey TW9 1SR

© Mary Nichols 2011

ISBN: 978 0 263 22508 2

Harlequin (UK) policy is to use papers that are natural,
renewable and recyclable products and made from wood grown in
sustainable forests. The logging and manufacturing process conform
to the legal environmental regulations of the country of origin.

Printed and bound in Great Britain

WINNING
THE WAR HERO'S
HEART

Chapter One

1816

Helen heard the hunt some time before it came into view. The dogs were yelping and the horn sounding a wild halloo, and there was the thunder of hooves which seemed to shake the ground at her feet. Surely they would not come galloping through the village? The road was narrow, flanked on either side by workers' cottages and their small gardens. And there were people on the street: woman gossiping at their gates, children playing, a cat sunning itself on one of the few days in the year in which the sun shone. Hearing the commotion, the women snatched up their children and disappeared indoors. The cat, its tail a wire brush, fled. Helen drew in her serviceable grey skirt and pushed herself against the fence of one of the cottages as the fox streaked past her. It scrambled over the gate and into a garden where a little boy was playing. It nearly knocked him over as it flew across the garden and through the hedge on the far side.

The dogs were in the street now, desperate to get at their quarry and the riders were not far behind. Afraid for the child, Helen moved swiftly into the garden, scooped him up and ran towards the house, but all she had time to do was press herself and the little one hard against the wall before the whole hunt was upon them. Dogs and horses milled about, trampling down rows of beans and cabbages and the currant bushes, wrecking the patch of grass and the few bedraggled flowers which had been growing each side of the path that ran between the rows and knocking over the hen coop and sending the chickens flapping and squawking to die under the horses' hooves.

And then just as quickly they were gone, flattening the neatly clipped hedge at the end of the garden—all except one rider, who pulled up beside her. 'Are you hurt, madam? Is your little one injured?'

Helen found herself looking up at the Earl of Warburton's son, Viscount Cavenham. She knew who he was because a great fuss had been made of him in the district when he came back from Waterloo, a wounded hero. He did not look wounded to her, sitting arrogantly on a huge black stallion, looking down at her with what she took to be contempt. True, she was wearing her grey workaday dress, a wool spencer and a plain chip bonnet and the child she held so close to her bosom was filthy and bawling his head off, but that was no excuse. Still, he was the only one of the hunters to stop and enquire, so she ought to answer him.

'No, we are not hurt, but the child is terrified. Have you no more sense than to come galloping all over other people's property, ruining a year of hard work? This was once a productive garden. Now look at it.' She waved an arm to encompass the mess.

'The dogs follow the fox, madam,' he said. 'And the riders follow the dogs. And unless I am mistaken, the property is not yours, but part of the Cavenham estate. The Earl may go where he chooses.'

'How arrogant and unfeeling can you be?' she demanded. 'How would you like it if someone trampled all over Ravens Park and terrified your children?'

'I have no children.'

'You know what I mean,' she countered.

His smile transformed his face from darkly brooding to almost human, but she was too angry to notice, too furious to take in his good looks, his thick dark hair curling below his riding hat and into his neck, his broad shoulders and the long elegant fingers holding the reins, not to mention a shapely thigh, clad in white riding breeches, with which he was controlling his restive mount. 'Perhaps. But I do not think anyone would dare invade the Park.'

'No, but why is there one law for the rich and another for the poor? And for your information, I am not the child's mother and I do not live here. I am simply an observer.'

'Oh.' He looked slightly taken aback, but recovered quickly. 'Then I suggest you reunite the child with his mother and mind your own business.'

'I intend to make it my business,' she said, as a woman came from the house, diverting him from a reply.

'Thank you, thank you,' she said, taking the child from Helen. 'I was upstairs when I heard the hullabaloo and in my haste to come down and fetch Edward indoors to safety, I tripped and fell. It winded me for a moment. If you hadn't acted so quickly…' She stopped, suddenly seeing the Viscount. 'My lord.' She curtsied and dipped her head.

The gesture infuriated Helen. 'He and his like have just frightened your little boy nearly to death and ruined your garden and you bend your knee to him. You should be angry and demanding compensation.'

'I can't do that,' she murmured, looking fearfully up at the man on the horse. 'This is a tied cottage and I work at the big house.'

Helen realised she would probably make matters worse if she went on, so she held her tongue. Looking from the woman to the Viscount, she caught him gazing at her with an expression of puzzlement. So, he did not know who she was. He would soon find out.

He turned his attention from her to the mother. 'Are you hurt, madam?'

'A bruise or two, my lord. It is nothing, I thank you.'

Helen could have kicked her for her meekness. No wonder men like the Earl and his son felt they had a God-given right to trample over poor folk, just as they had trampled over the garden.

'I am sorry about the garden,' his lordship said

softly, taking Helen by surprise. 'The dogs became too excited to control and there was nothing I could do.' He smiled again, though this time it was aimed at the other woman, not Helen. He reached into his waistcoat pocket and withdrew a coin, which he passed to her. She accepted it, thanked him and curtsied. Without looking at Helen again, he wheeled his horse about and rode off.

'Of all the arrogance!' Helen exclaimed, watching him go.

'He has given me a whole guinea,' the woman said in mitigation. 'And, to be fair, he didn't ride over the garden, did he? He was the only one who stopped.'

Helen was in no mood to see any good in the Earl of Warburton's son and did not respond, but accepted an invitation to enter the cottage for a cup of tea. 'It is only camomile,' the woman said. 'I do not have Indian tea.'

It was while she was waiting for the kettle to boil that she learned a little more about Mrs Watson. 'My husband died at Waterloo,' she told Helen, putting the baby on the floor while she set out a teapot and cups. 'Eddie was only a baby when he went off. He'd been all through the Peninsula without a scratch and he didn't have to re-enlist, but he would go because Viscount Cavenham went and he couldn't have the Earl's son going off and making him look a coward. Why are men so proud?'

'I don't know,' Helen murmured, thinking of her father. He was proud, too, and look where that had got him.

'I'm lucky the housekeeper at the big house gave me a job in the laundry,' Mrs Watson went on. 'While I have this cottage, I can manage. Having the garden helps with fruit and vegetables and eggs, though nothing was growing well this year. Do you think we will ever get a summer?'

'Let us hope so,' Helen said. 'I fear for the workers if the harvest is ruined.' The year so far had been uncommonly wet and cold. It had rained every day and there had been snow in London the week before. According to the London newspapers, which sometimes published news from the regions, there was snow in hilly districts only a little further north. Some crops were already rotting in the fields. Farm labourers were out of work and added to the numbers of soldiers returning from the end of the war with Napoleon. And yet the Earl must have his sport. Unlike some, he hunted all the year round.

'I'll have to see what I can salvage. Perhaps it's not as bad as it looks.' Mrs Watson broke in on

Helen's reverie. 'I have you to thank that Eddie was not trampled along with it. He could have been killed. That would have been far, far worse.'

'And I don't suppose the Earl would care any more about that than he cared about your dead chickens.'

Mrs Watson handed her a cup of tea. 'Is it just the Earl you dislike or is it all landed gentry?'

The question surprised Helen and for a moment she did not know how to answer. 'The Earl of Warburton is typical of his kind,' she said slowly. 'Arrogant, selfish, unfeeling. They seem to think money will buy them anything. It would do them all good to be without it for a while to see how everyone else has to manage.'

Mrs Watson laughed. 'My, you do have a chip on your shoulder, don't you?'

'I suppose I do,' Helen admitted. 'but I try not to let it show. Today I was so angry I couldn't help it.'

'You don't live in the village, do you?'

'No, in Warburton. My name is Helen Wayland.'

This evidently meant nothing to Mrs Watson so Helen did not enlighten her. In her experience, telling someone she owned and published the *Warburton Record* was a sure way to have them holding their tongues. They would not believe she did not intend to publish some calumny about them when all she wanted to do was publicise their plight.

'You are a town dweller, Miss Wayland, and cannot know what it is like to live in a small village, dependent on the local landowner for everything...'

'Perhaps you should tell me,' Helen said, picking the baby up off the floor and cuddling him on her lap. He began playing with her father's watch, which she wore as a fob. 'Then I might understand.'

Mrs Watson looked doubtful, but her visitor was so obviously fond of children and genuinely interested that she poured them both a second cup of tea and sat down to answer her questions.

Miles considered whether to catch up with the hunt or call it a day and decided he might as well go home. He did not want to be party to any more ruined gardens and he certainly did not want to have to justify himself to irate young ladies with fierce hazel eyes. Who the devil was she? Not gentry, that was evident from the simple way she dressed and the way she did not mind that grubby child dirtying her clothes, but none of that detracted from her proud demeanour. She had defied him and that was something he was not used to and his first reaction had been anger. But what she had said had troubled his conscience, not that he could do anything to prevent his father running the hunt over his own land. He was a law unto himself and as far as he was concerned owning the land and the cottages meant he also owned those who dwelt in them.

Did the defiant Miss Grey Gown come under that heading? She had undoubtedly saved the child's life and, in his opinion, its mother should not be the only one who was grateful because his father, as Master of the Hunt, should also give thanks that his dogs and horses had not trampled the little one to death. Had he even been aware of her or the child as he hurtled through the garden after the dogs?

And what on earth had the woman meant by saying 'I intend to make it my business'? It sounded like a threat, but how could a mere nobody, who could not be more than five and twenty, threaten someone like the Earl of Warburton? Miles was suddenly and inexplicably afraid for her.

He was walking his horse, deep in thought, and did not at first notice the man sitting on the milestone on the edge of the village. His attention was drawn to him when he stood up and took a step towards him, his hand outstretched. 'My lord...'

Miles pulled up. The man was in rags and painfully thin. 'Byers, isn't it?' he queried, not sure the vision who confronted him could be the big strong man who had once been employed as a gardener at Ravens Park.

'Yes, my lord.'

'What happened to you, man?'

'I came back from the war and there was no work to be had and my wife and children had gone to live with her sister. Will you give a coin or two to tide me over and help feed my little ones, my lord?'

Miles could tell how difficult it was for him to beg. 'Why did you not go back to Ravens Park when you were discharged?' he asked.

'The Earl had given my place to someone else, the cottage, too. He would not take me on again.'

'I am sorry to hear that.'

'I was a good worker,' Byers went on. 'No one ever found fault with what I did; I served my time for king and country and that's all the thanks I get for it.'

'I can understand your bitterness,' Miles said. 'But the garden at Ravens Park could not wait on your return, you know. And gardeners expect to be housed.' He paused. 'Did you see the hunt come through just now?'

'Yes, nigh on bowled me over, it did. Why do you ask?'

'It ran over Mrs Watson's garden and wrecked it. If you go and put it right for her, I'll pay you. Better than begging, don't you think?'

'Yes, my lord.'

'Off you go, then. When it's done, come to the house and ask for me. I'll have your wages for you.'

The man touched his forelock and Miles trotted on towards Ravens Park. Jack Byers wasn't the only one unemployed in the area. There were other ex-soldiers begging on the streets and they were adding to the agricultural labourers who were out of work on account of the dreadful weather ruining the crops. Times were bad for everyone, especially in a countryside that depended on farming for a living. He ought to try to do something to help, but what? Handing out money was not the answer.

He shook the problem from him as he cantered up the drive towards the house. His father, who had been Viscount Cavenham at the time, had had it built just before he was born, to replace an older building that had fallen into disrepair. It was meant to celebrate his marriage and his earldom. Miles's mother, Dorothea, only daughter of Earl Graine, was a catch for any man because of her ancient lineage, far superior to that of the Cavenhams. She was beautiful but frail and completely dominated by her husband. He was not physically violent towards her, but his tongue lashings often left her in tears. Miles loved his mother dearly and wished she would learn to stand up for herself. But he understood why she did not. She had been brought up in a culture in which the husband was head of the household and should be deferred to in all things and it distressed her when Miles argued with his father.

Their disagreements were usually over the way the Earl treated his people. He was like a petty king whose subjects were expected to bend the knee and obey his commands under pain of destitution. That only worked so far; sooner or later the people would rise up and rebel. Miles had seen what had happened in the army if an officer ruled by fear. It did not make for a happy and willing force, whereas justice tempered with mercy and a willingness to share in the men's hardship worked wonders for morale.

The last straw had been when Miles had defended the boot boy from a beating on account of his lordship's boots not being as shiny as he thought they should be. He had suffered the beating instead of the lad, which he did not regret, but as soon as he was old enough he had left home to join the army. He had come home to find his mother even more cowed than before and was shocked by how frail she seemed. Many a time he had bitten his tongue on a sharp retort for her sake. But it would be difficult to keep silent about the way Mrs Watson and Jack Byers had been treated.

Helen was taking her leave of Mrs Watson when Jack arrived to say he had been bidden to set her garden to rights.

'Who bade you do it?' Mrs Watson asked.

'The Viscount. He said he would pay me.'

'Then he's not as black as he's painted.'

'It's no more than you're due,' Helen put in. 'But it should have been the Earl who ordered it.'

'Don't matter who ordered it,' Byers said. 'I'm glad enough of the work, though it won't get me my old job back.'

'Why did you lose your job?' Helen asked.

'I went to war. It weren't as if I wanted to go, but the Earl hinted that if his son went, then I should not lag behind. I'd be a coward if I did. And then when I come back, my job had gone to someone else and the cottage with it. My wife and family had been turned out and gone to live with her sister in Warburton. She's only got a small house and they're cramped for room. I've been sleeping out o' doors.'

'You put my garden to rights and you can sleep in my outhouse,' Mrs Watson said. 'It's dry and there's straw for a bed. I'll give you a blanket.'

'Thank you kindly, ma'am.'

'I'll come back tomorrow and see how you got on,' Helen said as she bade them goodbye.

She would ask Jack Byers to tell his story and she would talk to other ex-soldiers; she would have something to say about the Earl and his guests riding roughshod over other people's gardens and their feelings. It would fill a page of the *Warburton Record* and perhaps she could stir up some influential consciences. She was already composing the article in her head as she walked the three miles back to Warburton.

Warburton was a bustling little market town with two churches, a chapel, a mill, a public school for those who could afford to send their children there and a dame school for those who could not. It had two doctors: Dr Graham, who looked after the elite who could afford his fees, and Dr Benton, who treated everyone else. The town also had a blacksmith, a farrier, a harness maker who also made and mended shoes, a butcher and provisions shop, a small haberdasher and the Warburton printing press, home of the *Warburton Record*, which was where Helen was bound.

The business occupied a building in the centre of the town. There was an office at the front and the printing press in a room at the back. Helen lived in an apartment above the shop with only Betty, her maid, for company. A sign hanging above the door proclaimed, 'H. Wayland, publisher and printer. Proprietor of the *Warburton Record*. All printing tasks undertaken, large and small.' The H. stood for Henry, of course, but it also served for Helen so she saw no reason to change it.

A bell tinkled as she opened the door and let herself in. At a desk to one side young Edgar Harrington was busy writing. Helen went to look over his shoulder. He was composing a report on recent court hearings. 'Committed to Warburton Bridewell for twelve months,' she read. 'John Taylor for stealing a pig from Joseph Boswell, farmer of Littleacre near Warburton.' And again. 'For stealing a peck of wheat from the barn at

Home Farm, Ravensbrook, Daniel Cummings was sentenced to six months in gaol.' There were several cases of poaching brought by the gamekeeper at Ravens Park. All had been found guilty and been sentenced to varying degrees of punishment, from prison to transportation, which Helen thought unduly harsh. No doubt the Earl, who controlled his fellow magistrates, had demanded they be made an example of. But if the poor men were hungry and had hungry families, who could blame them if they took a rabbit or two, or even a pig? It was different for the organised gangs, who came from the big cities to sell their ill-gotten gains to willing buyers. Those she condemned.

She moved through to the back room where Tom Salter was typesetting. Tom was in his middle years and had been working for the *Record* ever since Helen's father moved to Warburton eight years before. He was good at his job, though Helen suspected he had reservations about working for a woman. He looked up as she entered. 'A Mr Roger Blakestone came in while you were out, Miss Wayland. He wants us to print that poster.' He nodded to a large sheet of paper lying on another table. 'I said I'd have to ask you. It could get us into trouble.'

Helen picked the poster up and perused it. It was

notice of a rally to demonstrate the plight of the agricultural labourers, which was to take place on the common the following Saturday afternoon at half past two. 'The speaker will be Jason Hardacre,' it declared in large capital letters.

She understood why Tom was doubtful about accepting the job. Jason Hardacre was a known firebrand who went from town to town, urging workers to stand up to their employers and strike for more wages. He stirred up unrest wherever he went, inciting his followers to violence against the farmers, whom he called the oppressors, although the farmers were struggling to keep going themselves. He had had some initial success, but the labourers were too worried about losing their positions to support him wholeheartedly, especially when there were plenty of men ready to step into their shoes if they were dismissed. Publishing such a poster could be construed as seditious and the publisher liable to prosecution.

'How many does he want printed?' she asked.

'Half a gross.'

'Print them.'

'I'm busy putting the paper together.'

'Leave that. I've something new to put on the front page. I'll write it now and have it ready in an hour. You can do that poster in the meantime.'

'Miss Wayland, are you sure? You know how Mr Wayland was always in trouble for taking on work like that. The Earl had him prosecuted more than once, as well you know.'

'Yes, Tom, I do know. But my father was never afraid to do what he thought was right, even if it meant he was in trouble for it. He did not see why the Earl should dictate what he published and neither do I.'

'Very well,' Tom answered and set aside the page he was typesetting to begin on the poster.

The newspaper consisted of two large folded sheets and was on sale by lunchtime every Wednesday and Saturday. Helen kept the front for her own reports and for court announcements from the London papers. Her readers liked to know what the Regent and the nobility were up to in London. They wanted to know who had been granted a peerage, who had been made a knight and they keenly awaited a résumé of what was being said in Parliament. Earlier in the month she had copied the report of Princess Charlotte's wedding to Prince Leopold of Saxe-Coburg. It had been a joyous occasion in an otherwise miserable year.

The back page was almost all given over to advertisements: comestibles, livestock, agricultural implements and quack medicines. The inside pages were filled with local news: a farmer's stack set on fire—there had been several instances of arson lately, which were put down to the unrest among the labourers—a newcomer of note moving into the district, unusual happenings in the town, reports of the magistrate's sittings, who had been convicted, who let off with a caution for anything from petty theft and criminal damage to poaching and assault.

Helen skimmed through the latest notices of births, marriages, obituaries and coming events. Josiah Birdwood had died, aged seventy-six. He had been married three times and sired thirty children. Donations and prizes were needed for the races and various contests for the Midsummer Fair, held on the common every year. The Earl and Countess of Warburton and Viscount Cavenham would grace it with their presence and judge some of the competitions. There was to be a dance at the Warburton Assembly Rooms to celebrate the first anniversary of the Battle of Waterloo. Lord and Lady Somerfield's daughter, Miss Verity Somerfield, was to come out with a grand ball to be held at their ancestral home at Gayton Hall.

Helen took off her bonnet and sat at her desk to report the hunt and the destruction it had caused.

* * *

Gilbert Cavenham, first Earl of Warburton, flung the newspaper on the table and swore loudly. 'I thought I'd rid myself of that thorn in my side,' he said to Miles. 'But it seems his daughter is bent on continuing where he left off.'

'What do you mean?' Miles asked. 'What thorn in your side? Whose daughter?'

'Henry Wayland. He owned the *Warburton Record* and was always publishing libel. I had to bring him to court on more than one occasion, but neither fines nor prison seemed to deter him. Now he's dead, I'm getting the same sort of rubbish from his daughter. Whoever heard of a woman running a newspaper?'

'Why not?' Miles said. 'I suppose she inherited it and had no other way to support herself.'

'I doubt she'll carry it off. An appearance in court will soon dampen her ardour.'

'What has she said to annoy you so much?'

'Read it for yourself.' He picked up the paper and waved it at his son. 'Libel, that's what it is, defamation of character. She needs to be taught she cannot ridicule me and get away with it.'

Miles was busy reading and hardly heard him. It was all he could do not to smile. The lady, who-ever she was, had a witty turn of phrase. 'The noble lord, in order to please his guests, literally left no stone unturned,' he read. 'Everything was ordered for their entertainment. The hunt hallooed its way over hill and dale, down lanes and across fields, chasing a fox that had surely been especially selected to give the most sport. Reynard led them a merry dance into the village of Ravensbrook, scattering the population and trampling down the small garden of a poor widow and putting her baby son in mortal danger. The excuse given by the only rider who deigned to pull up was, "The dogs follow the fox and the riders follow the dogs." So we must blame the fox and no one else. But can a fox put right the damage that was done? Can the fox reset the rows of beans and peas? Can the fox revive dead chickens? Or still a child's crying? Does killing the erring animal exact just retribution?

'We must not begrudge the noble lord and his guests their *sport*, but who should pay for it? Surely not the poor widow endeavouring to provide for herself and her fatherless son. Not the fox, who was only doing what foxes do by nature and that is to run from its enemies. The dogs, perhaps? But they are trained to hunt the fox. Then we are left with whoever trained the hounds or caused them to be trained: the noble lord himself. But does he offer recompense, does he even apologise? No, because the land is his and he may ride over it whenever he chooses.

'There is surely something wrong with that premise. However humble, an Englishman's home is his castle and should be respected, even by those set above him, especially by those set above him. Responsibility should go hand in hand with privilege.'

Miles put the paper down with a smile. 'She doesn't mince her words, does she?'

'I'll send for Sobers,' the Earl said. 'He'll issue a writ for defamation of character on my behalf and we shall see if she is so sharp when it comes to reporting her own downfall.'

'That's a bit harsh, don't you think?' Miles said, wondering who had given the paper the information; it could have been Jack Byers or Mrs Watson, but it was more likely to have been Miss Grey Gown. Was that what her veiled threat had meant? 'Why not give her the opportunity to retract? I promised to pay Jack Byers to set the widow's garden to rights. If that were made public, she would have to put the record straight.'

'You did what?' his father demanded angrily.

'I found Byers begging and thought to give him a little work. It is sad to see a good, upright man reduced to holding out his hand for pennies. He always worked well when he was employed by the estate. Men like him should not be penalised for serving king and country. I gave him work and the widow will get her garden back.'

'I wish you would not interfere in matters that do not concern you, Miles. You have belittled my authority and added to the ridicule and that I will not tolerate.'

'So are you going to issue a writ on me, too?'

'Don't be ridiculous.'

Miles turned and left him. It had become more and more obvious that he and his father could not live amicably under the same roof, but he was reluctant to leave his mother. Since coming home six months before he had been looking for a property in the area where he could live independently and yet be close to her. He had found nothing suitable and had been considering buying Ravensbrook Manor, which stood just outside the perimeter of Ravens Park. It had been empty and derelict for years, but it was possible to see it had once been a substantial house. As a child, he had often crept through a broken window and played in it, his footsteps and laughter echoing as he ran from room to room, brandishing a wooden sword and pretending to capture it from an imaginary enemy. It would take time and money to restore it, but it was in an ideal position and so he had set about tracing its owner in order to make an offer. He said nothing to anyone of his plans and in the meantime continued to live at Ravens Park and tried not to be contentious for his mother's sake, even if it did mean turning his back on an argument.

He went to the stables and found Jack Byers there talking to the head groom. Seeing Miles, Jack turned to touch his forelock. 'I've done what you said, my lord. I've repaired the hedge and the hen coop, and some of the cabbages will survive, but there's no rescuing the peas and beans.'

Miles delved in his pocket for coins to pay the man. 'Your wages as promised and a little extra to buy half-a-dozen laying hens and new pea and bean seeds for Mrs Watson. There is time to re-plant, is there not?'

'If I get them in this week they should grow, always supposing the weather improves.'

'Have you found more permanent work yet?'

'No, my lord.'

'If I hear of anything, I'll let you know.'

'Thank you, my lord.' He pocketed the money

and took his leave. Miles ordered his horse to be saddled and set off for Warburton.

He found the offices of the *Warburton Record* easily enough, dismounted and went inside. A young man looked up as he entered and scrambled to his feet. 'My lord...'

'I wish to speak to Miss Wayland. I believe she is the proprietor.'

'Yes, she is. I'll fetch her.' He scuttled away.

Two minutes later he was surprised to find himself confronted by Miss Grey Gown herself. This time she was wearing a brown taffeta afternoon dress with a cream-lace fichu. Her rich chestnut hair was cut unusually short and fell about her face in soft curls. Her hazel eyes looked into his fearlessly. He smiled and bowed. 'Miss Wayland?'

She bent her head in the polite gesture she would have used to any slight acquaintance. 'My lord.'

He smiled. 'Miss Wayland, you have upset my father, the Earl...'

'Good.'

'Not good. He is determined to teach you a lesson and is sending for his lawyer to issue a writ for defamation of character.'

If she was upset by this she did not show it.

'Then you may tell the Earl I shall defend it. I wrote nothing but the unbiased truth.'

'Truth is not considered a defence, you know.'

'Then it ought to be.'

'Can you afford a court case and a heavy fine?'

'I shall win.'

'Better to retract. You heard me apologise to Mrs Watson and I asked Jack Byers to mend Mrs Watson's garden, which, if you had taken the trouble to discover, you would have known. That rather defeats your argument, don't you think?'

She had felt guilty about not mentioning that in her report, but she was not going to admit it. 'It is not relevant to the point I was making, that it was for the Earl to recognise his responsibility, not his son.'

'I represent my father.'

'I find it hard to believe the Earl sent you to plead with me.' She chuckled suddenly and the hazel eyes were suddenly full of humour, which changed her whole countenance. He realised with a start that she was beautiful and found himself smiling back. 'It would be entirely out of character.'

'He did not send me, but that is neither here nor there. Mrs Watson was recompensed.'

'That you did it is to your credit, my lord, but it

does not invalidate my argument. The Earl should be the one to make restitution and he should learn that even the humblest widow is a person deserving of respect. But I fear he is too set in his ways for that ever to come about.'

Miles was inclined to agree, but it would be disloyal to his father to say so and in his opinion family disagreements should be kept within the family. 'Nevertheless, restitution was made and it gives you the opportunity to reciprocate,' he said. 'Publish the true facts in your newspaper and the whole matter will be dropped.'

'Do you speak on behalf of the Earl?'

He hesitated and in that hesitation she had her answer. 'No, of course you do not. I wonder why you came.'

'To save you from your own folly,'

'Is it folly to stand up for the poor and oppressed? Is it folly to point out injustice when I see it?'

'No, I admire that, but if it leads to your own downfall…'

'Why are you concerned for my downfall? I should have thought you would rejoice at it.'

'I do not rejoice at anyone's downfall, Miss Wayland,' he said, smiling to soften the fierce look she was giving him. 'I suppose I like to think I am a just and fair person and you are—'

'A woman!' she finished for him. 'And not equipped to deal in a man's world, is that what you were about to say?'

'There is some truth in that.'

'Then I shall have to prove you wrong, my lord.'

'So you will retract?'

'There is nothing to gainsay. What I wrote was the truth. And I shall continue to write the truth, however uncomfortable it makes people feel.'

'Making someone feel uncomfortable is only the half of it,' he said. 'There is the consequence to consider.'

'A change of heart, perhaps?'

He did not think that would happen. 'I meant an appearance in a court of law.'

'I shall welcome the opportunity to have my say.'

'I would not advise it. You might make matters a hundred times worse.'

'Thank goodness I am not required to take your advice,' she retorted.

He smiled and changed tack. 'I believe your father and mine were often at loggerheads, Miss Wayland. Do you have to continue the feud, for feud I believe it was, though I have no idea how it started? It would be a pity to perpetuate it.'

'It was not a feud, it was simply that my father published the truth as he saw it and that did not please the Earl who saw, and still sees, his position as unassailable. But I think it should be challenged.'

She had spirit, he would give her that, but did she really understand the implications of taking up swords against his father? 'And you are determined to carry on where your father left off without even knowing why.'

'I do know why. I have just told you: justice and fairness for those who cannot stand up for themselves.'

'And who is to stand up for you?'

'I can look after myself, my lord.'

This was sheer bravado. He could see the doubt in her expressive greeny-brown eyes. Beautiful eyes, he decided, bright and honest-looking. He doubted she could lie convincingly. 'Then, as I cannot budge you, I will take my leave.' He bowed, turned on his heel and was gone.

She watched him stop outside and look at the large sash window in which she had stuck the pages of the latest edition of the paper. Poor people could not afford newspapers. With tax duty of four pence they had to be sold at sixpence or seven-pence at least, which put them out of the reach of the ordinary working man and left her very little profit. She was convinced the tax was high in order to keep the lower orders from learning of things the government and those in authority did not want them to learn and so she had begun the habit of putting the pages in the window, so that it could be read aloud by those who could read to those who could not. His glance moved from that to one of Roger Blakestone's posters advertising the rally on the common. As he walked back to his horse, she noticed he limped. She had read in the London paper that he had been wounded doing some deed of valour during the recent war with Napoleon and supposed that was the result.

Helen turned back to work, but the prospect of being sued was worrying. If she were heavily fined or sent to prison, then the *Warburton Record* and the printing business would have to be shut down and that meant no work for Edgar, who was the sole support of his mother, or Tom Salter, who had a wife and three children, or Betty, her maid, who was an orphan and whose only relation was a distant cousin too poor to help her. She had brought this on them in her pig-headedness.

Her father had spent six months in Norwich

Castle for speaking out against the Earl enclosing common land which the villagers had worked since time immemorial. His crime had been called seditious libel. He had returned home after he served his sentence, a shadow of the man he had been. He was gaunt and thin, his hair had turned white and he walked with a stoop. It was a long time before he stood upright again and put on a little weight, but it did not seem to have taught him a lesson.

The fire in his belly against injustice wherever he saw it, and particularly against the Earl of Warburton, had been as fierce as ever. She had watched him and worried about him, tried to tempt him with his favourite food, tried to persuade him to rest while she ran the paper, but to no avail. His pen was vitriolic. She had no doubt that if he had not died of a seizure, he would have been arraigned again. That was her legacy, not bricks and mortar, not printing presses, but his undying passion, a passion she shared.

'You are not going to let him bully you, are you?' Edgar said from his desk where he had been setting out advertisements, one for a lecture at the assembly rooms called 'At Waterloo with Wellington' being given by some bigwig from London, Mr West advertising his agricultural implements, and the miller his flour. Another was for an elixir of youth at sixpence a bottle. Goodness knew what it contained, but she did not doubt it tasted vile and could not live up to its name.

'I don't want to, but it's not only me I have to consider. There's you and Tom and Betty.'

'We'll manage, don't you fret.'

Tom came in from the back room in time to hear this. 'Manage what?'

'The Earl is threatening to sue me for defamation of character,' she explained. 'I am wondering if I ought to retract?'

'But you said nothing that wasn't true, did you?'

'No, but the Viscount tells me that is no defence.'

'He is only trying to frighten you. Call his bluff.'

'You think I should?'

'Yes, if you think you are in the right. Your father would have. We will stand by you.'

'Thank you, both of you, but I fear I have made an enemy of the Viscount.'

In any other circumstances and if he was not who he was, she could have liked the Viscount. He had none of the arrogance of his father, but he was his father's son nevertheless. Was he right about a feud? Her father had had no love for the Earl, but she had always supposed it was for altruistic reasons and not personal. But supposing there was something personal in their enmity, what could it possibly be? A wrong never righted? But why? Who was to blame? She sighed and went back to her work; she was unlikely to find the answer to that now.

Chapter Two

In spite of the overcast skies and threat of yet more rain, the crowd began gathering on the common by the middle of Saturday morning. Men, women and even children were milling about trying to find the best places to hear the speaker, for whom a flat cart had been drawn up to act as a platform. They were noisy and for the most part good-humoured, treating it as a day out. Stalls had been set up selling food and drink and favours. These were made of red, white and blue ribbon, no doubt leftover from the celebrations of victory the year before.

Helen, in her grey dress with a shawl over her head, mingled with the crowds. She had a small notebook and a pencil in her reticule, but did not bring it out for fear of being recognised. She wanted to report the proceedings anonymously. She was not the only one incognito, she discovered, when she found herself standing next to Viscount Cavenham. She hardly recognised him; he was dressed in yeoman's clothes, fustian breeches and coat, rough boots, with a battered felt hat on his curls.

'My lord,' she said. 'I never thought to see you here today.'

'Shh,' he said, looking about to see if she had been overheard. 'Not so much of the "my lord" if you please.'

'I could shout it,' she threatened.

'And have me lynched? I had not thought you so bloodthirsty, Miss Wayland.'

'And not so much of the "Miss Wayland" either,' she said.

He laughed. 'Then what am I to call you?'

'You do not need to address me at all.'

He ignored that. 'I believe your name is Helen. A lovely name and most suitable for one as beautiful and fearless as you are.'

'My lord, you go too far.' It was said in a fierce whisper.

'My name is Miles,' he said. 'Pray use it, then we shall be equal.'

'We can never be equal,' she said. 'You, of all people, should know that.'

'All are equal in God's eyes.'

'Then the Earl of Warburton must consider himself above God, for he would never accept that.'

'My father belongs to the old school, Helen. I doubt he could be persuaded to change his ways now.'

They were being jostled by the crowd and he put a hand under her arm to steady her. She resisted her first impulse to knock it away. It was firm and warm and rather comforting. 'And you?' she asked, turning to look up at him and found him looking down at her with an expression she could not interpret. It was full of wry humour, which she found unnerving. Her life until recently had been governed by her work with her father. The men she met were her father's employees, friends and business acquaintances and she dealt with them accordingly. Meeting and dealing with this man was outside her experience. For one thing they had not been properly introduced, which was absurd since they had already encountered and spoken to each other twice before. But it was not the lack of an introduction that confused her; it was the way he looked at her and his self-possession, which somehow seemed to diminish hers. She took herself firmly in hand. If she was going to fight the Earl, she had better learn to stand up to his son.

'I am my own man, Helen.'

'But you are also your father's son.'

'Oh, undoubtedly I am that.'

'So, why are you here?'

'Curiosity. I want to know why men risk everything to take part in meetings like this which could have them arrested and can have no favourable outcome.'

'Desperation, I should think.'

'And you, I presume, are here to report it for your newspaper.'

'Yes.'

'And can you do that without bias?'

'I sincerely hope not. It would be excessively dull and achieve nothing.'

It was not the answer he expected and made him chuckle. 'How long have you been producing the *Warburton Record*?'

'The *Record* was started by my father. He worked for a printing press in London, but when we moved to Warburton he set up on his own account as a printer; then he realised there was no way of disseminating local news except by pamphlets published by those with an axe to grind, so he started the *Record*. That was eight years ago.'

'I meant how long have *you* been doing it?'

'I used to love helping my father as a child and

learned the business along with my growing up, especially after we moved here. When he died last year, he left the business to me.' She did not add that it was all he had to leave. His many clashes with authority had left him almost penniless. No one was interested in buying the business as a going concern; the only offer she had ever had was for the machinery. She was not told who the prospective buyer was, but suspected it was someone who had no interest in running the *Record*, but rather wished to shut it down. Far from discouraging her, it had given her the impetus to keep going, especially as Tom and Edgar were both behind her.

'Why did your father choose to leave London and come to Warburton?' he asked. 'Norfolk is hardly the hub of government.'

'It was my mother's birthplace; as she was mortally ill, she wanted to die here where she had spent her childhood and where her parents had lived and died.'

'I am sorry for your loss,' he said softly.

'Thank you, my—' She stopped and corrected herself. 'Thank you, sir.'

He bent over and whispered in her ear, so close his warm breath was having a strange effect on her limbs. 'That's better than "my lord", but it's still not the address I asked for.'

She pulled herself together. 'Oh, I cannot use that. It wouldn't be proper.'

'Is it also improper for me to address you as Helen?'

'You know it is, but no doubt you will continue to do as you please.'

'But I like the name. It rolls off the tongue so readily.'

'Now you are bamming me.'

'No. That would be ungentlemanly.'

'Ah, but at the moment you are not dressed as a gentleman. Why the disguise?'

'Do you think I would learn anything in my usual garb? I would be hounded off the common. At least this way I can be an ordinary soldier back from the war, which I am.' He looked about him. 'I see a goodly number of those here, including Roger Blakestone. He was in my regiment, a troublemaker even then.'

'No one has said he is a troublemaker. He is out of work, as they all are. The farmers have stood the men off because the crops, if they ever grew at all, have been ruined by the weather; there's no work for the soldiers, either. There ought to be something they could do that is not reliant on the weather.'

'And how will listening to a man like Jason Hardacre help that?' he queried. 'He is for insurrection, which will surely make matters worse.'

'Oh, I do not think the people will be swayed by him. They simply want to make their voices heard and have a day out that doesn't cost them anything but a copper or two for a pie and a glass of cordial.'

The behaviour of the crowd seemed to bear that out. Many of them were in family groups, having a picnic. 'I never thought of sustenance,' he said. 'And I'm suddenly devilish hungry. Would you like something to eat, Miss... Oh, dear, it will have to be Helen, after all.'

'No, thank you.'

'I intend to have something. There's a woman over there selling hot pies. I think I will try one of those.'

He left her and she thought that was the last she would see of him; suddenly she felt rather alone, even with the noisy crowds pushing and shoving and threatening to topple her over. She made her way to the edge of the throng where she could breathe freely. Five minutes later he was beside her again. 'I thought I'd lost you,' he said, handing her a paper packet in which reposed a succulent meat pie.

'But I said no thank you,' she said. 'Do you never listen?'

'Oh, I heard you, but I did not believe you. We have been standing about an age and I was ready to wager you would eat it if it were put before you.'

She considered refusing, but the pie did smell rather savoury. 'I hate to waste it,' she said. 'Thank you.' She took a bite and realised she was indeed rather hungry.

They stood together, enjoying their pies and not speaking, until a flourish of a bugle heralded the arrival of Jason Hardacre. A cheer went up as he mounted the cart with Mr Blakestone. But even before the latter opened his mouth to introduce the speaker, a troop of militia rode onto the common at a fast trot, right into the middle of the crowd, who attempted to scatter in terror, but they were so close-packed it was almost impossible to escape. There were shouts and screams as people were knocked over by the horses or hit by the blunt edge of a sword or the sharp point of a spur. Even if they had wanted to depart, which most of them did, they could not get away. In turning from one horseman, they were confronted by another.

Miles was swift to act. He guided Helen into the shelter of an elder bush, then ran into the middle of the mêlée. Picking up two small children who were in danger of being trampled and tucking one under each arm, he pushed his way towards the lieutenant of the troop. 'Call your men off,' he commanded. 'Someone will be killed. This was a peaceful gathering until you arrived.'

'It is a seditious meeting,' the lieutenant said. 'Intended to encourage rebellion against the law of the land. I am empowered to put it down by whatever means I think fit.'

'By whose order?'

'His lordship, the Earl of Warburton, sitting as a magistrate.'

'And I am ordering you to call off your men before someone is killed.'

'And who are you to be giving orders?'

He had obviously not been recognised in his lowly clothes. It made him smile. 'My name is Captain Miles Cavenham of his Majesty's Dragoon Guards. As your superior officer, I order you to call off your men and ride slowly from the field.' His manner of delivering the order left no doubt he was used to command, even if he did choose to dress like every other man there.

The lieutenant obeyed reluctantly, but it was

some time before order was restored and the people had the common to themselves again. Roger Blakestone and Jason Hardacre had disappeared as soon as the soldiers appeared. Miles returned the children to their weeping mother and set about assessing the casualties. He was joined by Helen.

There were a few broken bones, some blood and many bruises, but mercifully no one had been killed. Helen put that down to the Viscount's timely intervention. He had undoubtedly also saved her, for there had been a horseman bearing down on them when he pushed her into the shelter of the bush.

'This is what happens when people hold unlawful meetings,' he said.

'This is what happens when men like the Earl order mounted soldiers against innocent women and children,' she retorted.

He knew she was right and did not respond. Instead he said, 'We need medical assistance. Will the doctor come?'

'I'll fetch him.'

'No, send a boy. He'll be quicker. I need you to help me with the casualties. We must separate those who can go home and look to their own wounds from those who need medical attention.

And we need pads and bandages. You do not faint at the sight of blood, I hope.'

'No, I am not squeamish.'

Looking about her for someone to send, she noticed a skinny fellow in rags watching them intently. It was difficult to tell how old he was—he had a childlike look about him, though he must have been in his thirties. He was grinning and dancing from one foot to the other, his eyes bright with excitement.

'Poor idiot,' Miles said, as he suddenly darted away. 'I hope someone is looking after him.'

Helen found a lad to send for the doctor and set about pulling up her skirt and undoing the ties of her petticoats and allowing them to drop to the ground. She picked them up and tore them into strips. They were busy binding some of the wounds when the doctor arrived and took over.

Those who had been bandaged were either sent home or to the town's small hospital in carts and carriages. When everyone had gone and the common deserted except for a scattering of waste paper, broken pies—which were being attacked by pigeons and dogs—torn clothing and churned-up hoof marks, Miles and Helen found themselves alone, their work done.

They stood and faced each other. He had lost his hat and his curls lay untidily over his forehead. His face was smeared with mud and blood; it was only when he raised his hand to try to wipe it that Helen noticed the long cut on his forearm. It had ceased to bleed, but there was a dirty crust of dried blood on it.

'You have been hurt,' she said, in surprise. 'Why didn't you say so?'

'It is nothing. I felt the edge of the sword of one of the militia. It is not deep.'

'It needs cleaning. And the doctor has gone. Come home with me and I'll clean it for you. It's nearer than Raven's Park.'

They walked back to the centre of town. It was crowded with people who had managed to escape the melee; they were standing in groups discussing what had happened. They watched Miles and Helen go past and that set them talking again. Helen could almost hear them: 'What's going on there? That's Viscount Cavenham or I'm a Dutchman. What is he doing dressed like that?'

'Did you see him scoop up those children?'

'And stop that lieutenant when he would have broken the head of everyone there. Seems a strange thing for him to do, seeing who he is.'

'And what is Miss Wayland up to? I wager it will be in the next edition of the paper. She is bound to be in trouble for sponsoring the meeting.'

'Well, if you want my opinion they are the most unlikely couple in Christendom.'

Miles must have realised it himself, for he was smiling as Helen opened the shop door and ushered him inside. She led the way through the front office to the printing room at the back where a basin and a jug of water were kept for the compositor to wash the ink from his fingers. She left him there while she ran upstairs to find ointment and bandages. When she returned he had already put water in the basin and was splashing the wound.

'It is only a scratch,' he said.

Nevertheless, he allowed her to sit him down and sponge it clean. This necessitated touching him and that set up a tumult inside her she could not understand. The warmth from his skin seemed to radiate from her fingers, up her arm and over her whole body until she felt as though she were on fire. Carefully she cleaned the cut, trying to ignore the heat in her limbs and hoping it did not show in her cheeks because it was the height of foolishness to be so affected. 'There, I think I have it clean. A little ointment and a bandage and you're done.' She was surprised how normal her voice sounded.

'Done,' he repeated and laughed. 'Perhaps you ought to turn me over and roast the other side, or perhaps stick me on a spit and set it turning slowly. I'll be cooked in no time.'

'And too tough to eat, I'll wager,' she said, answering him in the same way as she tied off the bandage. She could not pull down his shirtsleeve because it had been torn off.

'Will you report my little adventure in your paper?'

'What, tell everyone the Earl's son was the hero of the hour? I thought you wanted to be incognito?'

'So I did, so I do, but I did not think you would take any heed of that.'

'Oh, I think I will. Otherwise it would spoil my story of the Earl's infamy if his son turned out to be a hero. I fear he shall have to remain anonymous.'

'Why the Earl's infamy? He was not even there…'

'Of course not. He would not dirty his hands, but he was the one who ordered the militia out.'

He agreed with her, but he knew his father would have a ready answer to that. 'It was the lieutenant who did the damage,' he said, acting devil's advocate. 'My father will undoubtedly say he never condoned violence and the lieutenant acted on his own initiative and the lieutenant will maintain the populace started the fight by resisting an order to disperse. And if you write anything to the contrary it will be another writ, you can be sure.' He paused, then took her arm and added quietly, 'Can I not persuade you to retract over the widow's garden?'

'No. That would be cowardly.'

'Whatever you are, you are not a coward, Miss Wayland. Foolish, perhaps, wrongheaded, maybe, but not cowardly. I fear for you.'

'Why? It is nothing to do with you.'

'I seem to have got myself involved,' he said wryly. 'If only as a peacemaker. I have seen too much of war.'

Why he had disappointed her, she did not know. She could hardly have expected him to go against his father and openly condemn him. It was to his credit he had tried to make restitution to Mrs Watson and that was more than his father had done, and he had stopped the militia from causing even more harm than they had. Neither was enough to win her wholehearted approval. She stood back to allow him to stand.

He rose to his feet, six inches taller than she was, and she was tall for a woman. His disability was not obvious when he was standing, nor, she remembered, when he was on horseback. It was only when he walked that his limp became evident. She wondered incongruously if it stopped him dancing. She thrust the foolish thought from her and turned away, lest he read something in her expression she did not want him to know.

He took it as a dismissal, bowed to her and turned to leave. She accompanied him to the door and watched him go, striding with his ungainly gait down the road. Luckily the gossips had dispersed and the street was quiet.

After he had gone she set to work writing her report of the meeting that never happened, but she found it very difficult. The image of the Viscount and the memory of the warm sensation touching his skin had given her would not go away. She was afraid she was getting to like him a little too much and that was not good for her campaign against his father. The world must know how insufferably arrogant and unfeeling the Earl was. He had ruined her father without a qualm, because it was the worry of all the writs and his determination not to give in that had killed him in the end. If the Earl had his way, he would silence her, too. And she was determined he would not. She stiffened her spine, banished the image of the Viscount from her mind and picked up her pen. But after recording the foolishness of holding such a meeting in the first place, the cruel intervention of the militia on what had been a peaceful gathering, she felt obliged, in her honest way, to acknowledge the part played by Viscount Cavenham in saving the situation from becoming a real bloodbath.

Miles fetched his horse from the inn where he had left it and rode home in a contemplative mood. Miss Wayland was the most stubborn female he had ever come across. She was also resourceful and unafraid. But perhaps her lack of fear was simply ignorance of her true plight. He could not persuade his father to withdraw the writ and he could not persuade Miss Wayland to retract. He feared they were on a collision course. But, oh, how he admired her for it!

He found his mother alone in the morning room sitting at her embroidery. She had once been a great beauty, but that loveliness had faded over the years of being under the thumb of her domineering husband. Her hair, once so fine, was streaked with grey and her blue eyes were careworn. They lit up when she saw him, but catching sight of his torn sleeve and bandaged arm, she became alarmed. 'Miles, whatever happened to you? You look as though you have been in a fight.'

'I'm sorry, Mama, I should have changed before joining you. I will go and do so now and then I will tell you all about it. It is nothing for you to worry about.'

But when he returned, dressed more befitting a drawing room, in cream pantaloons, a brown-and-yellow striped waistcoat and a fresh shirt covering his bandaged arm, and recounted all that had happened, she was even more worried. 'Miles, when your father hears of this, he will be very angry. Don't you know better than to go against him? Think of me, if you cannot think of yourself.'

'Mama, I would, but I could not stand by and let the militia knock those poor people about, could I? There were whole families there, enjoying a day out. They were in mortal danger. The militia were laying about them as if they were enjoying it.'

'But why did you go there at all?'

'Curiosity. I wanted to hear the men's grievances and I wanted to see if Miss Wayland would go. I fear she will write it up to the detriment of the militia and whoever ordered them to prevent the meeting, and then she will be in more trouble.'

'And that is another thing—what is your interest in Miss Wayland? She is not a lady, is she? She earns a living in a way I cannot approve and upsets your father almost daily. How did you meet her?'

He had always felt able to confide in her, knowing she would not repeat it, so he told her about stopping when he saw the frightened woman and child cowering against a wall. 'She was so fiery against my father—it was more than just the incident of the hunt—and I wondered what had caused it. I did not know she was the proprietor of the *Warburton Record* then. I only found that out when I went to her business premises.'

'Whatever did you go there for?'

'I wanted to persuade her to retract what she had said about Father because he was going to sue her for defamation of character. But she would not.'

'Then you must let the law take its course.'

'Mama, the law is weighted heavily against her, my father will see to that.' He paused. 'There seems to have been some kind of feud between him and Miss Wayland's father and she is determined to maintain it. Do you know what it was about?'

'No, except Mr Wayland was forever publishing criticism of the Earl and he could not allow that, could he?'

Knowing his father, he sighed. 'No, I suppose not.'

She turned to look into his face, scanning its clean lines and handsome brow. 'You have not developed a *tendre* for Miss Wayland, have you, Miles?'

'No, of course not,' he answered swiftly without giving himself time to think.

'Good, because it would be disastrous.' She paused and, believing the subject of Miss Wayland closed, changed the subject. 'Invitations came this morning for the Somerfield ball in July. We are all to go. It is a come out for Verity, who has recently returned from some school or other that turns out young ladies. As if her mother could not do that perfectly well.'

Lord and Lady Somerfield had been friends of the Earl and Countess for many years, mostly because they were the only other titled people in the area considered high enough in the instep with whom they could associate.

'I haven't seen Verity Somerfield since I went into the army,' he said. 'She would only have been about thirteen then, if that. Long-legged and given to giggling, as I recall.'

'She has grown into a beautiful young lady with perfect deportment and manners and I have no doubt will attract many suitors, but I think Lord Somerfield is hoping you will make a match of it.'

'He may hope,' he said, 'but I am resolved to stay single.'

'Why, Miles? Is it because of your disability?' she queried. 'That is nonsense. It is hardly noticeable and I am sure if you were to ask the shoemaker he could raise one of your shoes a little. Heels are all the fashion, you know.'

'Yes, but is it the fashion to have one higher than the other? No, Mama, even if a lady were to disregard that, she would have to see the scars on my thigh.'

'Not until after you were married.'

'Yes, that could pose a problem,' he said, laughing to lighten the atmosphere. 'To keep such a sight until the wedding night would surely give any bride the vapours. And to show her beforehand would be highly improper.'

She understood the bitterness that went behind what appeared to be a flippant remark and reached out to put her hand over his. 'It is not as bad as all that, Miles, and if she loves you…'

'Ah, there's the rub. Who would have me as I am?'

'I am sure Verity Somerfield will. According to her mama, she is already well disposed towards you. She remembers you as being kind to her, which is to your credit. And since then, you have come back from Waterloo a hero.'

'I wish nothing had been made of that. I only did my duty as I saw it. I had no idea that fellow from *The Times* was taking notes. What they want sending a reporter out to war, I do not know. He only got in the way and the men made fun of him, which, to give him his due, he took in good part.'

'Nevertheless, it has raised your standing with those at home and with the Somerfields.'

'Mama, you are biased.'

She smiled. 'Perhaps. But you are a handsome man and there are other assets in your favour: your title and amiable nature, for instance. I am persuaded all you need to do is turn on your charm and Verity will be yours. It is time you married…'

'I will not impose myself on any young lady simply to provide the estate with an heir, Mama. It would not be fair to her.' He realised that one day he ought to marry, if only to produce the requisite heir, but he also realised the woman he chose must be strong and not squeamish, someone who could see further than an ungainly gait and scarred limbs to the man within, someone like Miss Wayland, who had not flinched at the injuries she had seen on the common. Knowing Miss Somerfield's delicate background, he doubted that she would have reacted in the same way. He cursed the war and the Frenchmen who had fired the cannon that had resulted in shrapnel becoming embedded in his upper thigh. It had been painful at the time and even more so when the surgeon had been working on him, but that was nothing compared to the way it had left him with a shrivelled thigh. His question, 'Who would have me?', had been heartfelt.

'But you will go to the ball?' his mother asked, forcing him back to the present.

'To please you, yes, but I shall not make a fool of myself by attempting to dance.'

'You could practise at home beforehand. I am sure you could manage some of the slower measures.'

'Perhaps.' Standing up, he bent to kiss her cheek and promised to be back in time to dine *en famille*. Then he left her.

He mused on the upcoming ball for a moment

or two, then put it from his mind as another idea
came to him. What the ex-soldiers and the out-
of-work labourers wanted was not hand-outs, but
work, something to keep them gainfully employed
and the wolf from the door. Farming was in the
doldrums and the farmers were not employing
labour to stand about idly waiting for the weather
to change, but what if the men were encouraged
to grow fruit and vegetables? If every man had
a strip of land, the sort of thing they had before
the enclosures spoilt it all, he could grow not only
enough for himself but for the market, too. If they
did not have to pay for the land or, initially, the
seed and plants, they would have a head start. It
would be a kind of co-operative venture with each
helping out the other with their own particular
skills.

He owned a few acres left to him by his maternal grandfather that he had never cultivated.
According to his father it was useless, no more
than scrub and fit only for rabbits, but would the
men work it? Not if they knew it came from him,
he decided. He needed to do it through a third
party and James Mottram came to mind. James
was a young man of his own age whom he had
met when they were both studying at Cambridge
University. James had since become a lawyer and

was already making his mark in the courts of justice, particularly in defence. He was a partner in a practice in Norwich. He would ask him, but first he would sound out Jack Byers about the project, ask him if he thought the men would agree to the plan and if he had any ideas to add to it. But he would swear him to secrecy.

He knew Byers was staying with Mrs Watson. He had his second horse saddled and set off for her cottage.

Helen had decided to visit Mrs Watson to see how her garden had been restored and how Mr Byers was getting on. She had promised herself she would find out his history and write a piece about the hardships of the returning soldiers and it might be a good opportunity to do that. The day was blustery and overcast; it looked as though there would be more rain, which bode ill for whatever crops had survived so far. She was wrapped in a long burnoose with the hood up and did not immediately recognise the man approaching her until he was standing right in front of her, his feet apart as if to detain her.

'Mr Blakestone, you startled me.'

'I want a word with you.' He sounded belligerent, which made her nervous.

'Say it, then.'

'Traitor!' He paused. 'You took my money for the poster, pretended to be on the side of the workers and all the time you were plotting with the Earl and that stiff-rumped son of his to betray us. It is fortunate for you that no one was killed today or you would have paid with your life.'

'The reason no one was killed was because the Viscount prevented it,' she retorted. 'Which you would have known if you had not run away like a coward.'

'Coward, you call me! I wasn't the one standing around in disguise waiting to enjoy the fruits of my betrayal. I was up there on the platform for all to see.'

'Until the militia arrived. It was miraculous how fast you disappeared then.'

'It was my bounden duty to protect Jason Hardacre from arrest and get him safely away. Thanks to you and the Viscount, he never made his speech and the people of Warburton are the poorer for it.'

'I doubt that.' She tried to pass him, but he dodged to prevent her. 'Let me pass, Mr Blakestone.'

'When I've done with you.'

'What do you mean?' She was becoming very alarmed and tried to push past him. He reached out and pinioned her arms to her sides. She tried kicking, but he held her at arm's length and she could not reach his legs.

'Struggle all you like,' he jeered, 'but hear this. We will not be so foolish as to advertise our next meeting, except by word of mouth, so if the Earl hears of it, we shall know where the blame lies. Your life won't be worth living.'

'Stand aside!' The voice was the Viscount's as he galloped up, threw himself from his horse and wrenched Blakestone from Helen. He had his crop in his hand and raised it to the man, ready to give him a beating, but Helen grabbed his arm.

'No, don't,' she cried. 'Let him go. I don't want violence done on my account.'

Miles lowered his arm, the white heat of his anger slowly subsiding. 'Get you gone,' he told Blakestone. 'And if I ever come across you offering violence to a lady again, it will be the worse for you.'

The man hesitated as if considering whether to stand and fight, but thought better of it and turned on his heel to march down the road, but not before he had uttered one more threat. 'You must watch your back, Captain. I ain't forgot you had me flogged and reduced to the ranks. A man don' forget that in a hurry. Watch your back at all times.'

'What did he mean by that?' Helen asked, as the man strode away.

'I caught him assaulting a Portuguese girl and hauled him off. He was put on a charge and was dealt fifty lashes and had his sergeant's stripes taken off him.'

She shuddered. 'I think flogging is barbaric. Surely there is another way to punish wrongdoing in the army?'

'I don't hold with flogging either, but it is the only punishment the men understand, and in war-time, under battle conditions, we do not have the facilities for imprisonment. Besides, the men are needed to fight.' He paused. 'But that doesn't ex-plain why he was manhandling you. What was that about?'

'He thought I had betrayed the meeting to you and that you had told your father, who ordered the militia. He was very angry.'

'I am sorry to hear that. You have helped him when you should not have done and he repays you with threats. Had I known I would have told him the truth.'

'He would not have believed you.'

'No, you are probably right, but be careful in

future, Miss Wayland. Do not go out unaccompanied.'

'Oh, it is nothing but bluster. I doubt he would harm me.' Now the man had gone she was full of bravado. It would not do to let Viscount Cavenham see how afraid she had been.

'I am not so sure. Where were you going?'

'To see Mrs Watson.'

'A happy coincidence. I was on my way there myself. We will go together.' He picked up the reins of his horse and walked beside her to the widow's cottage.

Mrs Watson was put in a fluster when she saw who had accompanied Helen and bowed and kept apologising for her poor home, until Miles smiled to put her at her ease and said he had come to talk to Mr Byers, whom he had spotted working in the garden, but he would enjoy a cup of camomile tea when he came back. And with that he was gone.

Relieved of his presence, Mrs Watson relaxed and bade Helen be seated by the hearth. The little boy was playing on the floor and Helen knelt down to play with him. 'How are you managing?' she asked the child's mother, picking up a crudely carved harlequin on a stick and tickling the boy with it. He chortled happily.

'Oh, we do well enough. I am thankful I still have my job in the laundry and Jack Byers has put the garden to rights as far as he was able. The Viscount gave him money to buy vegetable seeds in place of those I lost. Jack has sown them and planted new currant bushes for next year, but there will be no fruit this year. The guinea his lordship gave me is all but done and I cannot pay him. He is working for board and lodging.'

'I expect he thinks it is better than nothing.'

'Miss Wayland, you didn't ought to have writ what you did about the Earl. I didn't know you wrote a newspaper until Jack told me or I wouldn't have said what I did. It looks as if I were complaining and that weren't so. We could all be in trouble.'

'It's only me that's in trouble, Mrs Watson. The Earl is determined to close me down.'

'It don't do no good to go agin' him. What d'you do it for any road?'

'Because someone has to tell the truth and wake everyone up to what's been going on for generations. My father did it and I carry on in his memory.'

'And yet you be on good terms with the Viscount.'

'That's only good manners—underneath is a

different matter; he is like his father; arrogance is bred in him. Besides, I am also in trouble with the firebrands who would stir up unrest if they could.' She got up off her knees and scooped Eddie up to sit with him in the chair by the hearth. She loved all small children and this one was particularly fetching with his fair curls, blue eyes and chubby limbs, notwithstanding his clothes were patched and worn, probably bought second-hand from the market.

Mrs Watson put a cup of tea on the corner of the table where she could reach it. 'Seems to me you be in trouble all round,' she said. 'You will need the good offices of the Viscount before you're done.'

Helen did not tell her that the gentleman had already used his good offices to help her. She could see him through the window. He was talking earnestly to Jack Byers.

'What do you think, Byers? Would the idea find favour?'

'Anything that allows the men to work and keep their families from starving is a good thing, my lord. But where could we get the land? No farmer would let us have land, even if we could afford the rent.'

'I have a friend desirous of helping the unemployed, both old soldiers and farm workers, and he has a few acres not far from here that is uncultivated. You would be doing him and yourselves a favour taking it on. Of course, you need to get the men together and work out how it can be done. Some of you will have specialist skills: ploughing, drilling, looking after animals. And shooting. I believe the land is plagued by rabbits. My friend will supply seed and equipment, whatever you need to start you off.'

'Who is this friend of yourn?' Jack asked warily. 'What's he want from us?'

'He wishes to remain anonymous and he wants nothing from you. He is what you might call a philanthropist.'

'Supposing times get better and some of us are offered our old jobs back?'

'Then your piece of ground will go to someone else who needs it with compensation for the work you have done on it.'

'Sounds all right,' Jack said, still dubious.

'Get the men together and ask them. Vote on it if you like, but do not say I have a hand in it. I am only a go-between, you understand.'

'Oh, to be sure, I understand,' Jack said, grinning.

Miles left him to his gardening, knowing the man had guessed the identity of the philanthropist, but he would not say so, neither out loud to him nor to the men when he called them together.

He returned to the kitchen where Helen was nursing young Eddie, who had fallen asleep in her arms. She smiled up at him and put a finger to her lips. He sat down silently and accepted a cup of tea from Mrs Watson, not once taking his eyes off the woman and the sleeping child. The hard-nosed business woman who could write such vitriolic attacks on the nobility, who could get her hands covered in ink, stand firm in a mob and never turn a hair at broken limbs and bloody noses, was a nurturer at heart. The picture she presented, her grey dress dishevelled, her hair tousled by chubby fingers keen to explore, was one of domesticity. It gave him a lump in his throat. It was sympathy for her, he told himself, sympathy and at the same time unbounded admiration, nothing to do with the fact that he might never enjoy having a family like it himself.

Chapter Three

With the tea drunk and the child roused and taken from Helen, they took their leave. If she had expected him to ride away, she was mistaken. He insisted on escorting her home, walking beside her, leading his mount.

It was at least three miles and for a little while they walked in silence. She was acutely aware of him beside her, his height and strength, his warmth which was as unlike the coldness of his father as it was possible to be. His limp she hardly noticed—it was part of the man. 'Mrs Watson seems to be managing very well with Mr Byers's help,' she said. 'But she tells me he is working for bed and board only and that does not help his wife and family. And people who do not know the truth of it are gossiping. He really cannot stay there.'

'I know. I have a friend who has some spare land who has come up with an idea to help the unemployed men, which will give them work. The idea is that a strip is given to each man to work as a market garden, but lodgings are another matter. There is an old barn on the far side of Ravensbrook. I don't know if it is watertight, but if it could be made so, it could house several families.'

'Who owns it?'

'The man who owns the land,' he said evasively.

'Your friend is very generous.'

'No, simply wishing to help.'

'And what is the identity of this man, my lord?'

He laughed. 'Do you think I would tell you? It will be all over the next edition of the *Warburton Record*.'

'Why not? It would be good to publish some good news for a change.'

'I will tell you more about it when it is all arranged, then you can let the world know that Warburton and its neighbouring villages look after their men.'

'I wish the weather would improve,' she said. 'It would make all the difference, not only to the men's chances of working, but to their spirits, too. Some days it is nearly as dark as night and, what with the rain and gales, everyone is miserable. We need a little sunlight and then we shall all feel more cheerful. And market gardens will not flourish without it.'

'I know. I notice the parson prays for good weather in every service and the amens after that are louder than usual.'

'Let us hope his prayers are answered. If the men cannot cultivate the land they are given, it will not help them, will it?'

'No. I have been thinking about that. At Ravens Park we have a great glasshouse in which all manner of things grow regardless of the weather. The men could build some of those. I am sure my friend will provide them with wood and glass and there are bound to be carpenters and glaziers among them. They could grow more exotic things, which fetch more on the London markets.'

'The generosity of this friend of yours seems unending,' she said with a smile. She had already guessed the identity of the benefactor. It put her in a quandary. How could she maintain her antipathy towards him when everything he did was to his credit? She could only do it by reminding herself over and over again that he was his father's son, that when he inherited he would undoubtedly revert to type. How could he not do so with that great mansion and a vast estate to maintain, not to mention the society with which he would have to associate? She hoped that would not happen before the good he was trying to do came to fruition.

'If it keeps the men busy and stops them attending seditious meetings, that is all to the good, do you not agree?' he said.

'Oh, most certainly.' The clouds were darkening the sky again as they approached the town. 'If it rains again before you arrive home, you will be soaked,' she commented. 'Why not leave me? We are almost in the town. I shall be perfectly safe.'

'I will see you to your door, as I promised, and I always have a serviceable cloak rolled up on my saddle. I met weather worse than this in the Peninsula when we were on the march and am none the worse for it.'

'It must have been a hard time.'

'No worse for me than hundreds of other poor beggars. As an officer, I could ride when they had to march and officers had billets when the men had to sleep where they dropped, whatever the weather, sometimes so hot it was like an oven, at other times freezing with hale and snow and biting wind.'

'I wager you did not always take the billets, but slept with your men.'

He laughed. 'How do you know that?'

'Because I am coming to know the man,' she said simply.

He turned towards her in surprise, but decided not to comment. If she was beginning to look more favourably on him, that was all to the good. If they could work together and not on opposing sides, who knew what they could achieve? But he decided not to say that either.

They stopped outside her door. 'Thank you for your escort, my lord,' she said, wondering if she ought to invite him in for refreshment, but decided that would be going too far. She could almost see the curtains twitching in the house across the road. Instead, she held out her right hand.

He took it in his firm grip. 'Good afternoon, Miss Wayland. Take care now and if you need me, I am yours to command.' And with that he lifted the back of her hand to his lips.

Even through her thin glove, she could feel the warmth of his gentle kiss coursing through her and ending up in her cheeks. She was sure they were flaming. Was he simply being polite and behaving as a gentleman would to a lady? But she was not a lady and the situation in which they found themselves was not an occasion for the formal niceties of society. Oh, how she hoped the curtain twitchers had turned away at that moment.

She retrieved her hand, bade him a hurried fare-well and fled indoors, leaving him staring at the closed door.

He shrugged, fetched out his cape and put it on before mounting and cantering away in the rain. Had they or had they not established a rapport? He could not be sure. Nor was he sure why it mattered to him, except that, in spite of his father, she did have some influence through her newspaper and it was as well not to call down her wicked wit on his own shoulders, or he would never succeed in winning the men round.

On Monday he would take the carriage and visit James. He hoped his friend would act for him in the matter of the market gardens. And, if he could not persuade his father to change his mind, James might be agreeable to advising Miss Wayland over the accusation of defamation. It was strange how important it was to him that she should not be convicted, but he told himself severely it was only his sense of justice.

They were both in church the following morn-ing; Miles with his parents in their pew at the front, Helen in the body of the church with Betty beside her. Neither acknowledged the other. The lengthy sermon was all about knowing one's place and not aspiring to rise above it. A woman's role was to look after the home, to do good works and not set herself up as equal to a man. Helen smiled, realising it was aimed directly at her. She wondered if the Viscount, whose tall back was three rows in front of her, was smiling, too. The Earl was nodding vigorously as if he agreed with every word, having no doubt instructed the rector in his duty to point out the errors of his flock—and one in particular.

Helen did not linger about the churchyard afterwards, not only because it was another miserable day and everyone was hurrying home, but because Sunday was the day she did her accounts, prepared bills and planned the week ahead. Edgar Harrington was still learning and needed help with laying out the advertisements and copying some of the more important pieces from the London papers and she would spend some time with him the next day.

The accounts done, she fell to musing on the Viscount's idea for the market co-operative venture. Could it work? Would the men work together, or would there be lazy ones who would not pull their weight and others who worked harder than the others, but received no greater return? Viscount Cavenham undoubtedly meant well, but had he considered that? It would take a great spirit of willingness on everyone's part to bring it to fruition. And how would men like Blakestone react? It did not suit his purpose to have contented workers. She wished now that she had never printed his poster.

It reminded her it was still in the window of the shop. She went downstairs and removed it. Standing with it in her hand, she looked about her. The room was a large one and contained Edgar's desk and a large table at which she sometimes worked and where customers brought their advertisements and announcements to be printed in the paper. There were a few bookshelves, which housed some of her father's books. She noticed a well-thumbed one about the laws of slander and libel—she ought to study that—an English grammar, a copy of Johnson's dictionary, a book of maps, a timetable for the coaches leaving the Three Cups for London and Norwich each day and a bible. They hardly filled the shelves. And yet upstairs in what had been his study there were stacks of books on any number of subjects. And in her own room there were books she had bought or been given as presents throughout her childhood and growing up, some instructive, some purely romantic stories. Everyone should have access to books, she mused, and ran upstairs.

She was up and down the stairs all afternoon, bringing down books and arranging them on the shelves in the shop. Here was a veritable library and she would make it available to the towns-people. It might be that some of the men who were out of work could learn a new skill from one of them. And even if they did not, they might lose themselves in the printed word, adding to their education. She sat down and sketched out a notice to put in the window. The books would be loaned free so long as they were returned within two weeks in good condition. She stopped when Betty came to tell her that supper was on the table.

Immediately afterwards she returned to her task and made out individual cards for each book so that she could keep track of who had borrowed it. It kept her busy well into the evening and stopped her thinking of Viscount Cavenham and the strange effect he had on her. But as soon as she was in her bed that night, she found her thoughts returning to him unbidden.

What sort of a man was he? How sincere? What did he have to gain by his championing of the unemployed men? She found it hard to believe the Earl's son did not have an ulterior motive, but if he did, he hid it well. Why had he kissed her hand? He knew she did not have the social standing for such a gesture. Was he a rake, someone who took his pleasures among the lower orders, knowing no one would blame him? Hating his father as she did, it was easier to believe ill than good of the son. Her father, if he had been alive, would most certainly caution her about putting her trust in such a one. Her brain told her one thing, her heart another. Viscount Cavenham was helpful, generous and caring. He worried about the widow and her garden, about Jack Byers and the out-of-work soldiers and labourers, about preventing bloodshed and rebellion, and he was concerned that she should be safe. Those were not the attributes of a bad man. Was he as confused as she was about their respective roles? Surely her father could not have been wrong?

It was a question that would never be answered now. Sighing, she turned over to try to sleep.

Miles sat in James Mottram's office the following morning, discussing the market-garden project with him. James listened carefully and agreed that it was a worthwhile idea and he would help him all he could. It was after that discussion was finished that Miles told him about his father's threat to sue Miss Wayland for libel. 'I cannot persuade her to retract and my father is determined she shall be punished,' he finished. 'They are both being stubborn about it, but Miss Wayland has most to lose. I doubt she can afford a heavy fine and I cannot let her go to prison.'

'Why are you so concerned? Newspaper proprietors are notorious for stirring up dissent. It is what sells their papers.'

'I know that, but the trouble is, I agree with every word she says.'

'So you want me to defend her?'

'Yes, if it becomes necessary. As far as I know she has not yet been issued with a summons and my father might have a change of heart, though I doubt it.'

'It seems to me, my friend, that you are going to find yourself stuck between the devil and the deep. Is she worth it?'

It was a question he had been asking himself over and over again. Why was he so concerned? Why risk his father's wrath in a cause that could not be won? His mother had asked him to consider her because the Earl in a temper was something to be avoided for her sake. But he still wanted to help those in need. The ex-soldiers and out-of-work labourers were in need and so was Miss Wayland, even if she would not admit it. It was, he told himself, no more than that. He realised James was waiting for an answer to his question. Was she worth it? 'I think so,' he said, then added, 'but I do not want her to know who is paying for her defence if a case should come to court; she is obstinate and independent enough to refuse it.'

'Then I must be as philanthropic as you are,' James said with a smile. 'First I must give away land I do not own and provide tools, materials and seeds to a group of men I do not know, then I must defend a young lady who, by all accounts, is as stubborn as you are, from a charge for which there is no defence. You ask a lot, my friend.'

'I know, but you will do it, won't you?'

'For you, anything.'

'Good. And you will own the land because I propose to sell it to you for the princely sum of one guinea.'

'Why?'

'Because if the men know I own the land, they will be wary about accepting the idea. I want to stand apart from it. The only condition I make is that you use it for the common good.'

'And the seed and equipment?'

'I will open a bank account in the name of the society…'

'What name will that be?'

'I have not yet decided. I shall ask the men. It is, after all, their project.'

'Very well. I will wait to hear from you again.'

'Another thing,' Miles added as an afterthought. 'Have you discovered who owns Ravensbrook Manor?'

'Yes. Lord Brent. He lives in Cambridgeshire. I have written to him asking if the house is on the market; further than that I did not go. If he thinks you are keen to buy, he will undoubtedly ask a fortune for it and in my opinion it is not worth it, the state it is in. I have had no reply so far.'

Miles thanked him, took his leave and caught the stage back to Warburton and the Three Cups where he had left his mount.

He was riding out on to the road past Wayland's shop when he noticed Miss Wayland putting a notice in her window. He dismounted and went over to read it. She had seen him and gave a little nod in acknowledgement. He bowed in response and went closer to scrutinise the notice, then, tethering his horse to a post, he went inside.

He doffed his hat. 'Miss Wayland, good afternoon.'

'Good afternoon, my lord. What can I do for you?'

'Nothing, I thank you. I was intrigued by your offer to lend books.'

'Do you need to borrow a book, my lord?' She knew that was not at all likely, but could not think why he should come into the shop, unless it was to torment her.

He laughed. 'There are enough books at Ravens Park to stock a dozen libraries.' He went over to the shelves to peruse some of the titles. 'A very eclectic mix,' he said. 'And some of them must be valuable. Are you not afraid they will be stolen? The temptation to keep them or sell them to buy food and clothing will be great. And even if they are returned, they might be covered in dirty fingermarks, with the corners of the pages turned down.'

'I shall know who has borrowed each book and can remind them if they do not return them,' she said. 'As for dirty fingermarks, I would rather see a well-thumbed book than a pristine one. Books are meant to be read.'

'Is this another of your crusades—to get the populace reading?'

'Why not?'

'Why not, indeed? It is certainly safer than writing defamatory articles in your newspaper. I suppose it is no good trying once more to persuade you to retract.'

So that was why he had come! 'Not in the least.'

He realised it was said out of bravado, nothing more; she did not want him to know how worried she was. But he could tell from those expressive eyes that she was. 'Then I pity you, for I cannot see how you can defend your action.'

'I do not need your pity, my lord. I shall do very well without that.'

'Then I shall not waste it on you. Good day, Miss Wayland.' He replaced his hat on his head and left, wondering why he had even bothered to speak to her when she was so stubborn.

She could have told him she had decided to set the record straight over the widow's garden and how restitution had been made, though she had perhaps spoiled it from his point of view by implying it was done as a result of the publicity it had been given. The paragraph had been added to the account of the meeting on the common where she had said it had been the timely intervention of Viscount Cavenham that had saved the situation from becoming a bloodbath. 'It is to be hoped that the return of the Earl's son from the war will herald a change in attitude of those who have a responsibility towards lesser mortals over whom they hold sway,' she had ended. It was the closest she was prepared to go to admitting there was some good in the Viscount without, in any way, mitigating the behaviour of his father.

Miles rode out to the far side of the village on Wednesday morning to look at the land he meant to hand over to the workers. His father had no interest in it and it had been left uncultivated while he had been away and had become overgrown with bushes, brambles and rough grass. It would need a concerted effort on everyone's part to make it fertile. In the meantime, the men and their families had to live. There was so much more to the endeavour than he had first envisaged. He would have to finance it for at least a year, paying for everything the men needed and giving them enough money to live on until they could make a profit. His personal fortune, inherited, along with the land, from his maternal grandfather, was not huge, but fortunately his own needs were few. If the purchase of Ravensbrook Manor came to fruition, he might have to think again, but as such a move was not imminent, he did not regard it.

He called on Mrs Watson on his way home to tell Byers the project was to go ahead and there he encountered Miss Wayland again, interviewing Jack about his war service. He could see nothing controversial in that and joined in with a few of his own reminiscences. Their conversation of the day before was not mentioned, though it was in his mind. He wished he had not offered her pity; it was the last thing he should have done— sympathy, perhaps, but not pity.

'Tell me about Waterloo,' she said, doing her best to concentrate on Jack, though the presence of the Viscount was making her unaccountably nervous. Something intangible was drawing her to him and she did not know how to account for it or how to resist it. 'I believe Wellington said it was a close-run thing. And Napoleon Bonaparte fled the scene when he realised the day was lost.'

'So he did,' Miles said. 'I saw him briefly on a mound above the battle and then he was gone in that great coach of his.'

'He abandoned it to escape by ship, but it availed him nothing,' Jack said. 'He was forced to surrender and the coach was brought to London to be exhibited. Have you seen it, Miss Wayland?'

'No, it is some years since I was in the capital. What happened when the battle was over and you came home?'

'Nothing happened, miss, nothing at all. Not even a thank-you, much less a job.'

'But we hope to remedy that,' Miles put in. 'My friend is going forward with his plans to give all those who want it a strip of land to work in conjunction with others. The land is in poor heart, but can be made good and there is a barn that can be made into living accommodation for those who are homeless. The first year the project will be financed by my friend, but after that you must make it profitable.'

'Then we must pray for good weather,' Jack said.

'Are you going to tell me the name of this benefactor now?' Helen asked.

'No. He does not wish it revealed.'

'Then we must respect his wishes, but it will be good to publish some good news, even if we cannot say who is at the heart of it.'

'And if you drop a single hint that you think you know his identity, I shall take steps to have you stopped,' he said, looking sharply at her, making her more than ever convinced she knew.

He had left her talking to Jack and Mrs Watson and ridden home for nuncheon. The Wednesday edition of the *Warburton Record* had just been delivered and his father was hidden behind it. Miles kissed his mother's cheek and bade his father good morning before helping himself to food from the dishes on the sideboard. He began eating, waiting for his father to come out from behind the paper.

When he did the Earl's face was purple with rage. He flung the offending article down beside his plate. 'Are you determined to make me look a fool?' he raged. 'What, in heaven's name possessed you to go to that meeting? You knew I had ordered it to be broken up. Why the devil can't you mind your own business? That woman is enjoying humiliating me and I will not have it—especially I will not have it when my own son sides against me.'

'I am not siding against you,' Miles said, endeavouring not to raise his voice as his father was doing. 'I am not siding with anyone. I wanted to hear what was said and prevent trouble. That's what you wanted, surely?'

'What I want is to have that woman silenced. And for good.'

'What woman?' Miles asked mildly.

'Miss Helen Wayland, daughter of that mountebank, Henry Wayland, who encouraged her to be so mannish she has become unmarriageable. If she had been my daughter, you can be sure she would have been brought up very differently. She would have been a proper lady, learning to behave as ladies should. It's too late now, the damage is done and she must be dealt with.'

It was a strange speech and left more questions unanswered than it answered. That there had been a feud between his father and Henry Wayland he did not doubt, but it sounded as if his father regretted that Helen was not his daughter. If that were true, why did he persecute her?

'Dealt with?' Miles repeated. 'You mean dragging her through the courts and ruining her, I suppose.'

'It is the only way to teach her that she cannot hurl insults at me with impunity. I will not have my authority to do as I wish on my own land and with my own people questioned. That way leads to anarchy, and the Roger Blakestones and Jason Hardacres of this world will ruin a way of life that has held good since the dawn of time. Everyone has his place and should stick to it. And that is true for you, too, Miles. I wish you to curb your activities with the lower orders and behave as a son of mine should.'

Miles opened his mouth to protest that he did not appreciate being spoken to as if he were a child, but he saw his mother shaking her head and desisted.

Unable to provoke him, the Earl stood up. 'I am going to see Sobers about this. It is worse than defamation, it is sedition.' He left the room, taking the paper with him.

'What was in that newspaper to make him so angry?' his mother asked.

'I haven't seen it so I can only guess, but it was undoubtedly accusing Papa of sending in the militia to halt the meeting on the common and the fact that I stopped the troops laying about them and ordered them to leave the field. There were women and children there; I could not stand by and let them be battered to death.'

'Oh, Miles, will you never learn? I understand your sympathy with the lower orders, but you are not one of them and you cannot go wading into every cause that takes your fancy. And especially you must not appear to stand beside Miss Wayland against your father. She is not one of us and you know what he thinks of her.'

'I do and I wish I understood it. He may have had reason to hate Henry Wayland, that I do not know, but it is no reason to take his ire out on the daughter.'

'But he would not, Miles, if she did not provoke him so. I fear he is right and the only way to bring the conflict to an end is to have her silenced. You must see that.'

Unfortunately he did. If only Miss Wayland would silence herself there would be no need for a court case, but she was too proud, too convinced she was right, to do that. Now, it seemed, she had exacerbated her offence in his father's eyes by reporting the fracas on the common. And he did not doubt she had not spared the Earl and made matters between them worse.

'I am going to call on Lady Somerfield this afternoon,' his mother said, interrupting his thoughts. 'Will you accompany me? With all this unrest in the countryside against us, I am a little fearful.'

'Yes, of course. I will go and change.'

Half an hour later he returned, elegantly clad in a green single-breasted tailcoat, silk waistcoat striped in a lighter green and cream, a white-silk shirt with a starched white-muslin cravat elegantly tied and white pantaloons tucked into Hessian boots.

'Splendid,' she said, looking him up and down. 'I am sure you will impress Miss Somerfield.'

The idea had not been to impress Miss Somerfield, but not to disappoint his mother, but he let it pass.

Miss Somerfield, he had to admit when they were ushered into the drawing room of Gayton Hall, had become a dark-haired, dark-eyed beauty. The coltish schoolgirl was now an elegant young lady, with an enviable figure. After greeting Lady Somerfield first, as was correct, he bowed to Verity. 'Miss Somerfield, your obedient.'

'You remember Verity, do you not?' her mother said to him. Constance Somerfield was tall and upright in bearing and gave the impression she could not bend even if she wished to.

'Yes, indeed, my lady.' He smiled at Verity as he spoke. 'But it was many years ago and Miss Somerfield has grown in loveliness. I am persuaded she will have a string of suitors when she comes out.'

A faint blush stained Verity's cheeks. It was, he

noticed, nothing like the fiery red in Miss Wayland's cheeks when she was roused by something he said or did. He wondered why the newspaper proprietor had come into his mind just then. The two women were poles apart: one genteel, the other earthy. He supposed it was because he had been a soldier too long and acting the exquisite did not come naturally to him. He would rather be exchanging words with those who had to earn a living and knew what it was like to toil for their bread and the butter to put on it.

He was forced out of his reverie because his mother was speaking. 'Miles is settling down into civilian life now,' she said, 'but he has got out of the way of social intercourse.'

'Oh, I do not agree,' Verity put in with a light laugh. 'He has just paid as pretty a compliment as anyone who has been at the heart of society all along.'

He bowed to her. 'I spoke only the truth.'

'You will be coming to our ball, I hope?' Lady Somerfield said. 'We have sent out the invitations in good time, so that our guests do not find themselves booked elsewhere.'

'I am sure no one will turn down an invitation to Gayton Hall,' the Countess said. 'We shall certainly come. We are all three looking forward to it. It is why I called today, to bring our reply in person and so that Miles can become reacquainted with Verity.'

It implied he needed a head start over his rivals and Miles did not like that idea, but he could hardly contradict his mother, so he hastily changed the subject to the weather, which they all agreed was unprecedented in awfulness. Lady Somerfield said they had not been able to have even one picnic the whole year and had been forced to stay indoors and play cards. 'We have even lit the fires,' she said. 'And it will soon be June.'

'It has been the same at Ravens Park,' the Countess said. 'The garden is looking very bedraggled and hardly a flower to be seen.'

'It is hitting the farmers hard and throwing many good men out of work,' Miles put in, wondering if either woman understood the true implications of the bad weather. 'Already there is unrest and it can only become worse. Something needs to be done.'

His mother looked sharply at him. 'Miles is so used to being responsible for his men in the army, he cannot break the habit,' she explained to her hostess. 'Even when the labourers' problems are nothing to do with him.'

'It is to his credit,' Lady Somerfield said. 'But no one can help the weather.'

Miles did not like them talking about him as if he were not there and broke in with a laugh. 'I realise that, but I think something should be done to help the men. After all, when the weather improves we shall need them again, but if they are weak from hunger, they cannot work, can they? It makes economic sense to help them to stay fit and healthy.'

'Let us talk about something more cheerful,' his mother put in. 'Constance, would you and Verity take tea with us on Thursday afternoon?'

The offer accepted, the visit came to an end, Miles and his mother returned to their carriage for the journey home.

'I did not exaggerate, did I?' his mother said. 'Miss Somerfield is indeed a beauty.'

'Yes, but rather cool, I thought.'

'Cool?' she repeated. 'Whatever do you mean?'

'She is stiff and contained and she looks at her mother for guidance before she dare open her mouth. I cannot imagine her falling head over heels in love.'

'Falling in love, Miles? That is surely something the lower orders do. And it leads to all sorts of dangers.'

'Oh, Mama, where did you learn that nonsense?' He laughed. 'Did you not fall in love with Papa?'

'Certainly not!'

'No? Then how did you manage to live with him all these years and beget me into the bargain? Did Papa love you?'

'Miles, I do not think that is a subject to be discussed between mother and son.'

'Why not? It is something that has always puzzled me.'

'We were introduced to each other by our parents. My own parents pointed out what an advantageous marriage it would be for me and I trusted them. And in many ways it has been. I have the Earl's name and a place in society and I want for nothing...'

'Except love.'

'Oh, that is overrated. It is more important to be comfortable with each other.'

'Mama, you will never convince me of that. I want to be in love with the lady I marry, to feel she is the only one for me and I for her.'

'Then you had better set about falling in love with Verity Somerfield,' she said crisply, making him smile.

Chapter Four

They were driving through Warburton on the way home, when Miles noticed a small crowd outside the offices of the *Warburton Record*. 'What the devil's going on?' he murmured and called to the driver to pull up. He was out before the wheels had stopped turning. 'I will be back directly,' he told his mother as he left.

The crowd was, for the most part, made up of women, some with shopping baskets on their arms, some with children at their skirts. He did not need to speak for them to make way for him. There was a jagged hole in the glass of the window at the front of the shop and Helen was punching the rest out of it with a gloved hand and the end of the broom she carried.

'What happened?' he demanded.

'Someone threw a brick through the window.'

Her voice was flat, but he could detect the watery mixture of fear and anger in it.

'Are you hurt?'

'Luckily, no.'

'Who did it and why?'

'I do not know. I did not see anything. I was in the back room when I heard the glass shatter. Someone must have a real grudge against me. The Earl, perhaps…'

'Throwing bricks is surely beneath him.'

'He could have ordered one of his minions to do it.'

'You do not really believe that, do you? He doesn't need to stoop to such childishness.' He paused. 'But you have made other enemies besides my father, have you not? There was that fellow who accosted you on Saturday.'

'He believed I had betrayed him and was only warning me.'

'Perhaps this was to reinforce his warning.' He nodded towards the gaping hole. 'What are you going to do about that? You can't leave it open to the elements and anyone who takes a fancy to your belongings. All those books…'

'I'll find a piece of canvas and some timber. You go on your way. Your carriage is waiting.'

'Certainly not.' He turned to the women. 'Did any of you see who did this?'

They shook their heads.

'In that case, off home with you. There's nothing you can do. I will deal with this.'

They went reluctantly, muttering that no one was safe these days and it was a foolish thing to live alone like Miss Wayland did and carry on her father's business. Miles, who secretly agreed with them, ushered them away, then went over to his mother and told her what had happened. 'You take the carriage,' he said. 'I cannot leave Miss Wayland to struggle alone. When her shop is secure, I will come home.'

'Miles, must you? I am sure it is not a proper thing to do. Find a man to do it for her.'

'I will, but it must be one she trusts. She is very afraid, though she is pretending otherwise.'

'How will you get home?'

'Walk.'

'Three miles?'

'Mama, it is only a gentle stroll. I walked leagues more than that in the Peninsula.'

'That was before you were wounded.'

'The saw-bones assured me that walking would help to strengthen my muscles.'

'Very well, but do not be long. If your father finds out…'

'Mama, I am no longer a child to be ordered and scolded. I have become used to giving orders myself. I can deal with my father.'

'But when you quarrel there is such a bad feeling in the house, it makes me jumpy.'

'I am sorry for that, Mama, truly I am. If my father asks where I am, tell him you do not know.' He shut the door of the carriage and told the driver to take her ladyship home, then he returned to Helen, who had knocked out most of the remaining glass and swept it into a heap.

'Leave it and go inside,' he said, trying to take the broom from her, but she held on to it.

'My lord, if you think I am going to let you sweep the road outside my home and in that finery, too, you are mistaken. We would both be a laughing stock. It would not be good for my business or your image.'

'I cannot believe you are concerned about my image,' he said, ushering her into the shop, broom and all. A large brick lay in another heap of glass on the floor.

'I am not. But I have a business to run and it depends on the goodwill and respect of the townsfolk.'

He realised that, but it did not deter him. 'We must do something about this mess. Where is your young assistant?'

'I sent him to report the livestock auction in Swaffham. Farmer Harrison is selling his boar and it is enormous. Everyone wants to know how much it fetches. It was fortunate Edgar was absent, because the brick hit his table and showered it with glass before it slid across the floor. He would almost certainly have been injured, if not killed.'

'And the other one? The print setter.'

'Tom was in the back room, printing a poster.' She was staring down at the mess in a forlorn kind of way as if not knowing how to deal with it. It was unlike the forthright, practical woman he had come to know. He supposed everyone had their limits and maybe, after a year of struggling, she had reached hers.

'Not another seditious one, I hope.' It was said with a smile. Glass scrunched under his Hessians whenever he moved, so he stood still.

She managed a wan smile back. 'No, an advertisement for a dance at the Warburton Assembly Rooms to celebrate the anniversary of the victory at Waterloo. The proceeds are to go to the old soldiers.'

'And will you go?'

'I expect so. The Committee will expect a good report of it.'

'Then as it is such a worthy cause, perhaps I should put in an appearance, too. Where is Tom now?'

'He went off to deliver the posters and I told him he could go home afterwards. One of his children is sick and, as we don't print the paper today, I did not need him.'

It sounded as if she did not have enough work to keep them all busy and his sympathy for her increased. She was battling against overwhelming odds and he knew what that was like. 'You are alone in the house?'

'Betty is upstairs, but she is a timid soul and is terrified to come down.' She picked up the brick and put it on the table, then began sweeping the glass and torn paper into a heap.

'You need the help of a good strong man.'

She laughed. 'You, my lord?'

'Why not?'

'We are on opposite sides of the fence.'

'I am not on either side.'

'Sitting on the fence must be very uncomfortable, my lord.'

He laughed; she had retained her sense of

humour, so perhaps things were not so bad after all. 'I was thinking of asking one of the men to come in and help clear this up and do something about the window. And you need someone here all night…'

'My lord,' she gasped. 'You cannot possibly stay here all night. It would be most improper. We should never live it down. Betty and I will manage.'

'And if he comes back?' He spread his hands to encompass the mess. 'Some canvas and wood will not keep him out.'

'What makes you think he will come back? He has done what he set out to do…'

'Frighten you to death.'

'I am not frightened. I am angry.'

He did not believe her. 'All the same, you cannot be left here with only a young girl for protection. Who among the men do you trust?'

'I do not know whom I can trust. Any single one of them could have done this.'

'What about Jack Byers? Do you trust him?'

'Yes, but he is at Ravensbrook.'

He went to the gaping hole that had been the window and looked about him for someone to send. The women had all obeyed his instructions and gone home; the only man to be seen was the idiot he had seen on the common. He seemed to be watching the shop, grinning and dancing about from one foot to the other in boots far too big for him. Had he put the brick through the window? 'Hey, you,' he shouted, stepping outside. 'Come here, will you?'

The fellow fled as he had before. Miles shrugged and turned to look about him. Jack Byers's oldest boy was dawdling along the road with his hands in his trouser pockets. He called him across and despatched him to fetch his father as fast as he could. Then he went back to Helen.

'Thank you, my lord,' she said. 'I am sure Mr Byers will make the room weather-tight.'

If it was meant as a dismissal, he ignored it. He would not go until he had helped Jack make the place as secure as they could and arranged for him to keep watch on the place all night until the glass could be replaced the following day. 'I will wait until he arrives.'

'But, my lord, he might not be easily found and it is a long walk. It might be hours.'

'Oh, I am sure we can amuse ourselves. Do you think Betty will make us some tea?'

'Of course.' She left him to go upstairs to ask the maid to produce refreshments and bring them downstairs. She would not invite him into her living quarters; it was better for their reputations to stay in the shop in full view of passers-by. When she returned downstairs he had not only swept up all the glass and filled an empty box with it, but had taken every last shard from the frame so no one could be cut by it. It left the shop wide open and the wind was swirling about. The clouds were lower over the roofs, too, and it looked as though there would be more rain before long.

'I think it would be wise to move the books to the back of the shop,' he said, putting down the brush and shovel he had found in the back room. 'If the rain comes in, they will be ruined.' He began suiting action to words and she followed suit, piling the books on the floor as far from the window as possible.

'My lord, why are you doing this?' she asked. 'You must have other calls on your time.'

'Did you expect me to walk by on the other side of the road?'

'You were not walking. You could easily have driven past.'

He stopped, his arm full of books, to look at her. 'When I see a lady needing help and I am able to offer it, then I do so. There are times when a woman needs a willing man.'

She laughed. 'And you are willing?'

He looked sideways at her, a faint smile on his lips. He could so easily have misinterpreted her question. 'To shift books, yes.'

She realised his answer was meant to establish their relationship was nothing more than chivalry on his part. A son of the Earl of Warburton, chivalrous? That took some believing, except that he had never been anything else towards her. 'Then I thank you, but I really can manage.'

'Don't be so obstinate, Helen. You need help and I am here to help.' He paused. 'Unless you make it very clear you do not want me or need me.'

'Oh.'

'So?'

She hesitated; she had been frightened and was not sure, even now, that whoever had thrown that brick was not still watching her. Why he wanted to help her she could not fathom, but she would be a fool to reject his offer. 'My lord, I would not be so ungrateful.'

'Then let us finish moving these books.' And, as Betty came down the stairs carrying a tray, 'Ah, here is our tea.'

The girl put the tray on the table, bobbed a curtsy and scuttled back to the upper regions.

There was bread and butter and cakes on the

tray besides a pot of tea. They left the remainder of the books to sit at the table on the side furthest from the draught from the window and Helen poured the tea.

''Tis is like having a picnic,' he said, helping himself to bread and butter, knowing that a five-course meal was being served at Ravens Park. Somehow he knew he was enjoying this repast more. 'Do you like to go on picnics, Helen?'

She ignored his frequent use of her given name; to have made a fuss about it would only stir him into further impropriety and she was too exhausted and too muddled in her head to exchange that kind of banter with him. 'I rarely have the time. We used to go when my mother was alive. The fresh air was good for her.'

'How long since she passed away?'

'Six years. Papa died a year ago.'

'I am sorry, I did not mean to make you sad. Have you no other relations?'

'None that approve of me.' She gave him a wry smile. 'My father had no family and my mother's family are rather proper. They deplored the way my father brought me up. Mannish, they said, unmarriageable, and I am persuaded they were right.'

'That is nonsense,' he said, appraising her figure with appreciation. 'You are nothing like a man.'

'I am too tall and thin and my hair is too short for a lady.'

'What decided you to wear your hair like that?'

'I have no one to dress it—Betty is hopeless at it and I cannot spare the time to struggle with it myself, so I took the scissors to it.'

'It is very pretty. I like it. And as for being un-marriageable, I must disagree there, too. I am sure if you were to...'

She laughed while he struggled for words that would not offend her. 'Put myself in line, you mean? Make myself available?'

'Yes, I suppose that is what I meant, though I would not have expressed it so forthrightly.'

'Well, I will not do it. The marriage market is all so false, to-ing and fro-ing, tiptoeing around, following convention and making polite meaningless conversation. All for what? As far as the woman is concerned it is to become the property of her husband along with everything else she owns, to subject herself to his will however much it might run counter to her own. I prefer my independence, then I can at least try to do some good in the community, even if it is only pointing out wrongs.'

'Oh, dear, that has put me in my place.'

'Not at all, my lord. We were not talking of you, were we?'

'No,' he agreed swiftly. 'But would you never make an exception? There must be some merit in having someone with whom to share your problems and triumphs. Wanting to be with them no matter what.'

'When I meet such a one I will let you know, my lord.'

It put an end to that particular strand of conversation; as the food had all been consumed and the tea drunk, they returned to moving the books. Jack Byers had not arrived by the time they had finished and they sat down again to wait for him. Helen did not want to resume their previous conversation; it had been too personal for comfort. He had drawn things out of her that she had never told anyone before, but if she were honest with herself, there had been no one to tell: not Tom or Edgar or Betty.

'Have you heard what the men think of the market-garden idea?' she asked.

'No, although I believe Byers has arranged a meeting.'

'Will you attend it?'

'I have not made up my mind. I am only the

agent for the owner, after all, and must stand back from it. I do not want to interfere.'

She laughed. 'Viscount Cavenham, son of the Earl of Warburton, not wanting to interfere. That must surely be a first.'

'You do not always have to link my name with my father's, you know,' he said. 'I am perfectly capable of standing on my own.'

'Oh, I am sure you are and therefore to be held—'

'At arm's length,' he finished for her.

'I was going to say "in respect",' she said.

'That is a whisker. You have no more respect for me than you have for my father.' His once-pristine clothes had become dusty and smudged with dirt. White pantaloons and shiny black Hessians were not suitable wear for doing dirty jobs. He did not seem to mind, but then he did not have to clean them and, if they were past cleaning, he could easily purchase more.

'On the contrary, my lord. You have earned some respect. He has not. He has only ever earned fear. I wonder why that is?'

'So do I. It might help me to understand him.'

'Do you not understand him?'

'No, I do not think anyone does.'

She sighed. 'Do you think he really will take me to court?'

'I do not know. Let us hope he relents. He might, if you were to retract.'

They were back to that again, but she did not have to answer because Jack Byers had arrived and Miles turned to tell him what he wanted done. He was despatched to buy heavy canvas, some nails and wood. Miles turned to Helen. 'Do you have a hammer?'

'There will be one in my father's toolbox, I expect. He was always mending things. It's in the back room.'

She took him through to show him where the box was kept and he brought it back to the front of the shop and put it on the table. 'It will only be a temporary repair until you can call in a glazier,' he said, sorting through the tools to find what he wanted. 'Can you do that first thing tomorrow?'

'Yes,' she said, wondering how she was going to pay the man. Something would have to be sold. But what? Almost everything of any value had already gone.

'Ask for good-quality glass or you'll end up with inferior that will be broken again as soon as someone leans against it.'

She was suddenly angry again. Did he not know

how much the best glass cost? 'And if someone else decides to throw a brick through my window, will it avail me to have bought the most expensive glass?' she snapped. 'It will still shatter.'

He realised his mistake at once and called himself all kinds of a fool. He should have let her buy what she could afford and tipped the glazier to substitute a better quality. Too late now. 'Let us pray you are never subjected to this treatment again,' he said.

Jack returned, pulling a handcart containing a folded canvas, several good strong planks and a box of nails. The two men set about nailing up the canvas and then fastening the planks over it, so close together that even if someone ripped the cloth, they could not squeeze between the bars. The result was a shop in complete darkness. Miles left Jack finishing off outside and went indoors. In the dark, he bumped into Helen. She gave a little squeal of fright. He grabbed her to stop her falling.

'It's only me,' he said gently, feeling the softness of her in his arms. Whatever made her think she was mannish? he asked himself—she was every inch a woman. He could feel her heart beating erratically against his chest and realised she was far more frightened than she admitted. He put one hand up to the back of her head, which nestled comfortably in his shoulder. She made no move to back away and he did not put her from him. This woman, this lovely woman, needed him and who was he to complain about that? He hadn't had a woman in his arms since… Oh, since that brief affair in Lisbon. It had come to an end when Maria, visiting him in hospital after the surgeon had dug the shrapnel from his thigh, had seen the bloody bandages and fled in disgust, a foretaste of what he could expect in the future. It had made him very wary of close contact with women, yet here he was, embracing one.

Her curls were soft as a baby's and smelled of rose water. He wound one round his finger and let it spring away before stroking the back of his hand down her cheek and taking her chin gently between finger and thumb. She made no move to free herself and he was about to succumb to temptation and bend his head to find her lips with his own, when he suddenly came to his senses. Instead he said, 'You are safe now.'

'Yes, silly me.' She was shaking, sure that he had been about to kiss her and wondering why he had not. Chivalry again? Or the sudden realisation of how far beneath him she was? 'For a moment I thought it was Mr Blakestone grabbing me again. It could only have been you or Jack, couldn't it?'

'I am glad it was me.' She had still not moved backwards and he would not be the one to break contact while she was content to stay there. 'Do you think it was Blakestone who threw the brick? Or that idiot, perhaps? He seemed very interested in what was going on.'

'I do not know.' Slowly she backed away. His arms felt suddenly empty and he was tempted to reach out and grab her back again, but she was retreating into the darkness, talking as she went. 'It must have been something I wrote in the paper, though apart from writing about the hunt and Mrs Watson's garden, and reporting the militia riding onto the common and laying about them, I cannot think of anything. Your father has his own way of punishment, so it must have been the organisers of the meeting, or perhaps one of the soldiers. I did lambaste them rather heavily.'

He heard a flint being struck and then the room was feebly lit by a taper. He saw her hand reach out and put it to the wick of an oil lamp and then they could see each other again. Her cheeks were bright pink and her hair tousled. There was a spot of dirt on one eyebrow and a slight scratch on one cheek, but she was beautiful in the soft glow of the lamp. He felt his heart give a sudden lurch. She was dangerous, this one, dangerous and desirable. And not for him.

He pulled himself together as Jack joined them. 'That should hold out intruders and keep the place dry,' he said, fracturing the fragile moment. 'Is there anything else you want me to do?'

'No, I do not think so.' It was Miles who answered. Helen seemed not to have heard him. Her expression had a dreamy quality about it and her eyes were unfocused, as if she had only just woken from a dream.

'Thank you, Mr Byers,' she said, pulling herself together. 'If you wait, I will pay you.'

''Tis already been done,' he said. He touched his forelock. 'Goodnight, Miss Wayland.'

Jack left and Miles hurried after him, delving in his pocket for more coins. His inclination was to send him on his way and stay with Helen himself, but he knew that would be reckless in the extreme. She was right to say she depended on the goodwill of the townspeople. He could not, would not, do anything to jeopardise that. 'Can you keep an eye on the place tonight? The Three Cups is directly across the road. You could watch it from there. I'll have a word with the landlord before I go. And fetch the glazier for Miss Wayland in the morning.'

'Yes, my lord, 'tis a pleasure.'

Miles handed him some money and watched him cross the road to the inn, then went back inside.

'My lord, you must tell me how much I owe you,' Helen said.

'Nothing. Whoever did it should pay.'

'But we do not know who it was.'

'I will find out, if only to clear my father.'

'Oh.' She realised her accusation had rankled, but it had been said in the heat of the moment when he turned up so unexpectedly; she could not, in all conscience, imagine his lordship ordering anyone to throw a brick through her window. He had far more effective weapons.

'I will take my leave now,' Miles said, before she could put that into words. 'I suggest you lock and bolt the door after me and then go up to your rooms and rest. You have had a trying day. I will come back tomorrow and see the glazier has done his job properly. And you will need help returning the books to the shelves.'

'My lord—'

'I will hear no protests.' He took her hand, a grubby, careworn hand stained with printer's ink, and lifted it to his lips. 'Until tomorrow.' And then he was gone, leaving an emptiness behind him. The light flickered, casting strange shadows on the walls and over the stretched canvas, making her shiver. If only he could have stayed. She still felt nervous.

But her nervousness was not only because of the fright she had had, but because she felt something momentous was happening to her. It had begun when she fell against him and he had held her close for far longer than was needed to be sure she had safely regained her balance. She should have pulled herself away and maintained her independence. Instead she had clung to him, felt his gentle fingers tracing the outline of her face and didn't want him to stop. It had sent unexplained shivers down her body and a strong desire to press herself even closer to him. That was what was happening, she decided, her independence was being eroded. And she could not have that happen, could she? Not for worlds.

Just to prove she could resist, she took the lamp to her desk and began writing a piece about the plans to provide the unemployed men with land to work. The newspaper had to be printed the following day and she had not yet assembled all of it, something she always did the day before publication. The scratching of her pen seemed extraordinarily loud. All the sounds in the street were loud: footsteps, dogs barking, cats yowling, an empty bottle being tossed along on the wind, which seemed to be stronger than ever, rain pattering on the canvas. The Viscount would not be home yet; he would be soaked and catch a chill. The idea that he might be made ill on her account was worrying. Why had he stayed so long? And why did she wish he had stayed even longer? It was not only fear of whoever threw that brick; it was something far more profound than that.

She gave up and put down her pen. Picking up the lamp, she toiled upstairs with it, suddenly so tired her feet dragged with every step. Was it worth all this upset and hard work and animosity, just so that she could tell herself she was a purveyor of truth? It was a question she did not attempt to answer as she tumbled into bed. Her last thought before she dropped into an exhausted sleep was not of the *Warburton Record*, but of Miles, Viscount Cavenham, holding her in his arms.

Her sleep was disturbed by unusual sounds coming from downstairs. She rose, lit a candle, put on a dressing gown and, carrying the light in one hand and a poker in the other, went down, stopping on every step to listen, her heart in her mouth. The wind was gusting and rain was beating on the canvas, making it bellow in and out. The planks were creaking, but the nails were holding them. No one had broken in. With a sigh of relief, she put the candlestick and poker on the table and subsided into a chair beside it.

She should have gone back to bed, but she knew going back to sleep was impossible. There was too much going on in her head. She had made enemies, just as her father had, but she was no longer sure who they were. The Earl, yes, but what of the son? She did not understand him. He defended his father and yet everything he did belied that: helping Mrs Watson, preventing a riot, thinking of ways to help the unemployed. But that did not mean he was on her side, did it? His methods were far more subtle. He used kindness as a weapon and that was much harder to resist than hate and threats. But resist she must or he would weaken her.

In despair, she put her arms on the table and her head on her arms, only to be roused by a furious knocking on the front door. She rose and groped her way to it and was about to pull back the bolt, when caution made her hesitate. 'Who is it?' she called.

'Jack Byers.'

She opened the door and a gust of wind swept rain onto the mat as he stepped inside and stood peering into the room behind her. 'I saw a light flickering...'

'It was only me. I thought I heard something and came down, but it was only the wind and rain on the canvas. What are you doing here? I thought you had gone back to Ravensbrook.'

'No, his lordship asked me to stay and keep watch from the Three Cups.'

'He did?' she asked in surprise. 'Why?'

'Perhaps he thought the fellow would come back, though I doubt it myself. Foolish thing to do, that would be.'

'He said he wanted to catch him.'

'I doubt he'll be caught now, if no one saw him. But if you do not need me, I will go back across the road.'

'You could go home. I am sure I shall be safe now.'

'Miss Wayland, you forget, I have no home; as his lordship has paid for me to stay the night in the front bedroom of the Three Cups, I might as well take advantage of it. It will soon be dawn anyway. Lock up again after me.'

She was alone again, more confused than before. Why had the Viscount asked Jack to keep an eye on her premises? To catch someone who was probably miles away by now? Out of the goodness of his heart? Did a Cavenham have a heart? Oh, she knew he had because she had felt it beating against hers when he held her. Why did she keep remembering that and how it had felt? How warm and safe. She did not want to be warm and safe, she wanted to be cool and angry.

She bolted the door again, went upstairs and decided to dress and do some work. Sleep was out of the question.

Helen had taken a lamp downstairs and gone into the back room. It had a window in there, a window mercifully undamaged, and as she had worked, the sky had lightened and the lamp became unnecessary. She laid aside her pen, flexed her stiff fingers and stood up. It was time to open up. She unbolted the front door and propped it wide open, to let in the light and tell everyone that a little thing like a broken window would not deter her.

Tom and Edgar arrived at their usual time and she had to explain to them what had happened before they could get down to work. They were both shocked and said she should have sent to them for help. 'I had some help,' she said.

Betty came down, worried that her mistress was not in her bed, and was despatched to bring breakfast down for everyone. They were in the middle of eating it, sitting at the worktable, when Jack Byers arrived with a glazier. The two men removed the planks and canvas and set about repairing the window. Light streamed in. The rain had stopped, but the clouds were still too lowering for the sun to break through. Tom and Edgar began the day's work while Helen started to rearrange the books on the shelves.

She had barely begun when a skinny little man in a black suit of clothes arrived and thrust a sealed document into her hand, bowed and was gone. She knew what it was.

Chapter Five

Her hand shook as she opened it. She was summoned to attend the quarter sessions at Norwich on Tuesday, the eleventh day of June, to answer a charge that she, on Wednesday, the twenty-second of May, unlawfully, wickedly and maliciously did cause to be published a certain defamatory libel concerning his lordship, the Earl of Warburton.

She had been deliberately not thinking about it in the hope that the Earl might change his mind, but here it was and she had no defence. She knew there was a law that allowed defendants to engage an attorney to represent them in court, but she could not afford to do that and the scales of justice were weighted against her. And in spite of their support she must think of her employees. The answer was to retract publicly, humiliate herself in front of the judge and beg for leniency. Oh, how the Earl would gloat! And what would the outcome be? A newspaper that published only milk-and-water articles with no depth or fire and dare not say a word against the oppressors. She could almost hear her father admonishing her, 'Which is more important, to tell the truth as you see it, or let the Earl walk all over you? You are not my daughter if you let him bully you.'

She was torn in two. Bow the knee and grovel or try to defend her actions? What defence could she offer that a judge would accept? That she did not intend to defame the Earl; that he had misunderstood what she had written? That would be laughed out of court. Besides, it wasn't true. She had intended to humiliate him, to stir up the population against him. Not only that, she had exacerbated it by writing what she had about the behaviour of the militia on the common. 'Uncontrolled violence against innocents,' she had called it. 'Bloodlust.'

Somewhere, in the back of her mind, there stirred a doubt. What was she hoping to achieve? Had her father's hate and contempt spawned hate and contempt in her that had nothing to do with justice? Her mother would have deplored that. She had been a gentle soul, able to curb some of her husband's wilder statements. When she died, that influence had been lost and he became more vitriolic than ever. 'It is for the good of the towns-people,' he had told Helen. 'They have no one else to fight for them.'

Were the people of Warburton and its surrounds any worse off than those in the rest of the country? Life was hard for labourers and ex-soldiers everywhere. All over East Anglia there were riots, men marching, destroying machinery, burning barns, threatening the farmers, the parsons and the squires. Only the week before, there had been serious disturbances in Cambridgeshire and several arrests had been made. Before long it would reach Warburton and certainly would if Blakestone and Hardacre had their way. The government was terrified of revolution as had happened in France and the courts were being kept busy. What chance did she have in that kind of atmosphere? How was she going to pay a fine? How could she endure a spell in prison? It had as good as killed her father—would it kill her, too? And what ought she to do about Edgar and Tom and Betty?

She was still worrying about it when the Viscount arrived to help her restore the books to the shelves. His smiling countenance was more than she could bear. 'You...' She had a book in her hand. Before she knew it, she had thrown it at him. His reaction was swift. He lifted a hand and caught it deftly. 'I suppose that is one way to restore the books to the shelves,' he said, laughing and putting it on the shelf behind him. 'Shall we do them all that way?'

'You may laugh.'

'But you looked so furious. What has happened to put you in such a taking?'

'Nothing.' She did not want to hear him telling her it was her own fault for refusing to retract, which he would undoubtedly do if she told him about the summons. 'I was upset…'

'I am sorry to hear that. Is there anything I can do to help?'

'No, my lord. I shall recover directly.'

'What about the books?'

'Tom and Edgar will help me with them.'

'Then I will leave you and come back another time when you are more yourself.' With that he turned on his heel and limped away.

'You didn't oughta ha' done that,' Jack Byers said quietly.

'I know.' She wanted to rail at him, too, and at Edgar whose mouth was open wide enough to catch a whale, but it wasn't their fault. Mortified by her burst of temper, she took a deep breath to steady herself. 'Thank you for your help, Mr Byers. I can manage now.'

He left and she turned to her staff, calmer now, though no less worried. 'Come on, we have work to do if we are to get the next edition out on time. Edgar, finish that report on the market auction. Tom, the front page is ready so you can make a start on setting that up. Betty, clear away this tray and see to your work upstairs.'

Betty picked up the tray and fled to the upper regions. Edgar bent to his work and Tom disappeared into the back room. Helen put the writ to one side and set to work laying out the pages for the next edition. It took all her will-power not to look at the summons and keep her mind on what she was doing.

An hour later a stranger arrived in a spanking curricle. He was in his early thirties, she guessed, dressed in a black tailcoat, grey-and-white striped pantaloons, pristine white shirt and black waistcoat. He doffed a polished beaver hat. 'Miss Wayland?'

'Yes,' she answered warily, wondering if he might be delivering another summons.

'My name is James Mottram. I am an attorney.'

'I did not send for an attorney.'

'No, but I am interested in cases like yours.'

'What do you know about my case?'

His smile never wavered. He had a rather pleasant smile. 'I read the *Warburton Record* regularly and I saw the item about the hunt trampling the widow's garden and guessed you might be in trouble. It was borne out when the case for libel came into our office for prosecution.'

'And I suppose, like everyone else, you have come to ask me to retract what I said.'

'Not at all. I have come to help you defend it. Always supposing you wish to do that.'

'I am told it is indefensible.'

'Shall we see?'

'It will avail you nothing. I cannot pay a lawyer. And if you have been asked to prosecute, how can you act for the defence?'

'It is my colleague, Mr Sobers, who is prosecuting, not I.'

'It makes no odds, I still cannot afford a lawyer.'

'I do not require payment from you.'

She gave a shaky laugh. 'Lawyers never do things from the goodness of their hearts.'

He smiled. 'No, you are right. But funds have been made available for cases such as yours by those who value the freedom of the press and do not wish to see it eroded.'

'Who are these people?'

'They would remain anonymous.' He chuckled. 'They would hardly risk landing in the dock themselves for aiding and abetting, would they?'

'I suppose not.'

'May we sit down somewhere privately and discuss the matter?'

There was nowhere private on the ground floor, so she took him up to her sitting room. It was a large room, being the twin of the shop below it. It was comfortably furnished with good solid pieces, which had been there when they arrived from London, and her father had not seen fit to replace them. There were a couple of sofas, a table with some high-backed chairs around it, a bookshelf on one side of the fireplace and shelves containing china ornaments on the other. There was nothing elegant about it, except for the escritoire and the ornaments that had been her mother's.

She ushered him in, but left the door open so that Betty was within calling distance. It was done as a sop to convention, not because she believed herself in any kind of danger. She bade him be seated. 'May I offer you refreshments?' she said. 'Tea or coffee or something stronger?'

'Tea, if you please.' He flung up his tails and

sat in a chair at the table where he could spread out his papers.

She called to Betty to make tea and sat opposite him. 'I do not see what you can do,' she said. 'I know enough of the law to know that ignorance is no defence. Besides, I knew what I was doing.'

'What were you doing, Miss Wayland?' he asked mildly. 'What was your intention?'

'To make a certain person take notice and make amends.'

'To succeed in a complaint of defamation,' he said, 'it is necessary to show that the words used have exposed the plaintiff to hatred, contempt or ridicule. Did you intend to ridicule that person?'

She hesitated, considering her answer. Ridicule had not been in her mind—she had been too incensed to poke fun. 'No.'

'What about bringing that person into disrepute, making him the object of hatred or scorn?'

'Scorn? No, not scorn. And I do not need to tell anyone about his reputation—it is well known.'

He laughed at her evasiveness, perfectly understanding. 'But you did mean what you said?'

'I meant every word. The hunt should not be allowed to trample down poor people's gardens with impunity.'

'And that is the only point you were making?'

She hesitated, knowing, in her heart, that there was more to it than that, but he would not understand. 'Yes.'

'We might get you off on that.'

It sounded like hope he was offering, but she could not quite believe it. 'I doubt it will help because the article about the hunt is not all I have written against the Earl.' She reached for the latest edition of the newspaper containing the report of the fracas on the common and handed it to him to read.

'Dear me,' he said after perusing it. 'It could be claimed this is seditious, a far more serious matter.'

'And no doubt it has made you change your mind about helping me.' She could not disguise the hopelessness in her voice.

'I shall have to consult the people instructing me. It may be that I can continue to advise you, but he—they—might think it too serious.' He stood up to leave. As he reached the door, he turned back. 'Miss Wayland, why do you do this?'

She was still sitting at the table, her head in her hands. At the sound of his voice, she looked up. 'Because it needs to be said and the press needs to be free to say it.'

'Quite,' he said, placing his hat upon his dark

head. 'Good day to you, Miss Wayland. I will see you again.'

She heard him go down the stairs, bid good day to Edgar and leave the shop. Betty came in with the tea tray. 'Oh, has he gone?'

'Yes.'

'He's not going to help you, then?'

'Were you listening at the door?'

'No, miss, you left it open.'

There was no denying that. 'Then you know he has to consult whoever is paying him.'

'Who might that be?'

'I have no idea. Someone with grand ideas about the freedom of the press, but not the stomach to do anything about it themselves.'

James found Miles where they had arranged to meet at the old barn on the piece of land that Miles was going to donate to the men. He was inspecting the woodwork for soundness and considering how it could be divided up into living quarters for families. He had come straight here from his last confrontation with Miss Wayland. What he had done to deserve having a book thrown at him, he could not imagine, but whatever it was, it was something that had thrown her into a temper. My, she was magnificent in a temper, her hazel eyes flashing, her cheeks bright pink and her curls bouncing.

He turned as James approached on foot, having left his curricle in the lane. 'What do you think of this?' he said, indicating the building. 'We could put in a floor to make a second storey and walls to divide it into six little houses, three on each side, back to back.'

'If you say so. Have you costed it?'

'No, but I will do so.'

'You know, the way you are throwing your money at the project, it will never be profitable enough for the men to repay you.'

'Never mind that. It is enough that they have work and their self-respect. Did you see Miss Wayland?'

'I did.'

'And did she throw anything at you?'

'No, why should she?'

'I don't know.' He smiled at the memory. 'She threw a book at me.'

'Whatever for?'

'I have no idea. She was in a compliant mood last night, but then she had had a bad fright, but this morning she rediscovered her courage and let me have it.'

'So, do you want to withdraw your support?'

'No, of course not.'

'I ask because this morning she was served with a writ.'

'Oh, that explains it!' He laughed. 'She cannot throw books at my father, so she throws them at me instead. Poor girl. If I had known...' He paused. 'Just what has she let herself in for?'

'The summons is for defamation of character, but she showed me another article in which she condemns the militia for the way they put down a seditious meeting.'

'I know. I was there.'

'Will your father, the Earl, do anything about that?'

'I do not know. I hope he will consider the charge of defamation punishment enough.'

'So do you still want me to try to defend her?'

'Yes, of course.'

'Very well, but Miss Wayland would do better to plead guilty and throw herself on the mercy of the court. Given that she is a rather lovely young woman...'

'You think she is lovely, too, do you?'

'Well, she is or why would you be wanting to help her?'

Miles laughed. 'Why, indeed?'

'She could try weeping and promising not to do

it again. I have known people do that and get off with a shilling fine and a recognisance to be on good behaviour.'

Miles burst into laughter at this picture of Helen Wayland. 'Oh, you try suggesting that. I'll wager she will throw a book at you if one comes to hand. It might even be an inkstand. That could be rather messy.'

James sighed. 'If you were not my friend, I would not touch the case.'

'But you are my friend, are you not?'

'For my sins, yes. I had better go and do some probing. When are you going to start on this?' He indicated his surroundings with a movement of his hand.

'As soon as I have gathered the men together and discovered what they want.'

James went back to his curricle and Miles continued to look over the old barn, pacing out its dimensions and making notes. He was standing with his back to the lane, staring up at the roof, wondering if it would have to be rethatched when he became aware of a rustling in the long grass behind him and turned to see Miss Wayland picking her way towards him, holding her grey skirt out of the wet grass. He waited, wondering what sort of mood she was in before addressing her.

She stopped six feet from him, bent her head slightly, as politeness dictated. 'My lord, good afternoon.'

So far so good. He smiled. 'Good afternoon, Miss Wayland. You are somewhat far from home.'

'I came with the men who are come to look over the land.' She nodded her head backwards where a line of men walked round the field. 'We borrowed a farm cart from Mr Thomson.'

'You are welcome to attend the meeting, as long as you remain silent.'

'I will not say a word.'

'And do not throw things.' It was said with a broad grin.

'My lord, I am sorry for that. You caught me at a very bad moment…'

'Evidently.'

'I did not mean to hurt you.'

'I am glad of that..I dread to think what damage you could do if you really meant it.'

'Don't tease. I am trying to apologise. I am sorry, truly I am.'

'Then your apology is accepted and we will not mention it again.'

'Thank you. I also owe you for canvas and timber and nails and goodness knows what else. I discovered Jack Byers was staying at the Three

Cups to watch the shop at your behest. You did not need to do that, my lord.'

'Oh, but I did. Canvas and planks would not keep out a determined intruder. I could not stay with you...'

'I should think not!'

'Much as I would have liked to,' he went on, as if she had not spoken. 'I do so enjoy our little heart-to-heart talks.'

'Heart-to-heart,' she repeated. 'I would hardly call them that.' Even as she spoke she remembered being held in his arms and feeling his heart beating close to hers. She felt the colour flare in her face. 'We have nothing at all in common.'

'I don't agree,' he said calmly. 'We have much in common. For instance, we are both concerned about the plight of the out-of-work labourers and want to do something to help, even if we go about it in different ways.'

'Of course we do. I cannot afford to hand over land and barns and goodness knows what else. Besides, that only helps a few. What they need is help from the government so all may benefit. To get that they need publicity, a general outcry...'

'Such as provided by Blakestone and his friend Hardacre. I think not. That is anarchy.'

'I meant newspaper publicity.'

'But does that work?'

'It would if I were left to do it, but, no, I have to be hounded like a criminal.'

'A criminal, Helen?' His voice was gentle. 'Surely not?'

'Yes, thanks to your father. Today I was served a writ to appear at the quarter sessions to answer a charge of defamation of character.'

'Ah, that was the reason for pelting me with books, was it?'

'It was only one book and you said you would not mention it again.'

'So I did. Now it is my turn to be sorry.'

He did not sound a bit sorry, but was smiling at her. 'It is easy for you to smile,' she said. 'You do not have a summons hanging over you. The Earl would have me ruined.'

'Would it ruin you?'

'Imprisonment or even a heavy fine certainly will. I cannot pay my workers if the business is not a going concern; without me, I do not see how it can be. Tom and Edgar cannot run it on their own.'

'But that did not stop you writing what you did. You must have known that it would bring trouble down on your head.'

'Is that a good enough reason for not doing what

you believe to be right, my lord? Or mayhap you think it is? I imagine you would buckle under for a peaceful life.'

'No, or I would never have gone to war.'

'I was not speaking of war; that is a different thing altogether. I was speaking of justice. Do you think I will get justice?'

'I should like to think you will.' He searched her face, the bleak worried eyes, the pallor, the slightly parted lips that made him want to kiss the breath out of her. The fire had gone out of her and he longed to take her in his arms and tell her he would make it all right again, but he could not make it right. The law would take its course. 'What do you propose to do about it?'

'I am not going to grovel, you can be sure of that.' Briefly the fire flared up again. 'And I have been offered help.'

'Good.'

'Do you know a gentleman called James Mottram? He says he is an attorney.'

He hesitated before answering. 'Did he say he knew me?'

'No, I just wondered. He told me he is representing a group of people anxious to maintain the freedom of the press and is prepared to defend me, at least against the defamation, though he was not so sure about anything else.'

'I am sure he will do that, too, if you allow it.'

'How do you know?' she asked sharply.

'As it happens, I am acquainted with Mr Mottram. He is the gentleman who owns this land and barn.'

'He is?' she queried in surprise. 'But I thought…'

'You thought it was me?'

'Yes, I suppose I did.'

'I am sorry to disappoint you. I am not the philanthropist you thought I was.'

'I should have known better. A Cavenham a philanthropist!' She gave a brittle laugh. 'Hell will freeze over before that happens.'

He had really cooked his goose now, he decided. They were back to where they were when he had pulled up in Mrs Watson's garden. She was just as furious as she had been then, and he just as misunderstood. It was all very well to do good by stealth, but when it alienated the person he most wanted to please, he began to wonder if it was worth it. He was in a cleft stick. His philanthropy would infuriate his father; though he did not trouble himself too much about that, he knew it would upset his mother and bring on one of her bad turns, so he would not risk making it

public. On the other hand, he hated being at odds
with Helen. They did have much in common: their
compassion for those in need and their love of
justice and fairness. He admired her courage, the
passion she showed for the causes she adopted,
her loveliness and her vulnerability. He had held
her in his arms and he could not forget that. He
wished he could do it again now and soothe her
prickliness away. She would be outraged if he did
and who could blame her?

'Are you going to let the gentleman help you?'
he asked.

'I might as well. No one else will.' And with
that she turned from him to the men who were
making their way towards them.

She watched Miles usher the men into the barn
out of the wind and followed them, standing a
little apart, listening to what they had to say. It
would take the rest of the summer to make the
land good, they told him. The scrub would have
to be rooted out, the larger stones removed and
the soil turned over and fertilised before anything
could be made to grow in it. It would be spring
before they could sow seed.

'Yes, my friend realises that,' Miles told them.
'He has authorised me to say you will be given a

subsistence while you are doing that, but he expects you to rear some pigs and chickens to help out and keep careful accounts. And this…' he indicated the barn around them '…needs converting into living quarters. It will make six homes for those of you with families. Is there anyone with building skills among you?'

'We can turn our hand to most things,' Jack said. 'Leave it to us.'

'Good.'

'I i'n't sure about the accounts, though,' someone said. 'None on us hev had to do nuff'n like that afore.'

Miles looked across at Helen. 'Perhaps Miss Wayland can be persuaded to do them for you?'

Helen had stopped listening some time before. She was hurting inside, hurting badly, and all because he had turned out not to be the knight in shining armour she had imagined him to be. How could she have been such a fool? She became aware that they had all turned to look at her and Miles was smiling, waiting for an answer to something he had said. She shook herself. 'Sorry, what did you say?'

'The men were asking if you can do the accounts for them, Miss Wayland. They must keep records of what they spend and any income they receive.'

'Oh.'

'Go on, miss, say you will,' Jack said. 'We'll all be too busy to struggle with figures.'

'Very well.'

They all clapped. 'You be one of us,' one of the men said. He was an ex-soldier, tall and upright, but far too thin. 'An' it be good to hev you on our side.'

'This is not a war,' Miles reproved him.

'It feel like it to me,' another said. 'Us ag'in the toffs, beggin' your pardon, my lord.'

Miles laughed. 'What do you propose to call this army of yours? It needs a name.'

Dozens of suggestions were put forward and they finally settled on the Ravensbrook Market Co-operative, then they decided how the land was to be divided, some saying it should be done equally, others that those with families ought to have a larger strip, but Miles pointed out their resources were to be pooled and if a man was married and had a family it did not mean he could work more land than the others, so he was in favour of everyone being given an equal piece of ground, then there could be no arguments and the rent for each strip would be a penny for the first year. With their agreement on this, the meeting was brought to an end and they returned to the horse and cart which had brought them. Helen turned to go with them, but Miles called her back.

'Miss Wayland, we need to discuss the accounts. When will it be convenient to call upon you?'

She hesitated. Did she really want to be so often in his company? He had disappointed her, inexplicably considering she had known all along that he was his father's son, but she had hoped… Oh, she did not know what she had hoped. They were not in the same stratum of society. It could only end in tears. Tears on her part, not his. But in his defence she had to admit he was doing his best to promote the well-being of the men, even if he had not donated the land, and that was something close to her own heart. Whatever else was close to her heart, she repressed.

'Not tomorrow—I shall be busy preparing the paper for publication and the day after is publication day.'

'Monday then. I will call on you on Monday. Shall we say eleven in the morning?'

'That will be convenient, my lord.' By then perhaps she would have talked some sense into herself and remembered who he was: the son of her bitterest enemy, an enemy who thought nothing of throwing her into jail and three good people out of work. 'I must go, the men are waiting for me.'

Miles watched her go, stiff-backed, head up, too proud and unbending for her own good. He hoped sincerely that James would manage to get her off. It would infuriate his father, but that could not be helped. He was glad he had thought of asking her to do the accounts. He would have an excuse to see more of her. Why he wanted to do that, he would not allow himself to conjecture. He only knew that his heart started beating a little erratically when he looked at her, that he enjoyed the cut and thrust of their debate and would not, for the world, have her anything but the fiery campaigner that she was.

He heard the cart rumble away and went to find his horse, which he had tethered in the field. He could not let the animal roam free because the hedges were not secure and that was another thing the men would need to do. He mounted up and five minutes later was cantering home.

His mother was waiting for him and so were Lady Somerfield and Verity. He had forgotten they were coming for tea. And here he was in riding clothes and muddy boots. They were pristine, her ladyship in forest-green taffeta and a huge bonnet and Verity in pink muslin with a high waist, puffed sleeves and a scooped neckline, filled with a scrap of lace. A pink straw bonnet, set back on her head and tied with ribbon, framed a perfect oval face.

'I am sorry I am late,' he said, bowing to them. 'Something urgent cropped up I had to deal with. I will go and change at once.'

Half an hour later he rejoined them, wearing a green coat, white pantaloons, a spotted waistcoat and an elaborately tied muslin cravat. He repeated his apology, which was graciously accepted, though he noticed Lady Somerfield was sitting stiff and unbending, no doubt taking umbrage that he should neglect her and her daughter for something that had 'cropped up'. He must try to restore her good opinion of him or he would earn a jobation from his mother. While the Countess dispensed tea, he set out to charm.

'Allow me,' he said, taking the cup of tea from his mother and carrying it to Lady Somerfield, bowing as he handed it to her. 'I am truly penitent that you have had to wait for this, my lady,' he said.

She nodded, but did not speak. He did the same

thing for Verity, but she had a smile for him. 'I am sure you would not have neglected us for anything less than a matter of great importance,' she said. 'And truly we had not been here very long before you arrived.'

He took his own tea and sat down on the sofa next to her. 'Are you looking forward to your ball, Miss Somerfield?' he asked.

'Yes, though I am a little nervous.'

'Oh, there is no need to be nervous,' he said. 'I am sure everything will go off swimmingly. How could it not? Your mama is famous for her entertainments and this ball will be extra special. It is not every day one brings out a beautiful daughter.'

Her cheeks were faintly tinged with pink as she answered. 'You are too kind, my lord.'

'Not at all.'

'Have you chosen your gown?' the Countess asked her.

'Oh, yes, we have had that for ages, but there are ribbons I must buy and a little lace to go in the neck.'

'Perhaps such things can be bought in Warburton,' her mother suggested. 'It would save us having to go all the way to Norwich or Lynn.'

'I believe there is a haberdashery in the town,'

he said. 'Though how good it is, I do not know, having had no cause to patronise it.'

'Miles, why not take Miss Somerfield to War-burton and see if she can find what she needs?' the Countess suggested. 'The day is fine. You could go in your curricle.'

He looked at his mother in astonishment. The young lady ought to have a chaperon, but there was no room for one in the two-seater carriage as his mother well knew. She was throwing him at Verity. He wanted to refuse to take her, but could not do so without being intolerably rude. 'It will be my pleasure,' he said. 'But will you be warm enough, Miss Somerfield? It is true the sun is shining, but there is little warmth in it.'

'Verity has a shawl in our coach,' her mother put in, convincing him it was a conspiracy between the two ladies. 'Perhaps you would fetch it for her.'

'Certainly.' He put his cup and saucer on the tray and rose to his feet. 'I will order the curricle to be harnessed at the same time.'

Helen was pasting a notice about the free library in the shop when she saw the carriage draw up at Mrs Green's haberdashery shop next to the Three Cups. She watched as Miles jumped out, secured the reins to a post and turned to help an elegant

young lady step down. She was beautifully at-
tired; her bonnet was tied beneath her chin with
a wide satin ribbon and framed a delicately pale
face. Helen did not know who the lady was, but,
judging by the fuss the Viscount was making of
her, she must be someone special. She felt a dull
thud inside her as her heart plummeted.

'That be Miss Verity Somerfield,' Edgar said
beside her. 'You know, daughter of Lord and Lady
Somerfield, the one the ball is for. Grand affair
that's going to be by all accounts. I did hear tell
there might be an announcement...'

'Announcement?'

'Yes, you know—a betrothal. The Viscount and
her.'

'Oh.'

'Mighty cosy they look, don't they?' he went
on. 'And her with no chaperon. Seems like the
rumours are true or why are they out together like
that?'

'I don't know,' she said. 'Let's get back to work
or there will be no paper on Saturday.'

He sighed and went back to his desk. Miss Wayland was in a strange mood these days, sometimes
as chirpy as a cricket, other times down in the
mouth and snapping at everyone. He never knew
how to take her. Not that she didn't have some-

thing to be down in the mouth about, what with the court case and worrying about the cost of repairing the broken window, but she didn't ought to take it out on her staff. And she should never have thrown that book at the Viscount, though he had laughed it off. It was bad enough having the enmity of the Earl without inviting that of his son. She was going the right way to have them all thrown into jail.

Helen knew perfectly well what Edgar was thinking and knew he was right, but she didn't seem able to do anything about it. Her head was so muddled, her emotions so confused, she could not think straight. It would be a miracle if the paper came out on time. Forcing herself away from the window, she returned to her desk to begin writing a report of the meeting in the barn. At least something was being done to help the unemployed men and she meant to tell the world about it, even if she did have to withhold Mr Mottram's name. Better to do that, than mope about a man for whom she was nothing more than a nuisance.

Chapter Six

'Bellamy tells me the men have been gathering on the wasteland over by the brook,' the Earl said over dinner that evening. 'I reckon they're going to have another of their infernal meetings. Do they never learn? It is up to you to stop it, Miles. It is your land.'

Miles had safely delivered Verity back to her home, but declined to go in for refreshment, saying he was expected at home for dinner at five. He was beginning to wonder if it might have been better to stay away. His father was in one of his grumpy moods, but it did not sound as if the bailiff had seen him with the men, for which Miles was thankful. 'No, sir, it is not. I sold it.'

'Sold it. Whatever for?'

'You said it was useless, unproductive, so I rid myself of it.'

'Unproductive or not, it is land. No one sells

land unless the dunners are at their door and then only as a last resort. You are not pinched in the pocket, are you?'

'No, sir.'

'Who bought it?'

'A gentleman called James Mottram. I knew him at Cambridge.'

'What does he want with it?'

'I imagine he means to cultivate it.'

The Earl laughed. 'He will come home by weeping cross, then. The man must have more money than sense.'

Miles shrugged. 'That is his affair.'

'What were all those men doing down there?'

'Perhaps he means to employ them.'

The Earl roared with laughter. 'Oh, that is a joke,' he said. 'The land is useless and the men will have worked for nothing. But still, that is neither here not there. They will soon realise their mistake.'

'It is better for the men to be employed than holding seditious meetings,' Miles said.

'Oh, no doubt of it,' the older man agreed. 'Did you say the man who had bought your land was a James Mottram?'

'Yes. Why?'

'I am sure that is the name Sobers mentioned. Is he a lawyer?'

'I believe he is.'

'Strange, that. Sobers tells me he has been roped in for Miss Wayland's defence.'

'Has he?' Miles tried to sound indifferent.

'Do you know anything about it?'

'I know nothing of Miss Wayland's affairs; as for getting mixed up with lawyers, I leave that to you, sir.'

'There is something smoky going on here. How can someone like her afford a lawyer?'

'She has a thriving business.'

'Thriving? Pah! She is barely making ends meet and people are becoming bored with her way of giving them news. There is nothing of interest in that rag of a paper, no court news, very little reporting of national affairs. It is all her complaining and stirring up trouble and telling people what they know already. It is about time she began behaving like a female and gave the whole thing up. What she needs is a husband. That would shut her up.'

Miles was not sure it would and the idea of Helen with a husband inexplicably unsettled him.

'Someone is behind this,' his father went on.

'And I mean to find out who it is. Mottram must be persuaded to drop the case.'

'Why? Do you think he might win it for her?'

'Of course not. I shall win. Never doubt it.'

'Miles,' his mother said, 'I think we have said enough about Miss Wayland and court cases for one day. Will you ring for Rivers to clear away these plates and bring in the next course?'

Miles obeyed, but he wondered if his father could stop James. Mr Sobers was his senior and could make life difficult for him if he had a mind to. Would he give in? And if that happened, what chance did poor Helen have? She was constantly in his thoughts. He found himself at odd times of the day wondering what she was doing, imagining her in her plain grey gown, sitting at her desk surrounded by shelves of books, writing furiously. Or getting her fingers covered in ink as she helped Tom work the printing machine. At other times his imagination placed her in Mrs Watson's cottage, nursing the sleeping Eddie. That little domestic scene had touched a chord in him and he could not get it out of his head. If only… But what was the use of dreaming?

The paper had come out as usual on Saturday and on Sunday Helen and Betty went to church.

They were in their pews some time before Miles and his parents and she made sure she did not turn towards them as they entered, but kept her gaze straight ahead. Thankfully the sermon was not directed at her this week, but to men who put their faith in false promises instead of trusting in the Lord. She supposed he was referring to the men taking up the promise of the land, which meant the Earl must know about it. She wondered if the Viscount had told him. When the service ended, she slipped past the parson who was standing in the porch talking to the Earl and his wife, gave a brief nod to the Viscount and made for home, thankful to escape.

Once there, she set about her accounts as usual. They made worrying reading. Circulation was down; if that went down, so would the advertising revenue. When she checked she realised they were printing fewer pamphlets and notices. Many of her customers lived in property owned by the Earl or worked directly or indirectly for the estate—were they afraid to be seen supporting her? It was lucky she owned the freehold of her shop and the apartment above it, but without a steady income it did not help to keep body and soul together or pay her employees' wages. The citizens of Warburton might achieve what the Earl wished before any case came to court.

She was still in the suds when Miles arrived on Monday morning to talk to her about the Co-operative's accounts. There was very little work to do downstairs and, having made sure both Edgar and Tom were gainfully occupied, she had gone upstairs to wait for him in the drawing room. Her chair was near the window, which looked out on the street, so she saw him ride up and dismount. A minute later Edgar showed him up.

'Why so glum?' he asked when her greeting of him was less than cheerful and he had been invited to take a seat. He chose to draw a chair up to the table and she sat opposite him. 'Not more writs, I hope?'

'No, thank goodness. One is enough.'

'It is worrying you, is it not?'

'Wouldn't you be worried if you were me?'

'Yes, I expect I would.' He did not think it was wise to remind her that she had brought her troubles on herself—there was a handy vase on the table. 'Are you going to allow Mr Mottram to help you?'

'Yes, if he still wishes to.'

'I am sure he will. I have heard he is fond of a challenge.'

She gave a wry laugh. 'And it is certainly that.' She did not want to talk about the writ because that would remind her that he was the son of her adversary and she should not be associating with him at all. In spite of that his presence was soothing. When he was near, nothing seemed so bad as it did when she was alone and the cloud hanging over her seemed to lift a little, only to descend again as soon as he left her. 'The Co-operative will be a challenge for him, too, so let us get down to business.'

He had brought a ledger with him, in which she was to enter all the expenses and income for the Co-operative. 'Mr Mottram does not wish the men to have to bear the expense of the setting up of the venture,' he said. 'And there is no need for them to know how much that amounts to, so we will not enter things like bricks, timber and glass for the conversion of the barn and the building of the hothouses, but we will put down the purchase of the pigs and chickens, fertiliser, seed and oil for heating. Do you understand?'

'Yes, I understand. Mr Mottram wishes to leave the men with their pride. They must believe they are paying their way and looking after their families.'

'Yes.'

'They are not stupid, you know. They will ask.'

'Then we shall tell them that any new structures and alterations to the barn are putting value on the land and do not count.'

'Are you saying that on the instructions of your friend?'

'Naturally I am.'

'My lord, I cannot help but feel that you have more than a hand in it.'

'I am a go-between, nothing more, and do not even hint of that in your newspaper. My father is already suspicious…'

'And you must not upset your father,' she said sharply.

'No, I must not upset my mother. She has a weak heart and is very delicate. The least upset could trigger an attack and I would not, for the world, bring one on.'

'I am sorry. I did not know. She does not give the appearance of being ill.'

'Most of the time she is not, but that is because everyone is so careful of her. It is particularly important now because she has set her heart on going to the Somerfields' ball.'

'I understand that is going to be a very grand occasion.'

'Yes. Miss Somerfield's come out.'

'I believe I caught a glimpse of the lady the other afternoon when you brought her into town. She is very pretty, is she not?'

'Delightful.'

The heaviness in her heart increased. No one had ever called her delightful. If anyone praised her, it was for her strength and strong will, her forthrightness and common sense, all traits she had learned from her father. They had stood her in good stead until now. It was her forthrightness that had got her into trouble and her strong will that made her refuse to buckle under when confronted with injustice. Her father's words had become a kind of mantra to her: 'Do not let anyone browbeat you into denying the truth, daughter.' And there was another truth she could not deny. She had become far too fond of Miles, Viscount Cavenham, and if she were not careful it would break her heart.

'Our little dance in the Assembly Rooms will seem tame by comparison,' she said, keeping her voice light.

'I do not see why it should. When I was in the army, the men's entertainments were always more enjoyable than those arranged for the officers and their ladies. The other ranks did not have to remember to stand on their dignity and their womenfolk were as gusty and gutsy as they were.'

Gusty and gutsy—was that how he saw her? She supposed it was. 'Did you mean it when you said you would attend?'

He had not been thinking very clearly when he suggested going, or he might have thought twice about it. It was all very well to tell her he might go, but did he really want to make a fool of himself by trying to dance? But he ought to go, if only to support the cause of the destitute old soldiers. 'Yes. It is, after all, to commemorate a victory in which I was privileged to take part and many of the town's ex-soldiers will be there. It behoves me to put in an appearance.'

'I think everyone will appreciate that,' she said. 'Will you bring Miss Somerfield?'

He chuckled. 'I cannot imagine her wanting to come. What about you? Who will be escorting you?'

'I am going to report the proceedings, not to dance.'

'What a pity,' he said. 'I was looking forward to hopping round with you.'

This was too much for her; the picture of him

hopping made her want to laugh. She picked up the ledger and stood up. 'I will keep this here, shall I?'

He stood up, too, realising she was bringing the meeting to an end. 'Yes, please. Keep it safe. No doubt Mr Mottram will wish to see it.'

'No, we must not forget Mr Mottram, must we?' she said with heavy emphasis, as he departed.

Mr Blakestone did not advertise the venue and time of the next rally, but relied on word of mouth. Consequently, Helen did not hear of it until the day itself, the day before her court hearing, and that was through Edgar, who had heard it from Jack Byers. 'Two o'clock,' he told her.

'Where? The Common again?'

'No, I do not think so. I have been told everyone is to make their way to the crossroads on the Ravensbrook road and there will be someone there to direct them. If anyone asks, they are going to see a quack doctor who has arrived with all his medicines.'

'I expect that is their way of making sure no interlopers manage to attend and no one tells the militia.'

'No doubt. But you will not be going, will you?'

'Yes, I will, but it will mean a little subterfuge.'

'I beg you will not. You know what happened last time.'

'Yes, but if militia are absent, there won't be any trouble, will there? And I must report what is said.'

Helen could not be dissuaded and so, dressed in a nondescript skirt and blouse, her head covered with a shawl and wooden patterns on her shoes to keep her feet dry, she had made her way to the crossroads by going down back alleys and over a field and watching from behind a hedge dripping with moisture as a whole host of people, almost all of them men, arrived and the way was pointed out to them. Keeping out of sight until the cross-roads were behind her, she followed, mingling with everyone else.

She was astonished when she realised where they were heading. One by one they arrived at the barn on Mr Mottram's land and were let in. Did Mr Mottram know of it? Did Viscount Caven-ham? Helen found herself looking about for him and wishing he were there. She was decidedly nervous.

When everyone who was coming had crowded into the barn, the doors were shut and Blakestone stood on a box to call the meeting to order and introduce Jason Hardacre, but suddenly he caught sight of Helen. 'There are enemies among us,' he said, pointing at Helen, making everyone turn towards her. 'I refer to the Viscount's spy. If it were not for her, we would have had a peaceful meeting on the common and no one would have been hurt.'

'Throw her out!' someone yelled.

'And have her alert the militia again?' Blakestone retorted. 'No, we will hold her until the meeting is concluded and everyone safely away.'

'I am not proposing to go anywhere,' Helen said angrily. 'I am not a spy. I am here to report proceedings truthfully.'

Hardacre jumped up onto the box, displacing Blakestone. 'We do not want our proceedings reported. We do not want the farmers and parsons and the bigwigs in the town notified of what we intend.'

'What you intend?' she echoed, thoroughly alarmed, but trying not to show it. 'I thought this was to be a peaceful meeting, simply an airing of your grievances. Surely you wish those to be published?'

'We have gone beyond airing grievances,' he shouted. 'We are for action.'

'What action?' This was Jack Byers. 'I don't condone no violence.'

'Then what are you doing here?'

It was something Helen had been wondering herself.

'I am here on legitimate business to do with the land you are standing on,' Jack said. 'Some of us are trying to help ourselves. If others here were to do the same, there'd be no need for meetings of this like. I reckon you're naught but a trouble-maker, Jason Hardacre. You don't even belong in the town.'

'We don't want to hear about what you soldiers are a-doin',' someone yelled from the back. 'You've come back here and took what jobs are goin' and left us land workers with naught.'

'We were labourers, just like you, before we enlisted,' Jack retorted. 'And I do not have work either.'

'An' we served king and country and kept you all safe from Boney,' one of the other soldiers added. 'We deserve better 'n to be thrown on the midden heap.'

'This ain't helping anyone,' Hardacre roared. 'Listen to me and I'll tell you what we'll do.'

Once he had their attention, he put forward an idea to march *en masse* from farm to farm, and to the parson and anyone else they thought owed them a living, and demand money and bread; if it were not forthcoming, then they would take it by force. This started another vociferous argument and scuffles broke out between those who favoured this idea and the men who wanted to work the land Mr Mottram was offering. Helen, caught up in it, was unable to move for the crush of flailing arms and clenched fists. She was pushed unceremoniously aside and only just saved herself from falling. Ducking and pushing, she finally made her way to the edge of the melee and wished, for once, the militia would turn up. She pulled at the doors, intending to go for help, though they were at least two miles from any habitation, which was no doubt why the venue had been chosen.

Tumbling out at last, she fell into the arms of Viscount Cavenham. Not realising who he was, she struggled ineffectually. He held her tight, taking in her tousled appearance, her frightened eyes and the noise behind her. 'Stop fighting me,' he commanded.

She obeyed him, faint with relief. 'Oh, it's you. I thought…'

He did not release her, but stood with his arms

about her, leaning back to look into her face. 'What's going on in there?'

'One of those seditious meetings. And this time it really is seditious. Mr Hardacre is talking of violence towards the farmers and parsons, but they don't all agree. Those in favour are fighting Jack Byers and the men who belong to the Co-operative. I don't know how to stop them.'

He smiled. 'I shouldn't think you do. Nor do I, for the moment. How many are there?'

'Fifty, at least, though how many on each side I cannot be sure. Oh, Miles, we must do something. There will be bloodshed for sure.'

It was the first time she had called him Miles and he savoured it for a moment, while trying to think of a way of bringing the conflict to an end. Still with an arm about her shoulders, he led her to where he had left his horse. He had been out shooting and there was a shotgun across his saddle. He picked it up. 'Sit on the stile over there,' he commanded. 'And do not move until I come for you.'

Reluctantly she took a step away from him. 'What are you going to do?'

'Put a stop to it.'

'You cannot do it single-handedly. They will turn on you. Oh, Miles, please, fetch the militia.'

'There is no time. And it was the militia that caused the trouble before. If I can get Jack and the other Co-operatives to my side, we can restore order. Now do as you're told and sit over there. You are still shaking.'

She watched him go back towards the barn, but he did not go to the big doors she had opened, but round the side of the building. There was another small door there and he must be heading for that. As soon as he was out of sight, she crept back to the open doors from which some bloodied participants were making their escape. She edged round them and went inside to make her way to the side door to make sure it was unbolted, then she went looking for Jack. She found him about to deal a blow to one of the militants, which knocked the man clean out of his senses. As he crumpled to the floor, Helen tugged on Jack's arm. 'The Viscount is coming by the side door to rally you. Be prepared. Pass the news on.'

She left him and repeated her warning to others and gradually they congregated towards the side door, so that when Miles entered, firing his gun towards the roof, they were ready to stand by him. The shot echoed loudly in the confined space. It silenced everyone and they stopped what they were doing. Some turned towards him. Others thought it was the militia arriving and fled.

'Go to your homes, all of you.' Miles raised his voice so that they could all hear. 'Fighting among yourselves will achieve nothing. And this is private property. Do you want to be hauled before the justices for trespass and affray? Will that help you find work? You would do better to talk to Jack Byers about joining the Co-operative. Do that or go home before the militia arrive.'

'And you will tell them where to find us, no doubt,' someone called out.

'No. If I had wanted that I would simply have waited until they arrived and let them do their worst. You have been given the chance to disperse peaceably—I suggest you take it.'

There were a few murmurs of dissent, but in the end they trooped away, leaving Miles facing Helen. 'Do you never do as you are told?' he demanded. 'I said stay by my horse.'

'Is that the thanks I get for unbolting the side door and rallying the men?' she retorted. 'They were so busy fighting they would not have heard you arrive.'

'You could have been hurt.'

'But I wasn't and neither was anyone else, not seriously, anyway. There will be a few cuts and bruises and certainly some dented pride, but that is all.'

He stepped forwards and took her arm. 'Come, I will take you home.'

She wrenched herself away, as angry as he was now the danger had passed. 'I can take myself home.'

'And do you know where Blakestone and Hardacre are?'

'No. They must have left as soon as they saw you.'

'How do you know they are not lying in wait for you? This is the second time their meeting has been stopped. They are not going to take that lying down.'

'Oh.'

'Come, do not be so obstinate.' He took her arm again and this time she allowed him to lead her to his horse. He used the stile to mount. 'Get up behind me.'

'I cannot do that!'

'Of course you can. Caesar is as docile as a kitten. There is nothing to be nervous about.'

'I know that. It's just...' She floundered.

'Do as you are told for once,' he commanded. 'Or I shall have to get down and throw you over the saddle. Very undignified that would be.'

'You wouldn't.'

'Try me.'

Not sure if he really meant it, she stood on the stile and he reached down and, putting his arm about her, hoisted her up behind him.

The only way she could stay on was to put her arms tightly about his waist and clasp her hands in front of him, which meant the side of her face was hard against his back. He put one big hand over hers to make sure she was safe and set the horse to walk. She giggled suddenly. 'I hope you do not intend us to ride into Warburton like this.'

He chuckled. 'That would put the cat among the pigeons. I would love to see the gabble-grinders' faces when they caught sight of us.'

'My lord, I cannot afford the scandal even if you can. I beg you set me down before we reach the toll or I shall die of mortification.'

'I would not have you die of mortification, or indeed of anything,' he said. 'I would rather have you alive, fiery temper and all.'

'I do not have a fiery temper,' she said, though his words had raised her spirits.

'No? I seem to remember having a book thrown at me.'

'That was because I was upset and I have apologised more than once for it. What more do you want from me?'

'Now let me see,' he said, pretending to consider the question seriously. 'You could try doing as I ask without argument, especially when I am only thinking of your safety. And you could promise to dance with me at the Assembly Rooms on the fifteenth.'

'I don't know about that. Had you forgot that court case? I might be in gaol by then.'

'I do not think your misdemeanour is bad enough to warrant that, even if you are found guilty, which I doubt. I have every faith in Mr Mottram.'

'I pray you are right.'

'So, promise or I shall ride through the streets with you clinging to my back. Not,' he added, 'that I am not enjoying the feel of you there, so cosily attached to me. Are you comfortable, by the way?'

'Perfectly,' she said, though it was decidedly uncomfortable on the rump of the horse with no saddle. On the other hand, Miles was strong and warm and his closeness was making her yearn for something more. A dance, perhaps?

'We are approaching the crossroads and you

have not answered my question. Will you dance with me at the Assembly Rooms?'

She pulled herself together. 'I am not going to dance at all. I told you that.'

'Then there is nothing for it but to keep going,' he said, continuing over the crossroads towards the toll. Luckily the gate was open and the gatekeeper nowhere in sight.

'No, no, Miles, let me down. I agree.'

He pulled up and she slid to the ground. He dismounted. 'There, that was not difficult, was it?'

'No, because I am not as sure as you are that I will be in a position to keep such a promise.' She busied herself, straightening her clothes and trying to rake her fingers through her hair. 'I shall go home over the field and down the back alleys,' she said. 'With luck I shall meet no one. You may safely leave me.'

'I am to be dismissed?' he queried, laughing. 'Just like a servant or a lover you have tired of. I beg to remind you, madam, I am not so easily set aside. I am…'

'Viscount Cavenham,' she finished for him. 'Son of the Earl of Warburton, my adversary.'

'That does not make *me* your adversary,' he said,

opening the gate into the field and leading his horse through it. She was tempted to disconcert him by changing her mind and carrying on along the road, but, acutely aware of her dishevelment, followed him into the field and walked beside him as he took the path that went round its boundary. The field was sown with barley, but the crop was blackened and great swathes of it were flattened by wind and rain. It was the same everywhere. It was no wonder the men were in despair.

She sighed. 'Perhaps not, but that summons fills my mind to the exclusion of all else.'

'I can understand that. When must you go?'

'Tomorrow.'

'Allow me to take you.'

'Certainly not. You must remain sitting on the fence.'

'Ouch,' he said and laughed, then added more seriously, 'but the writ is not the beginning of the feud, it is its result. What started it?'

'I am not convinced there ever was a feud. It was simply that my father and yours never saw eye to eye on how to treat the lower orders. Your father calls himself a justice, but he deals neither in justice nor mercy.'

'And do you think you are being fair to him?' It

was his own sense of fairness that made him say it, but it roused a sharp response.

'Is he fair to those poor devils that are brought up before him for poaching? Their families are hungry and they are desperate. Was he fair to Mrs Watson? Or Jack Byers? Is he fair to me?'

'Perhaps he would be if you were not so stubborn.'

'Oh, we are back to asking me to retract, are we?'

'No, I will not waste my breath.'

They had come out onto one of the meaner alleys of the town. The little hovels were lop-sided, with peeling paint and broken windows. Skinny, half-naked children played in the gutter; grubby washing hung from lines strung overhead between the houses. Frowsy women stopped their gossip to watch Miles and Helen pass. And the idiot was there, dancing along behind them, his arms flailing out of the ragged sleeves of his shirt. Miles turned and tossed him a coin, which he caught deftly and darted away.

'Who is he?' she asked. 'Why does he seem so interested in us?'

'I don't know that he is interested in us particularly. No doubt he is sly enough to know who is most likely to give him money. He must live by begging, for no one would employ him, especially when there are so many others out of work.'

'It is your father's opinion that such is ordained by God and nothing can or should be done about it. He pays his poor rates and that is the extent of his involvement.'

'How do you know so much about my father's opinion?'

'He makes no secret of it. Now, here we are on the market place and I am brought safely home. I thank you, my lord.' She stopped to turn and curtsy to him. Their encounter had been a strange mixture of familiarity, the addressing of each other by given names, touching and holding and worrying about the safety of the other. It had ended in a stiff formality as if they had emerged from one world into another. He was again the Viscount to be addressed as 'my lord'; she was the one causing trouble.

'We will continue this discussion another time, Miss Wayland. It intrigues me.' He smiled, bowed and remounted. And then he was trotting away.

She watched him for a minute and then turned and went into the shop, back to the business of producing a newspaper, wondering, as she did so, if this might be the last edition of the *Warburton Record* ever to be printed.

Miles rode home, feeling strangely dissatisfied, the clopping of his horse's hooves a rhythmic accompaniment to his thoughts. Women, in his experience, were timid creatures who fainted at any sign of violence, who obeyed when told to keep out of it. They sat at their sewing, drank tea and gossiped about fashion and the latest *on dit* and left the men to govern and keep order among the people for whom they were responsible. Helen Wayland was not a bit like that. She plunged in where others feared to go and spoke her mind when she would have done better to remain silent. How could you tame a woman like that? Why, in heaven's name, did he want to tame her? She was not his wife. She was not even eligible to be his wife.

Why, then, did he enjoy their meetings so much? Why did he savour the cut and thrust of her debate, even welcome her fiery temper? He remembered his mother looking sideways at him and asking him if he had developed a *tendre* for her, and his sharp denial. Now, if she asked him again, he would not know how to answer. Miss Helen Wayland had him in thrall, so much so that he had been fool enough to ask her to dance with him. He had not danced since he had been wounded and did not know if he could. And what would she make of it if he found he could not? Why, in heaven's name, had he said he would go?

Chapter Seven

'Miles, what are you going to wear for the Somerfield ball?' his mother asked at breakfast the next morning. 'You really should be thinking of it, if you want something made up.'

He had been trying not to think of the ball, but he supposed his mother was right. Like it or not, he was committed to going, so he would have to do something about clothes. 'I haven't decided. The evening clothes I had before I went to war no longer fit me and are no doubt out of date. I would be glad of your advice.'

'If you are not busy today, we could go into Lynn and choose something,' she suggested.

'Very well,' he said. 'That is, if we may have the carriage.'

'I was going to take it to the Assizes,' his father said. 'The verdict is a foregone conclusion and I wouldn't go, but Sobers thinks I ought to put in an appearance, even if I do not give evidence.'

'I had forgotten about that,' the Countess said. 'We could go another day.'

Miles had certainly not forgotten it. He had changed his mind about going himself several times over the last twenty-four hours, but finally decided that if he did, Helen would almost certainly assume he was there to support his father, and that was far from the case. He needed something to try to take his mind off it and going shopping with his mother might help.

'No, you go,' the Earl told his wife. 'I can take the curricle. The ball is an important occasion for everyone and I want Miles to make a good impression, so do not stint.' He paused to look his son up and down. He had come in from an early morning ride and was wearing riding clothes. 'Do not have your breeches made too tight, Miles.'

'Shall I wear cossacks?' he queried with a smile.

'Those monstrosities! I should think not. And while you are out go and see Dr Graham and ask him to give you a clean bill of health.'

'There is nothing wrong with me.'

'Nothing wrong? You hop about with one leg shorter and skinnier than the other and say there is nothing wrong.'

'Nothing can be done about that,' Miles said, keeping his temper with an effort. He did not need to be reminded of his shortcomings—they were with him night and day. 'My thigh is scarred and has lost some muscle, but not all, and the more I exercise it, the stronger it becomes. It does not affect my general health, nor my ability to do whatever I want physically.'

'Glad to hear it. Get Graham to confirm it. It would be a pity if Verity Somerfield rejected you on the grounds you cannot perform. She will need reassurance, or rather her father will.'

Miles's hold on his temper snapped. 'You take too much for granted, sir. I have not said I will offer for her. I will choose my own wife in my own time, and when I do, I shall be open about my shortcomings to the lady herself. I do not wish it to be made a feature of the marriage settlement. You may tell her father that.'

'Very well, but you are not making it easy for yourself.' He stood up. 'I'll go and order up the carriages.'

Miles watched him go, still so angry he could hardly contain himself. 'He is insufferable,' he told his mother. 'I will not be treated as if I were some monster. There are men back from the war much worse off than I am and they are not required to produce certificates of manhood.'

'Would it hurt you so much to do it?'

'Hurt?' He barked a laugh. 'No, it will not hurt anything except my pride, but I will not do it.' He paused, unwilling to argue with his mother as forcefully as he had with his father. 'Let us say no more about it,' he said.

'As you wish.'

The Countess went off to change and Miles went to his own room to divest himself of his riding clothes and put on pantaloons and tailcoat. He felt calmer, but no less determined not to be dictated to. Verity Somerfield was pretty and amiable, but he did not love her. And in spite of his mother's assurances, he felt sure she did not love him. He knew many marriages survived perfectly satisfactorily without love, including that of his parents. His mother and father lived in the same house, but they had separate spheres of influence within it and different ways of passing their time. His mother was dominated by his father and would not have dared to contradict him, however outrageous his statements. Miles did not want a marriage like that.

He wanted to be at one accord with his wife, able to discuss his problems and ideas with her, to listen to her own ideas and share their life together in every sense. And that was his problem. Ladies like Verity Somerfield would not understand that, any more than they understood about his scars or how they affected him. Lord Somerfield was excessively wealthy and he might be prepared to pay handsomely to marry his daughter to the heir of an earl, limp or no limp, provided, of course, he could do his duty as a husband. Miles knew he could, but that was not the point. The point was how the lady he chose was likely to behave when she caught sight of his damaged thigh. How could he be sure she would not flee in horror as Maria had done?

An image of Helen bandaging his arm came unbidden into his mind; she had never once questioned him about his limp or even appeared to notice it. What, in heaven's name, was he thinking of? It could not be. He shook himself and went to join his mother.

The journey to Lynn was accomplished in just over an hour and during that time he conversed amiably with his mother, but his thoughts were miles away. What was happening at the quarter sessions? Was Helen following James's advice or firing up in a temper to repeat her defamation?

Or was she being sensible and remembering other people relied on her for employment: Tom, Edgar and Betty, as well as the news carriers who delivered the paper. If she were fined, would she allow him to pay it? He doubted it. She would be furious if she knew he was paying James for her defence.

He pulled himself together as they arrived in the town and left the carriage at the Globe before setting off on foot to visit the shops. They spent an hour or two choosing fripperies for his mother's ball gown, which had already been made, and then went to the tailor to order clothes for him. He rejected bright colours and fancy waistcoats and instead picked an evening coat in black superfine, black kerseymere breeches and a white-brocade waistcoat embroidered with silver thread, a silk shirt, white stockings and black dancing shoes with silver buckles. Returning to the inn, they had some refreshment before setting off home.

'You will have all the young hopefuls green with envy when they see you standing up with Miss Somerfield,' his mother said, when they were on their way.

He was so on edge he felt like telling her he was not in the least interested in Verity Somerfield, that if she did not remember Helen was standing trial, he had and he could think of nothing else. But, as ever, he was polite and careful of her and let her rattle on.

Helen had never felt more isolated or more vulnerable, even though the courtroom was packed with people: clerks, counsel, witnesses, the sheriff, an usher, the twelve jurors, and many others whose roles she did not know. Her only support was James Mottram and Betty, who had accompanied her on the early morning stage and had spent the whole journey weeping. Helen had become exasperated with her and then regretted it and apologised. As soon as they arrived, Betty had been directed to the spectators' seats and Helen had been sent to a back room to wait until she was called.

The formalities dealt with, she stood in the dock while Mr Sobers listed her many crimes against the Earl of Warburton, culminating in her scurrilous attack on him over the hunt. He read that aloud and caused a few titters in the public gallery, which were quickly silenced by Mr Justice Phillips.

'Do you deny you wrote that?' he asked her.

'No.'

'And caused it to be published?'

'I don't deny it.'

Sobers did not try to disguise his satisfaction at this. 'My lord, the accused condemns herself out of her own mouth.'

'My lord.' James rose to his feet. 'There is the question of intent.'

'Quite,' the judge said, annoyed at being reminded of that requirement. He turned to Helen. 'What have you to say for yourself? Did you intend to write what you did?'

Helen was shaking with nerves and it was all she could do to stop it showing. 'Of course I intended it.'

'But my client did not intend defamation,' James interposed before Helen could spoil her own case.

'What did you intend?' the judge asked her.

She took a deep breath, remembering the discussion she had had with Mr Mottram about her evidence. 'To point out that the hunt should not be allowed to trample down poor people's gardens with impunity.'

'The hunt? Not his lordship, the Earl, particularly.'

A warning look from James made her answer carefully. 'I meant any hunt that ran over other people's property and caused damage, not necessarily the Warburton Hunt. Restitution should be made in such cases.'

'I believe, in this case, it was.'

'Only after I had pointed out the harm done.'

Mr Mottram was shaking his head. She refrained from adding more.

The judge went on. 'Was that your only intention? Did you intend to make the honourable Earl an object of derision? Or bring him into disrepute?'

'No. If it had been any other than the Warburton Hunt, I would have said the same thing.'

'Then the jury must retire to consider their verdict.' He turned to address them. 'There is no dispute over who wrote the article in question. Miss Wayland admits they are her words and she caused them to be printed and distributed. What you have to consider, and consider carefully, is what she intended. Was it a direct attack on the Earl of Warburton? Or was it, as she maintains, a general complaint about hunts trampling down gardens?'

They filed out and Helen was allowed to sit while they considered their verdict. They came back in less than an hour and the foreman was asked if they had reached a verdict.

'We have, my lord.'

'Is the defendant guilty or not guilty?'

'Not guilty, my lord.'

A huge cheer went up from the public gallery. James Mottram was smiling, the Earl was fuming and Helen was looking dazed. Had she heard right? Had the man said, 'Not guilty'?

'Miss Wayland, you are free to go.'

Still in a daze, Helen left the dock and was joined by James. 'Well done,' he said.

She shook herself. It was all over and she was still free, not even a fine to pay. She could hardly believe it. 'I have you to thank and whoever it was who paid for my defence,' she told him. 'I wish I could thank them personally.'

'You know I cannot tell you that,' he said, as they made their way to the door where Betty stood waiting. 'Suffice to say, you have been vindicated. Now go home and carry on with your daily life, bring out your paper as usual, but I advise caution in what you say against the Earl. There are other ways to make your point.'

She thanked him again and, taking Betty by the arm, went to take the stage back to Warburton. 'Did you see the Earl?' Betty said, happy again. 'He was that angry his face turned purple.'

Helen did not want to talk about the Earl. She wondered why the Viscount had not been in the public gallery. Was he not even a little curious about the outcome?

Miles was not only curious, he was on tenterhooks all the way home. As soon as he set eyes on his father, he knew the outcome. The Earl's face was like thunder and he was in a terrible temper.

'That woman got off scot-free,' he said, banging his fist down on the table at which he was sitting, making the coffee pot and cups on it rattle. 'Scot-free! Not even a fine. Not even a reprimand or an order to watch her step in future. Phillips must be off his head; he cut proceedings short and more or less directed the jury to find her not guilty. She walked out of court free to do it all again.'

'Do you mean Miss Wayland?' Miles asked. His heart was joyful and full of gratitude to James. It would be worth whatever he charged to see Helen smiling again.

'Of course I mean Miss Wayland. Who else would I be talking about? She need not think she has got away with it. There is still the business of the militia on the common.'

Miles's heart sank. 'Must you pursue that? Surely you have done enough? Miss Wayland has no doubt learned her lesson.'

'But don't you see?' his father said, as if explaining something to a recalcitrant child. 'If she had been punished, given a small fine and, more to the point, made to apologise, I would have let it drop, but the very fact that she has escaped punishment has made me look more ridiculous than ever. I need to make my point. That is Sobers's advice and that is what I pay him for, after all.'

'It is in Mr Sobers's interests to keep it going,' Miles said. 'You pay him handsomely. If you had not sued Miss Wayland in the first place, the whole business might have died a natural death.'

'And who are you to tell me what I should do and not do? I am beginning to think that young woman has you under her thumb. And why is that, I wonder? Do you fancy her for a *chère amie*?'

'Certainly not! She is a lady.'

'Of course she is, but you would never know it. That is the influence of her father. He has ruined her, especially since her mother died.'

Miles remembered Helen telling him her mother had been brought up in Warburton. 'Did you know her mother?'

'Of course I did. Everyone knew the Brents. They lived at Ravensbrook Manor.'

'Ravensbrook Manor?' he repeated, trying to keep the surprise from his voice. 'But that's derelict.'

'It wasn't then.'

'What happened to it?'

'There was a fire. The old couple died in the blaze and the house was left to go to rack and ruin.'

'Old couple? You mean Miss Wayland's grand-parents?'

'Yes. Lord and Lady Brent.'

'Good Lord!'

'You are surprised?'

'In a way, yes.' He had had no idea when he asked James to find out who owned the Manor that it was in any way connected to Helen. 'Is Miss Wayland aware of it, do you think?'

'I have no idea and it makes no difference. It's all in the past and I don't want to hear any more about it.' He stood up and walked out of the room.

It was such a sudden ending to the conversation that it left Miles more puzzled than ever. He turned to his mother, intending to ask her what she knew of it when he noticed that she was very pale and struggling for breath. He knelt at her side, annoyed with himself for arguing with his father in front of her. 'Mama, what is the matter. Have we upset you? Shall I send for Dr Graham?'

'No, I shall recover directly. Ring for Annie, will you?'

He did as she asked and the maid soon arrived and helped the Countess to her room, leaving Miles to ponder on what had happened in the past. Why had his father left the room so abruptly? Talking about the Brents had undoubtedly upset him. Did Helen know that her grandparents were titled and had lived at Ravensbrook Manor? If she had, she had given no indication of it. There was more to be learned about Miss Helen Wayland, much more. He told himself firmly that his interest was to bring the feud to an end so that everyone could live in peace, that looking after the poor and helping them to find work and keep their pride was more important that pursuing vendettas which benefited no one. But he knew in his heart there was more to it than that.

The Wednesday edition of the *Warburton Record* contained an account of the trial. Helen had written it herself in the third person and was scrupulously accurate. It went alongside the article about the Ravensbrook Market Co-operative. She did not mention the meeting in the barn, having decided she would give Hardacre no more publicity.

On Wednesday afternoon, with the paper out and the cloud of the court case lifted from her, she was able to give her mind to the dance at the Assembly Rooms. She had been speaking the truth when she told Miles she was only going to report proceedings and intended to go in a simple gown and take her notebook, but the prospect of dancing with Miles was too enticing to resist. She ransacked her wardrobe for something suitable to wear.

She had nothing herself, but there was a chest in her father's room that contained one or two gowns of her mother's and it was to that she turned. Some of the garments were moth-eaten, some too out-dated even for the Warburton Assembly Rooms, but there was one she thought could be altered. It was of aquamarine silk and was so outdated it had many yards of material in the skirt, enough to make a dress in the latest classic style. She lost no time in unpicking it and cutting out the new shape.

For two days she and Betty plied their needles; by Friday evening, the gown was finished. It had a high waist gathered into a broad velvet ribbon, which was tied with a bow beneath her bust and had long floating ends. More of the same ribbon bound the edges of the little puffed sleeves and the boat-shaped neckline. Trying it on, she danced about her bedroom, watched by an admiring Betty. 'Oh, Miss Wayland you will knock them all out, you surely will.'

She did not want to knock them all out, only one in particular. She knew she was playing with fire, that there could be no possible liaison between her and the Viscount. She was twenty-five years old and resigned to spinsterhood and doing what good she could for the community in which she lived. He was an aristocrat, the son of her implacable enemy who wished only for her ruin, and by all accounts was courting Miss Verity Somerfield. She was laying herself open to having her heart broken if she did not keep herself and her emotions in check.

She could hardly concentrate on getting Saturday's paper out, for thinking of the evening to come. She could not remember the last time she had been to a dance—certainly not since her mother died. Life since then had been nothing but work with the occasional lecture or tea party, nothing so grand as a ball. She was filled with trepidation. Would she be making a fool of herself? Perhaps she ought to revert to her original intention and go in the interests of the paper and nothing else. All day she wavered, right up to the time for getting dressed. She stood in her bedroom in her petticoat and looked from the shimmering bluey-green gown draped across her bed ready to put on, to Betty who was standing ready to help her into it. 'I can't do this,' she said.

'Whatever do you mean, miss? You ha' spent two days making that gown and it hev turned out as good as any that I hev seen in the *Ladies Magazine*. What's wrong with it?'

'Nothing,' she said. 'But will everyone think it pretentious of me to go dressed in such finery and expect to dance when I am only there to report proceedings?'

'You can do both. Come on, miss, let me help you into it.'

Helen allowed herself to be persuaded and when at last she was ready, her hair brushed and a tiny headdress of silk flowers fastened in her curls, she had to admit she looked very well. In her mother's trunk was a small box containing a few trinkets and she took from it a necklace of green stones in a silver filigree setting. She did not suppose they were real gems, but they went well with her dress and she fastened them about her neck. A gossamer shawl of her mother's completed the look. Slipping into her shoes and picking up her reticule, she went downstairs and into the street to join the crowds flocking to the Assembly Rooms. Luckily it was a fine night.

The largest room had been decorated in bunting and little flags of the various regiments that had been at Waterloo. There was a large portrait of Wellington on the wall above the dais where the musicians were gathering and tuning their instruments. Large vases were filled with flowers, which must have denuded the gardens of the committee members. In a second room, plates of cakes, pies and buns supplied by the committee ladies were being laid out on tables, alongside a punch bowl containing she knew not what. For those who did not care for punch there was ale and cordial. The ills of the country, the dreadful weather and the prospect of another bad harvest were to be set aside for one night.

The tickets had been expensive and there were those who could not afford to attend, but any profits the evening made were to go to the relief of the poor, though how they were to be distributed Helen did not know. She looked about her. The dancers were for the most part from the middle orders: farmers, shopkeepers, Dr Benton and his wife and daughters, the two millers and their families, gentlemen and officers, both army and navy. And a few ordinary soldiers like Jack Byers, who had brought his wife. But there was no sign of Miles. Her disappointment was profound. He had not meant it when he said he would come. He had been teasing her when he said he wanted to dance with her. She should have known better than to believe him. No doubt Miss Somerfield had claimed him. The little green god sat on her shoulder and tormented her.

The dancing began and she was soon inveigled into joining in a country dance by Edgar, who had smartened himself up, slicked back his hair and cleaned the ink from his fingers. 'I'm glad you came,' he said. 'I feared I might have no one to dance with. But I felt I had to come to support a worthy cause.'

'I am sure there are any number of young ladies with whom you can take a turn,' she said, hoping he did not expect to monopolise her, though if the Viscount did not come, she would have no other partner.

As the dance ended she saw Miles. He was standing just inside the door and looking about him. His arrival caused a sudden silence to descend on the room; even the music faded and everyone turned towards him. He had chosen to wear his dress uniform and magnificent he looked in it. The red jacket with its yellow facings, its gold epaulettes and gold buttons and the white breeches and stockings would have made him stand out in any crowd, even if he had not been so tall.

Aware of the tension, he smiled. 'Carry on dancing,' he said. 'Do not mind me.' Then he crossed the room to join the mayor and mayoress, who were sitting in seats reserved for the dignitaries near the dais. Helen watched him go as a concerted sigh went up from all the ladies.

'My, he do look grand,' Edgar said.

'Does look grand,' she corrected him. How could she expect him to write good reports if he persisted in using the local dialect?

He could not have liked being corrected out of working hours and drifted away. The master of ceremonies announced a country dance and Helen found herself once more on the floor, this time with Jonathan Benton, one of the doctor's sons.

Miles watched from his seat beside Alderman Warner, the Mayor. He had spotted Helen as soon as he came in the door. She looked so lovely in that gown she took his breath away. If it had been the grandest ball of the London Season, she would not have been out of place. She was tall, graceful

and ladylike. Considering the previous occasions
when he had been in her company, the transforma-
tion was unbelievable. Miss Grey Gown, who did
not mind getting muddy, or nursing grubby children, who could fight like a wild cat, who threw
whatever came to hand in temper, had become as
ladylike as you please. And uncommonly beautiful. His heart gave a sudden and unexpected lurch.

He wanted to dance with her, but he did not dare
attempt the more robust of the country dances
for fear of looking foolish. Neither did he want to
single her out before all the other ladies, knowing she would hate that. When the more sedate
dances were announced, he stood up with Sarah
Benton, one of the doctor's daughters, and then
with Mrs Byers, which had that lady blushing
and stumbling, but which pleased Jack no end.
And then the master of ceremonies announced
a waltz. Miles made his way over to Helen and
bowed before her. 'Miss Wayland, will you dance
this waltz with me?'

She took the offered hand and he led her onto
the floor. He bowed, she curtsied and then his
right arm was about her waist and his left hand
clasping her right and they were moving to the
rhythm of the music. She was in a kind of seventh
heaven of delight, a setting aside of reality for a

dream and was hardly aware of the whispers of the matrons who were sitting on the sidelines, making barbed comments. He really should not be holding her so close, she knew. Twelve inches was the accepted distance.

'You are looking very beautiful tonight,' he whispered, so close to her ear his breath made her shiver, but it was not cold but warmth that spread all over her body.

'You are bamming me.'

'Goodness, no. I meant it. Has no one ever told you how lovely you are?'

'No, and it would not be true. I beg you to desist.'

'Very well. I will not pay you compliments. Will insults do in their stead? Let me see, how can I insult you without having something thrown at me? Do you know, I cannot think of a single one? I fear we shall have to dance in silence.' But he was laughing and so was she.

They continued to waltz and he discovered he had not forgotten how, but he was struggling not to let his limp hinder him as he guided her into the turns. 'Miss Wayland, I beg your pardon. I am clumsy.'

'You are far from clumsy, my lord, just a little out of practice, I think.'

'Bless you for that. I have not dared to attempt to dance before tonight, but you have inspired me to try.'

'Have I?' she asked in surprise.

'Oh, yes. You are the only person who has never commented on my limp. You do not tread warily round me as if I am different from everyone else because if it.'

'I do not regard it,' she said. 'Why should I? You have shown me in any number of ways that you can do whatever you want to do.'

'Even dance?' he queried with a smile.

'Even dance.'

'All the same, shall we take a turn about the room instead?' He stopped dancing, took his arm from about her waist and offered it to her. 'It will be easier to talk.'

'Do you wish to talk, my lord?'

'It is always a pleasure to talk to you.' She laid her fingers on his arm and they left the floor to perambulate its perimeter. 'May I congratulate you on the outcome of your court case,' he said. 'I knew if anyone could get you off, James could.'

'Thank you, my lord. I was mightily relieved, but I wish I knew who paid for my defence. I should like to thank him personally.'

'I thought it was a group of people.'

'So Mr Mottram said.'

'There you are, then. I am sure James will pass on your message.'

She let that pass. 'The Earl was not pleased.'

'No, he was not.' He paused before continuing. 'I wish I knew why he and your father were so at loggerheads.'

'As I told you before, I thought it was my father's zeal in championing the downtrodden that did not please the Earl, who saw it as a personal criticism.'

'Which it was.'

She chuckled. 'Yes, I suppose you are right, but not without justification.'

The music had faded and the dancers were moving towards the refreshment room. As neither of them had come with a partner, they drifted there together. He found two seats at a small table in an alcove and left her to fetch food for them both. When he returned, he sat down and continued the conversation as if there had been no break. 'We will not argue about the rights and wrongs of what both parties did, but I am curious as to why it became so personal.'

'I have no idea.'

He watched her eating for a minute or two, ignoring the food on his own plate because he had dined with his parents before coming. They, of course, would not have dreamed of attending anything like a dance at the Assembly Rooms to which anyone with the price of a ticket could go. 'My father told me that your mother's parents lived at Ravensbrook Manor. Did you know that?'

'The Manor?' she repeated in surprise. 'Are you sure?'

'That is what he said and he would know.'

'Yes, I suppose he would. Whoever lived there would have been his neighbour.'

'You never knew your maternal grandparents?'

'No, nor my father's parents, for he became an orphan when very young and was brought up by a spinster aunt in Yorkshire. I met her once when I was small, but the journey became too much for her in later years and she died before my father.' She paused. 'Why are you asking me all these questions?'

'Because I am interested in everything about you. You are not what you would have us believe.'

'What do you mean? I have deceived no one.'

'You have not, but perhaps others have. Your grandparents' name was Brent, was it not?'

'Yes, but I know nothing at all about them. Some of the family came to my mother's funeral, but they did not stay for the refreshments afterwards.

I was surprised how grand they were. They hardly spoke to me and ignored my father, though he was very cast down by his loss and needed consoling. He and my mother were devoted to each other. They seemed not to need anyone else.'

'How lucky they were. It is rare to find such felicity in a marriage. Do you know why your mother's family behaved like that towards your father?'

'No, except that they must have thought themselves above him because of what he did for a living.'

'Your mother must have given it all up for love.'

'Perhaps. She never gave any sign of regretting it.'

'It is wonderful what love can do,' he said softly. 'It can overcome all obstacles.'

She looked at him sharply; his voice had sounded so wistful. 'You believe that, do you?'

'Of course. Don't you?'

'Yes, I suppose I do, but I have never been asked to put it to the test, so I cannot be sure.'

'Has there been no young man eager to make you his wife?'

She laughed. 'If there was, he never declared himself. Besides, I have been too busy learning the business, looking after my mother and, when she died, housekeeping and helping my father.'

'But now?'

'Now, my lord, I have been much occupied, as you know, what with the *Record* and the Co-operative and lately the court case…'

'That is over now.' He paused, wondering whether to say anything of his father's latest threat, but he knew it would worry her and spoil the evening. 'Do you think that was where the feud started? At the Manor, I mean.'

'My lord, I have told you before I am not sure there was a feud.'

'I am persuaded there was. Are you not curious to find out what caused it?'

'Until you spoke of it, I was unaware of anything of the sort. I have grown up not knowing and since I have been on my own, I have been too busy with the present to think about the past. The newspaper occupies me to the exclusion of almost everything else.'

'More's the pity,' he said softly. 'Tonight you have shown me a different Miss Wayland, as far removed from a newspaper proprietor as it is possible to be, a lovely, feminine woman any man would be proud to escort. You should have time to dress up and enjoy yourself occasionally, meet new people, go visiting…'

'I can do all those things and have done so recently,' she said, trying to keep the tremor from her voice. 'I have met Mrs Watson, the men who are going to work on the Co-operative land, even Mr Mottram and you, my lord. And tonight I am enjoying myself.'

'I am glad to hear it. So am I, more than I would have thought possible.'

She turned to look at him and found herself looking into brown eyes that were far from mocking. There was a message there she could not interpret. Not for the first time she wished there was someone to teach her how to cope with the attentions of a gentleman. The conversation was becoming too deep for her and she could not gauge how much of it was sincerely meant and how much meaningless flirting. Not knowing how to answer, she concentrated on the food on her plate, though she had no appetite and all she did was push it about.

'Have you ever been inside Ravensbrook Manor?' he asked suddenly.

'No, why should I go there? I did not know my mother's family had lived there.'

'It must once have been a lovely home. It seems

a pity that it has been let go to ruin. If it could be restored, it would make a capital home. I need to set up my own establishment and have been thinking of buying it.'

The idea of him setting up home reminded her of Miss Somerfield and the rumour that they were to wed and it quite ruined the evening. What a fool she had been. He was not interested in her, but in the history of a building. No doubt, given its condition, he expected to buy it cheaply. That thought set her to wondering who did own it. Her mother had had a brother, she knew that because he had been at her mother's funeral, along with his wife, a son and two daughters. All had been expensively dressed in the latest fashion. William, the son, was an adult, recently married, the girls just about ready to come out, something Helen herself had never done. Printers' daughters did not aspire to such frippery.

She had never felt deprived until now when she would have given anything to be a little higher up the social scale. Then perhaps Viscount Cavenham might treat her seriously. As it was, she was simply someone he could argue with, set to work as a bookkeeper and to tease. And, oh, how he teased her! Every minute they were together and much of when they were not, she felt teased and confused by him. She could not make him out. What went on in his head? Was he deliberately seeking her out or was it simply coincidence that they met so frequently?

Had there really been a feud between their families? Was she unwittingly perpetuating it? No, she told herself, her criticism of the Earl had been honest and fair. And the judge and jury had agreed with her. As for the Earl's son… She shook herself. She must not think of the son; she must put him from her mind, forget he had ever called her beautiful, forget he had held her in his arms, forget she had ridden up behind him, clinging to his waist, her cheek against his broad back, forget it all.

'The dancing is resumed,' she said, pushing her plate away from her and standing up, obliging him to get to his feet, too. 'I must not forget why I am here. I must return to the ballroom and make notes of who is here and what they are wearing. My readers will want to know.' And with that she made her way out of the room, along the corridor and back into the brightly lit ballroom. With an effort to keep her runaway emotions in check, she took her notebook and a pencil from a drawstring bag on her wrist and sat down at one side of the ballroom and began to write. She described the

room and its patriotic decorations, then the townsfolk who were dancing past her, the music and the
refreshments, but the account was flat because
she felt flat.

She was about to give up when there was a stir
at the door and Roger Blakestone came in with his
wife. The man was dressed in regimentals with
the three yellow stripes of a sergeant on his arm.
Helen remembered him saying the Viscount had
caused him to lose his stripes, so he must have
regained them or was wearing them when he had
no right to them. He stood looking about him and
then led his wife over to a group of other soldiers
who were standing not far from where Helen sat.

He appeared not to have seen her or did not
recognise her in her finery. Whichever it was,
he barely lowered his voice as he greeted them
by name, introduced his wife and then added, 'I
see the gentry are here. I wonder why. Spying, I
shouldn't wonder, trying to trap us into an indiscretion. But we'll have him yet. He needn't think
his fine clothes will save him.'

'What you got ag'in him?' one of the others
asked.

'Plenty,' he said. 'He had me flogged.'

'Why, what d'you do?'

'Me? Nothing. There was a little Portuguese

lady he had his eye on, but she preferred me and he did not like that. But I'll get him for it.'

Helen found that hard to believe and preferred Miles's version. She rose and wandered away, fearful that they might have seen and recognised her. But no one stopped her and she went in search of Miles to warn him. He was nowhere to be found and she supposed he had left. She decided to leave, too.

Outside the wind was whipping along the street, stirring up rubbish as it went. It was going to rain again. She pulled her shawl closer about her shoulders and put her head down to hurry home. It was a good job her window had been mended, even though it had cost her the price of two of her mother's figurines. She feared she might have to sell more of them if the paper was to survive.

She heard footsteps behind her and increased her pace. Whoever it was did the same. She was almost running when a hand took her arm. She squealed in alarm as he pulled her round to face him, then realised it was the Viscount and let out her breath in relief. 'Oh, it's you, my lord. You gave me a fright.'

'I am sorry for that, but did you not remember me telling you not to go out unaccompanied?'

'You may tell me whatever you wish, but I do

not have to take heed. It is but a step from the Assembly Rooms to my door.'

'Why did you not tell me you wished to leave?'

'I could not find you.'

'I had only stepped outside to smoke a cigar.'

'Then you did not hear Mr Blakestone making threats against you. It is you, not I, who should not go out unaccompanied.'

He laughed. 'I have survived threats before and shall do so again. It is all bluster.'

'I hope you are right. I should hate to think of you lying unconscious in a ditch somewhere.'

'Should you?' His voice was low, seductive, increasing her confusion.

'Of course.'

'I promise you I shall be alert to danger.'

They had reached her door and she turned to face him. 'Thank you for your escort, my lord.'

He took her hand from his sleeve and put it to his lips. She felt the familiar warmth coursing through her and lifted her face to his. The wind whipped a cloud across the sky and for a brief second the street was bathed in moonlight and she could see his face. He was regarding her over their clasped hands as if drinking in the sight of her, moving his gaze from her eyes to her lips and back again to her eyes. He seemed to be looking right inside her, revealing things she did not want revealed: her uncertainty, her weakness where he was concerned, her longing to have him put his arms about her. Another cloud obscured the moon again and they were once more in darkness. She felt his lips brush her forehead. 'Goodnight, my dear,' he said softly, letting go of her hand.

She was trembling all over as she let herself into the shop and shut the door behind her. How dare he take such liberties? How dare he? She had not given him the least encouragement. Or had she? She was in a ferment. She ought to have given him his rightabout, made him realise how affronted she was. But how could she? It had been such a gentle brushing of his lips against her brow, not lustful in any way—brotherly, perhaps, nothing more. To have made a fuss would have blown the incident up out of all proportion. So she told herself, but it led to a wakeful night as she relived the evening over and over again.

Chapter Eight

Jack Byers had been put in charge of ordering supplies for the Co-operative and he had instructed the bills to be sent to Helen. One arrived for timber the following Monday. She told herself that to do the job properly, she ought to see what had been delivered and check it against the invoice and if she were to come across Viscount Cavenham there she would act with cool disdain.

The wind was still blustery and cold and she walked quickly, glad that the rain was holding off for once. Perhaps, after all, they would have a summer. That would make everyone more cheerful. She was surprised and delighted when she arrived at the site to find so many men at work there. They had allocated the plots and were busy clearing the scrub. Some were already digging, though the ground was saturated and muddy. On one side there was a pile of timber and men were busy sawing it into lengths. Jack Byers was among them and she went over to him. 'You are making headway, I see.'

'Yes, we are going to make glasshouses on this patch. When we've got the frames up, we will order the glass for them.'

'What about the barn?'

'Getting the land in good heart and the hothouses up is our first concern, Miss Wayland. We need an income as soon as possible. Some of us are sleeping in the barn just to keep an eye on things. We don't want anyone to make off with the timber and tools, do we?'

'Very sensible. Did you hear Mr Blakestone making threats against Viscount Cavenham at the dance on Saturday?'

'Yes, he spoke so loud, everyone did. That's one of the reasons why we decided to put a guard on the place. He is a troublemaker, that one.'

'Do you think he will try to harm the Viscount?' He shrugged. 'His lordship don' think so.'

'You have spoken to him about it?'

'Yes, he's in the barn with Mr Mottram. Why don't you go and say how d'you do?'

Helen's heart skipped a beat. Did she really want to speak to him? She was only laying herself open to more heartache. That brief kiss had set her pulses racing, stirred the woman in her and opened the gate to a longing for something more, something she could not have and she was afraid it would show. And yet she found her feet taking her to him, ignoring her brain.

He was busy with a tape measure, a pot of paint and a brush, drawing the ground plan of the houses he had envisaged on the hard earth floor. She stood and watched him for a moment. He was dressed in plain riding breeches and an even plainer waistcoat over his shirt. He wore no coat or hat and his dark curls nestled in his neck and across his brow. His cravat was a simple neckerchief. You would never tell, looking at him, that he was a member of the aristocracy. She knew he liked to work alongside the men and that could not be done in fancy waistcoats and pantaloons. But the clothes did not detract from, but rather enhanced, his muscular physique. When he was working like that, his disability hardly showed. Mr Mottram in his fine city clothes was standing watching him.

Miles looked up and saw her. 'Miss Wayland, good morning. Have you come to see how we are getting along?'

'Yes. Good morning, my lord. Mr Mottram.' She acknowledged them in turn. 'I thought I would write a diary for the paper of each day as the work progresses. It might inspire others to think of joining forces for the common good.'

'Good idea. Self-help is better than relying on charity. If everyone did that, the country would soon come out of its doldrums.'

'It would not please men like Mr Blakestone and Mr Hardacre.'

'No, but Mr Hardacre has moved on, so I have been told, and Mr Blakestone is a lone voice. Few people are taking any notice of him.'

'Including you, my lord, even though he threatened you.'

'And you, too, as I recall. We shall have to watch each other.' He gave her one of his disconcerting smiles as he spoke, his eyes seeming to pierce what little armour she had left. She felt the colour flare in her face and tore her eyes away from his, only to find herself meeting the gaze of James Mottram. He seemed amused.

'I received this bill for timber this morning,' she said, proffering the invoice to him. 'I'll give it to you for payment, shall I?'

She intercepted a look between him and the Viscount, which set her wondering all over again. Mr Mottram seemed momentarily surprised and Miles gave him an almost imperceptible nod before James took the invoice from her. 'Yes, of course. Send all the bills to me.'

'His lordship has instructed me not to include building materials in the men's ledger,' she told him.

'I told Miss Wayland it was a capital outlay and increased the value of the land, so should not be put down to the Co-operative account,' Miles put in. 'That is what you intended, was it not?'

'Yes, of course.'

Helen looked from one to the other. Why did she think they were acting out a charade for her benefit? Who was the benefactor and who the middle man? It annoyed her to think they did not trust her with the truth.

'I will leave you now,' James said. 'Everything is going on as it should and I have an appointment in Norwich later this afternoon. Good day to you, Miss Wayland.'

And he was gone, leaving Miles holding a pot of paint in one hand and a brush in the other. 'What do you think of it, Helen?' he asked, waving the brush and spattering paint on the floor.

'You mean the barn?'

'All of it. The men are working with a will, but I thought I would help them by planning out their homes. You see what I have done?'

She laughed. 'Covered everywhere in white paint, including yourself, my lord.'

He looked down at himself; his riding breeches were spattered with paint. 'So I have.' He put the can down in a corner and stood the brush in a pot of water. 'I was just leaving. I do not want the men to think I am standing over them all the time. They do not need that. Are you ready to leave? We can walk together.'

'Do you not have your mount?'

'Caesar, yes. Would you like to ride up behind me again?' It was said with a twinkle in his eye, which made her smile.

'No, thank you. I prefer to walk.'

They turned and left the building. He stopped to speak to the men, so Helen set off on her own. He soon caught up with her, leading the black stallion. 'It is not far to Ravensbrook Manor,' he said. 'Shall we go and look at it?'

'Why?'

'Are you not a little curious?'

She sighed. 'I suppose I am a little, but I cannot see how my curiosity can be satisfied. A house will tell us nothing.'

'Nevertheless, will you humour me, please? I would like to know if you think it will make a good home.'

She wondered why he did not ask Miss Somerfield that question, if he was going to marry her.

'Very well, if you insist.'

'If it is the only way to get you to agree, then I do insist.'

When they reached the crossroads, they left the Warburton road and took a narrow lane that went round the wall of Ravens Park grounds. In a mile or two they came to a gate leaning drunkenly on its hinges. It led to a weed-infested drive at the end of which stood a substantial house. It was a square building covered in ivy, which hid the fact that the walls were scorched and obscured the broken windows.

'I knew the place was here,' she said, 'but I have never been up the drive. It looks as though it was destroyed by fire.'

'Yes, that was the start of it, but since it was abandoned it has become worse. I used to play here as a boy. I would run off and hide from my tutor and pretend I was a general commanding an army and had to capture it from the enemy.' He laughed. 'I had a wooden sword and an empty pistol.'

'Did you have no siblings to play with?'

'No. My mother was unable to have more children. It has always been a source of sadness to both my parents, particularly my father, who wanted more sons. My mother would have liked a daughter. Unfortunately, they have had to make do with me.'

She detected a wistfulness in his voice, as if he knew he had been a disappointment to them, and she felt herself sympathising. Being wealthy and having a title did not necessarily make for happiness. She had worked hard all her life and they had never been more than comfortably off, but she had been happy, secure in the love of her parents.

He pushed open the creaking front door and they stepped into the entrance hall. It was dark as pitch. She dare not step forwards. 'I should have brought a lantern,' he said, taking her hand to lead her. 'It will be lighter in the drawing room.'

She screamed as something brushed against her face and then she was in his arms and he was holding her tightly. 'Something touched my face,' she said from the depths of his chest. 'Was it a bat?'

'No, only a cobweb.' He brushed it from her face with gentle fingers. She shivered, but it was not from fear, it was the sensation his touch was stirring in her. He put his finger under her chin to lift her face and the next moment his lips were on hers. And this was no brotherly kiss, this was a kiss full of passion and she allowed it, not only allowed it but welcomed it. She knew, as surely as she knew the difference between night and day, that she had fallen hopelessly in love with him. And it *was* hopeless. Afraid she had betrayed herself, she drew away. 'My lord…'

'I am sorry,' he said contritely. 'I did not mean that to happen. It was too much of a temptation to resist. I beg your forgiveness.'

He did not mean it to happen. He was simply tempted and succumbed. That hurt most of all. She was breathless and trembling and did not answer.

'Please,' he pleaded, 'I should hate to think my indiscretion made you think the less of me. We have become friends, have we not? We have so much in common and work well together. I should be unhappy if I had spoiled that. Say you forgive me and we can go on as before.'

There was no going on as before in her heart, but she could not tell him that, could not tell him how much she was hurting. 'I forgive you,' she murmured. She could easily forgive, but not forget. How could she forget what it felt like to be in his arms and feel his lips on hers, stirring a passion that had looked set to overwhelm her, and would have done if she had not suddenly come to her senses? 'We will not mention it again.' She forced herself to sound unconcerned.

'Good. Now stand still while I pull some of the ivy away from the window and we can see where we are going.'

He left her with empty arms and an aching heart and the next minute the room was light enough for her to see it. It had no furniture, carpets or curtains and the woodwork was scorched, but it was a spacious room with high ceilings and long windows. They went into more rooms. All were the same with varying degrees of fire damage and rot, which meant some of the floorboards were unsafe and they had to be careful where they put their feet. 'It must once have been a lovely home,' she said, forcing herself back to reality.

'Yes, and I believe could be again.'

They could not go upstairs because the stairs had gone, so they made their way towards the back of the house where the kitchen, dairy and laundry were situated. 'I used to climb up the servants' stairs when I was a boy,' he said. 'They were damaged by smoke and water, and some of the steps had gone, but to an adventurous boy that was all the better.' He pushed open a door. 'This was the morning room and, being on this side of the house, was not so badly damaged by the fire. I made it my headquarters in my games.' Then, as the interior was revealed, 'Someone has been in here. Look at that.'

The ivy had been pulled away from the window and there was light enough to see the dust on the floor was covered in footmarks. Cold ash spilled from the grate; a saucepan and a kettle stood in the hearth, alongside a burned-out candle set in a tin candlestick. In a corner was a ragged blanket. Miles picked up the kettle and shook it. There was water in it. 'Recently, too.'

'A tramp, perhaps,' she ventured.

'I expect so. So, what do you think of the house?'

'It will take a prodigious amount of money to restore. You would be better building something new.'

'But there is history here.'

She was shivering. True, the house was cold, but it was more than that. It had a dreadful atmosphere of decay and, though she was not given to fancies, she felt a kind of ghostly presence that added to her nervousness. 'And tragedy too, I can feel it. It is oppressive.'

'But that is only the darkness caused by the ivy.

Given more light, rebuilt and refurnished, it would be entirely different.'

'Perhaps. Let us go, my lord. I have seen enough.'

They turned and went out by the front door, shutting it carefully behind them. Miles untethered his horse and they returned the way they had come. Neither had much to say until they reached the crossroads, where he stopped and turned towards her. 'Where do you go now, Miss Wayland?' She was Miss Wayland again, no longer Helen. So be it.

'Back to Warburton. I have the first entry of the journal to write and I promised to print posters for the Midsummer Fair on Saturday and I must see how Tom is getting on with them. The ladies of the committee are hoping for a record attendance.'

'With all the work going on at the barn, I had quite forgotten the fair. We must certainly do our best to make it a success. I believe Ravens Park has donated a pig for the bowling and prizes for the races. Will you be there?'

'Of course. I must write it up.'

'Allow me to escort you home. You never know…'

'No need,' she said brightly. 'Here comes Joseph Taylor and Jack Byers. I can walk with them and talk to them about what they have been doing and their plans for the next stage as we go. I thank you for the escort, my lord.' She spoke politely, a little stiffly, unable to return to the easy relationship they had enjoyed before that kiss.

'As you wish.' He stood holding his horse's reins until she joined the men. She did not look back or she would have seen him staring after her.

The two men were eager to tell her all they had been doing and planning, but it was an effort to concentrate on what they were saying. She could not help reliving that kiss. In some ways she savoured the memory and in others wished it had never happened, then she would not be longing for something so far out of her reach. It was not an exaggeration to say it had changed her whole outlook on her life. A knowledge and acceptance of who she was and what she was had suddenly become a matter of uncertainty and discontent. Apart from that, why was the Viscount taking such an interest in her family? She did not believe in ghosts, but that deserted house had given her the shivers. If it could talk, she wondered what it would say. In spite of what she had said to the Viscount, she could imagine it in its heyday, light and airy. What had started the fire? Had anyone been hurt? Why had the Brents left it to rot? The questions came one after the other, but overriding all of them was the biggest of them all—why had Miles kissed her?

Once in Warburton, she bade goodbye to the men and went into the shop, back to the world of work and printer's ink, which was where she belonged. She must not let herself forget that.

It rained most of Friday night. Helen could hear it spattering against the window of her bedroom as she lay sleepless. The wind was howling in the chimney, too. It did not bode well for the Fair. Never had there been such a bad summer; some days it hardly grew light at all. Usually the weather could be relied on for the Midsummer Fair and rarely had it been necessary to curtail or cancel the events, all of which took place out of doors. There was bowling for the pig, which was always hotly contested, running races, trials of strength, boxing matches and horse racing, as well as stalls selling everything from fruit and vegetables, ribbons and buttons, sweetmeats and pies, cheap ornaments and second-hand clothes, religious tracts and quack medicines. The Warburton Fair was renowned for its racing and its prizes, not to mention the gambling that went on when large sums changed hands. The labourers and domestic servants also relied on it to help them find new jobs when their contracts came to an end, because that was where employers went to find staff.

Employment prospects were not good and that set her thinking about the men of the Co-operative. They were enthusiastic and working hard, grateful to whoever it was who was financing the project. Was it Mr Mottram or Viscount Cavenham? Who were that pair deceiving? The men? Or her? How many times must she remind herself that the Viscount was his father's son and heir and way above her touch? Just because he was kind to her, just because he liked talking to her and had flattered her into disclosing more about herself and her family than she meant to, did not mean he saw her as anything more than what she was: the proprietor of a country newspaper and one who seemed to have a talent for getting into scrapes. It amused him to tease her and kiss her. The truth was hard to bear, but she had never been one to deny the truth or she would not publish the things she did, so now was the time to face up to reality. But when she remembered what it was like to have his arms about her, to hear his soft voice paying her compliments and his lips on hers, she was ready to burst into tears.

This will not do, she told herself sternly. *You are not a delicate flower, which can only bloom in the hothouse of a man's love and attention, you are stronger than that. You are a sapling, strong enough to bend with an ill wind and not break. The wind will die down and so will the ache inside you.*

It was nearly dawn. She lit a candle, washed and dressed and went into the kitchen to make herself a dish of chocolate and spread some butter on a hunk of bread by way of breakfast. She did not disturb Betty, who was a heavy sleeper. Then she went down to the shop and checked the piles of newspapers waiting to be delivered. Tom had done it the night before when he had finished printing it and it did not need doing again, but she had to keep busy.

As soon as it was fully light, she wrapped a cloak about her and went up to the common. The rain had ceased and a watery sun was trying to break through. It was going to be fine after all.

Already there were men setting up stalls and others marking out the track for the races. The handyman from Ravens Park was there helping to construct the dais from which the Countess would declare the Fair open and on which she and the

Earl would be seated to watch the events. Others came, bringing chickens, eggs and produce to sell. The sun rose as Helen wandered round, making notes, and more people arrived to wander about and see what the stalls had to offer and to listen the banter of the stall holders as well as look over the horses and place their bets.

Helen went to the enclosure where the horses were being groomed and talked to their owners, noting the names of the runners. It was here she saw Viscount Cavenham. He was standing watching his groom brushing Caesar until his already glossy coat shone like ebony. She was about to leave without speaking when Miles turned and saw her.

He bowed. 'Miss Wayland, good morning. You are here early.'

'Good morning, my lord.' She acknowledged his bow with one of her own. 'I did not want to miss anything. It looks as though it might stay fine.'

'Yes, thank heavens. If it had been raining, my mother could not come and open it. She has not been well lately.'

'I am sorry to hear that.'

'Thank you. She is well looked after, but I worry about her.'

'Of course you do.' She paused. 'Are you entering Caesar for the races?'

'Yes. Do you think he will win?'

'I could not even hazard a guess,' she said. 'I know nothing of horses. But if being handsome is a guide, then he most certainly should. He looks magnificent.'

He laughed and addressed his groom. 'Did you hear that, Burrows?'

'Yes, my lord. Handsome is as handsome does. He is becoming a little restive—shall I walk him round?'

'Yes, do that. I will meet you here again at noon, in good time to prepare for the first race.' He turned to Helen. 'Come, Miss Wayland, let us see what is on offer.'

She ought to have made an excuse that she had other things to do, but instead she fell into step beside him.

They strolled round all the stalls; though some were open for business, others were waiting for the official opening at eleven o'clock. The men in charge of the running races were taking the names of contestants. 'I used to enter the races when I was a boy,' he said. 'Before I joined my regiment.'

'And did you win?'

'Sometimes. It was often between me and Ralph Somerfield in the end. We were great rivals.'

'Is he related to Miss Verity Somerfield?'

'He was her brother. He died in Spain in one of the bloodiest battles of the campaign.'

'How dreadful. So many good men died and were injured and it is sad to see how the survivors are treated now they are home again.'

'I agree, which is why I am determined to do what I can to help them. I was lucky. I might not be able to run races again, but I can ride and in all other ways I have a good life...' He stopped as a cheer went up as the Cavenham carriage turned in at the gate. 'I must go,' he said. 'Cheer me on this afternoon.'

She watched him limp over to where the carriage had stopped next to the dais. He opened the door and let down the step before helping his mother to alight. When she was standing beside him, he turned back to the carriage and offered his hand to a second lady. Helen's heart plummeted when she saw it was Miss Somerfield, elegant in a blue silk gown and dark velvet pelisse. Her bonnet was bedecked with artificial flowers and ribbon bows. The Earl and another gentleman emerged behind the ladies and all five made their way to the platform and took their seats.

Helen, comparing her drab brown walking dress and plain chip bonnet with Miss Somerfield's finery, wanted to flee, but was rooted to the spot as if watching Miles making sure Verity was comfortable, speaking to her and smiling at her, would be enough to set her free from her obsession. All it did was make her miserable.

A bugler blew a few notes to gain everyone's attention and then the Master of Ceremonies climbed the steps to the dais and made a speech of welcome, praising the Earl for his generosity in sponsoring the event and the Countess for graciously agreeing to open it.

The Countess looked frail as she rose to declare the Warburton Midsummer Fair open, but she smiled and spoke in a clear voice before sitting down again between her husband and son. The cheer that followed was the signal for proceedings to begin and every one of the stall holders began shouting their wares. Miles rose and helped his mother down; taking her arm, he conducted her round a few of the stalls with Verity on his other side. Helen turned away.

She was immediately caught up in everyone else's excitement and thrust her unhappiness to one side as she took her turn at pinning the tail on the large drawing of a pig while blindfolded, throwing quoits over pegs stuck in the ground, neither of which won her anything. Leaving those, she wandered round the rest of the stalls. She bought a pin cushion and a length of ribbon and exchanged banter with the stall holders, pretending to enjoy herself and stopping every now and again to take out her notebook and jot down details she might otherwise forget. When the first of the running races was announced she went to the winning line so that she could record the winner. This was her life and yearning for another would not make it come about.

The Countess was too frail to walk round all the stalls and soon tired. 'You have done as much as can be expected of you,' Miles told her, looking round for his father, who had disappeared. 'I will take you home.'

'Would you, dear? I am afraid your father has found some of his friends and will not be ready to leave yet. No doubt he wants to see the horse racing.'

'No doubt,' he agreed. 'What about you, Miss Somerfield? Shall you return to Ravens Park with my mother? I have to come back because I have entered Caesar in the races and he has a good chance of winning.'

She considered this, looking down at the mud on her dainty shoes and spattered along the hem of her gown. 'I think I will stay with the Countess. We can have a comfortable coze over the tea cups until you come back.'

'Very well. I will find my father and tell him I am taking the carriage and will bring it back for him.' He escorted them to where the carriage waited, saw them comfortably ensconced and went in search of the Earl. He found him in a tent that had been set up to dispense beer and spirits. He had a glass in his hand and was talking to Captain Fitch of the Warburton Militia and his lieutenant who had led the charge against the gathering on the common. He stopped speaking as Miles approached

'Mama is not feeling up to the mark,' Miles told his father, after he had nodded a greeting to the others. 'I am going to take her and Miss Somerfield home. I will bring the carriage back for you.'

'Yes, yes, do that,' his father said impatiently. 'I have business here. Will you be back in time to race Caesar?'

'Yes, I shall come straight back.'

'Good, because I have a considerable sum on him winning.'

Miles left him and returned to his mother, wondering what the men had been talking about. His father had stopped speaking very abruptly and they had all looked slightly uncomfortable. He supposed it had something to do with the wager he had put on Caesar. He hoped it was not too much; he could not be certain of winning and, for all his appearance of wealth, he did not think his father could afford to lose a vast amount. It might be one of the reasons he was so keen for him to marry Verity. The running races were just beginning as he made his way back to the carriage and he caught a glimpse of Helen standing against the ropes at the finishing line. She had flung back the hood of her cape and her curls were blowing about her face. He saw her lift a hand to brush them out of her eyes and was filled with regret that he had been so foolish as to spoil the rapport they had established by kissing her. For spoil it he had.

He ordered the driver to go back to Ravens Park and climbed in the carriage with the ladies.

Miles had seen them safely indoors and set off back to the Common. With luck he might see and speak to Helen. He could not understand why he kept thinking about her. He told himself it was the mystery that surrounded her past which had intrigued him. Something dreadful must have happened for her mother's parents to have cut off all contact with the family. But it was more than the mystery; it was the woman herself. In his mind's eye he pictured her with her windblown curls, her expressive hazel eyes and lips inviting to be kissed. And he had kissed her. And been surprised by her response. She should have been outraged, but instead she had simply looked bemused. He should not have done it; it had spoiled everything. He had never been tempted to kiss Verity like that. He smiled to himself as he imagined her reaction. She would be outraged and no doubt her father would insist on him marrying her at once. Helen did not have anyone to protect her in that way, which made his behaviour all the more reprehensible.

The carriage had rolled to a stop close to the dais and he left it with Greaves, their coachman, to go to the horses' enclosure to prepare for the first of the races. There were so many entrants the organisers had arranged eight heats with eight horses in each. The first two in each would race again in two more heats and the first two in those would race again to determine the finalists. Spread over a mile and a half, the course was a test of stamina as well as speed and energy, which had to be conserved if the horse was to qualify for the finals and win. On the other hand, for a rider to hold too much in reserve risked him being knocked out in the heats. It needed fine judgement and an exceptional horse. He thought he had one in Caesar, who had carried him on many a gruelling campaign. He wanted to win for all sorts of reasons: to please his parents, to prove to one and all his disability meant nothing when he was on a horse, to show the men he was one of them, but most of all because he loved the thrill of competition.

Helen was standing on a knoll where she could see the start and the finish. It was a popular viewing platform and she was being jostled by other people eager to see as much as they could. They were noisy and good-natured, picking out their favourite. 'I've backed the Viscount's Caesar,' someone said behind her. 'Stands to reason his lordship can afford the best mount and I hear he won many a race on the stallion in Spain.'

'You'll lose yer money, then,' another voice growled. 'I'll wager he don' even finish.'

Helen recognised that voice. She was sure it was Blakestone, but she dared not turn and look.

'What make's you think he won't?' the first man asked.

'I knows what I know,' Blakestone said. 'If you don't believe me, take my wager.'

'Right, I will. Ten shillin' say he finish.'

'Easiest ten shillin' I ever earned.' Blakestone laughed, a sound that chilled Helen to the bone. She wriggled her way out of the crowd and sped across the enclosure where the horses were being held.

Miles was standing at Caesar's head, stroking the horse's nose. 'Keep calm, me beauty. That noise is no worse that the clash of battle and you didn't mind that, did you?'

Helen approached carefully. It was not that she was afraid of the stallion, but he seemed a little restless and she did not wish to startle him. 'My lord.'

He turned at the sound of her voice. She seemed agitated; her eyes were bright and her breathing erratic. 'Helen. What is the matter? You are breathless.'

'I had to run and find you before the racing started.'

'You have found me. What can I do for you?'

'Nothing for me. I came to tell you Blakestone

is in the crowd and boasting that you and Caesar will not finish the race. He is taking wagers on it.'

He seemed unperturbed. 'That is foolish of him. I have every intention of finishing. And winning.'

'I am sure he has some evil plan in mind to prevent it. He was laughing. He said, "I know what I know".'

'What do you think he means to do?'

'I do not know. Could he get at Caesar and harm him in some way?'

'No. My groom has been with him since we brought him this morning and I have been with him while Burrows has some refreshment.' He smiled. 'Blakestone was probably trying to lengthen the odds. If he backed Caesar himself and persuaded other people not to, he could win a great deal of money…'

'I cannot help worrying about his threats.'

'He will do nothing in a crowd, my dear, there would be too many witnesses.'

The first heats were called as he spoke. He reached out and put his finger under her chin to raise her face to his. 'Come, wish me luck.'

'Oh, I do, I do.'

He flung himself into the saddle and trotted out to the start line. Helen watched him go and went to find another vantage point. The knoll was too crowded and she did not want Blakestone to see her. She prayed she was wrong and Blakestone was being his usual arrogant self and nothing bad would happen. But she would not be easy until she saw Miles and Caesar at the finishing line. She pushed her way to the ropes that marked out the course just as the starter's flag fell and they were off.

The runners could be seen for a hundred yards or so and then they disappeared into a small copse of trees and were out of sight for some minutes. They came out of the wood and galloped across the far end of the common, which was heavy going where the ground was always soft but which was now saturated and boggy. Then they turned for home. Some of the spectators dashed after them to see them emerge from the wood and others moved from the start to the finishing line. Helen was with the latter and breathed a sigh of relief when she saw Miles and Caesar reappear, easily in the lead. He reined in and dismounted, handing the horse over to Burrows to rub him down and prepare him for the next heat, and walked over to Helen, who was coming towards him.

'I am back safe and sound.'

'Thank goodness. But there are still two more heats and the final.'

He smiled. 'I do believe you are worried about me.'

'Of course I am. I do not trust Blakestone. Oh, how I wish you had never gone to that meeting on the common. It is all because of the way you intervened.'

'If I had not been there, the militia would have done a great deal more damage. And I would have missed talking to you and getting to know you.' He looked closely at her. 'Do you wish that had never happened?'

She felt the colour flare in her face. 'No, my lord…'

'There you are, Miles,' said a voice. Both turned to see the Earl bearing down on them. He glared at Helen. 'What are you doing here?'

'Reporting for my newspaper, my lord.'

'Go and do it then.' Having dismissed her, he turned to his son. 'I'm going to fetch your mother and Verity. They will want to be here for the prize-giving.'

'Mama was not well, sir.'

'If she is not well enough to return, Verity can distribute the prizes. She might as well learn what will be expected of her when she is your wife.'

He had spoken loudly enough for anyone in the vicinity to hear, including Helen, who was moving away. Even though she had heard the rumours about a pending engagement, the knowledge that it was more than a rumour was enough to sear her through and through. It was all very well to tell herself he was not for her, that anyone of his exalted rank would not look twice at a woman who had to work for a living; it was another to make herself believe it. Now she had to. That kiss in the dark was all she was going to get. It had meant nothing to him and everything to her. What a fool she had been. Fighting back angry tears, she made her way back to the crowds watching the racing. But the day was spoiled for her now.

The next heats went by in a blur; she hardly noticed which of the runners came first and second, hardly heard the roar of the crowd, until she saw Miles lining up for the final. Suddenly afraid, she looked round for Blakestone, but he was nowhere to be seen. Perhaps he had realised his bluff had failed and had taken himself off. The crowd roared as the last four horses set off on the gruelling course for the fourth time. But when they reappeared, galloping towards the finishing line, Miles was not with them. Helen did not even trouble herself to find out who had won, but made a dash for the trees where the course went out of sight. Something had happened to Miles, something dreadful.

She was not the only one; several men tore past her. She arrived to find them squatting by an unconscious Miles, endeavouring to bring him round. Caesar lay close by, struggling to get to his feet. No one took any notice of the horse. Helen was aware of it, but dashed through the men so that she could see Miles. He had a gash on his head that was bleeding, but he was coming round, shaking his head as if to shake off the dizziness. He grinned ruefully when he saw her bending over him. She fished her handkerchief from her pocket and dabbed at the cut. 'It's not deep. What happened?'

'I'm not sure. Caesar suddenly stumbled and seemed to go head over heels. I felt myself flying through the air.'

'The horse has broke his leg,' someone said.

Miles sat up at that and tried to get to his feet. He was prevented by the arrival of his father, Burrows and two men carrying a stretcher, which they put on the ground next to him. He laughed. 'If you think I am going to be carried off on that, you are wrong,' he said. 'I can walk, but first I have to see to Caesar.'

'Leave him to me,' the Earl said. 'Let the men put you on the stretcher.'

Miles was having none of it. Shakily he found his feet and went over to his horse. 'Poor fellow,' he murmured, as the horse neighed in distress. 'You did not deserve this, did you?' He knew what he must do and it would break his heart to do it, but he could not leave the stallion in agony and he could not leave the job to anyone else. 'Has anyone a gun?'

Someone handed him a pistol. 'I was going in for the shooting competition,' he said.

'Let me do it,' the Earl said.

'No.' Miles was adamant. 'Leave me, all of you. Leave me to see him off.'

They turned away and all but the Earl, Burrows and Helen trudged back to the Fair. They walked a little way off and waited. Helen was struggling to control her tears. Caesar was a lovely animal; she had ridden on his back behind Miles and she knew how much the horse meant to him. There was a single shot that made her wince; after a few moments Miles staggered through the trees. His face was white and his eyes over-bright. Helen's heart went out to him.

'For God's sake, it was only a horse,' his father said, then turned to Helen. 'As for you, madam, go about your business. If you print one word of this, you will come to regret it, I promise you.'

'Don't speak to Helen like that,' Miles said angrily.

'Helen, is it?' The Earl looked from one to the other. 'I thought as much. She's no better than her whore of a mother. Like mother, like daughter…'

'How dare you! How dare you speak ill of my mother?' Helen said, her sympathy for him evaporating as quickly as it had come. 'It is you who should be in court, answering a charge of defamation. And if I hear you repeat that anywhere else, I shall certainly do something about it. Good day to you, my lord.'

She turned and hurried away. She was so furious that, if she had had the pistol which was still in Miles's hand, she would have cheerfully shot the Earl on the spot. Blinded by her fury, she stumbled unseeingly through the trees and almost stumbled against Verity Somerfield coming to see what had happened to Miles. Helen brushed past her without a word and did not stop walking or fuming until she was safely in her own sitting room, when she collapsed onto the sofa and burst into a torrent of tears.

* * *

Miles watched her go with a heavy heart and then turned on his father. 'That was uncalled for, sir, and as cruel a thing as you have ever done. What harm has she done you, that you can hate her so fiercely?'

'Made a fool of me, that's what, just as her mother did, just as she is like to do to you. Cut her out, Miles, cut her out before you get caught in her net. There are plenty of other bits of muslin for you to amuse yourself with.'

'I was not amusing myself with her, nor ever will.'

'I am glad to hear it.'

Miles turned as Verity approached them and ran to Miles. 'My lord, what happened? Are you hurt? Oh, your poor brow is cut. Has a doctor been sent for?'

'He don't need a doctor,' his father said contemptuously. 'Unless it be a head doctor to make him see sense. And he's lost me a great deal of money, letting himself be thrown just like a novice.'

'It was no accident,' Miles said, wondering how Helen's mother could have made a fool of his father. 'Caesar would not have tumbled over like that unless something had been put in his way, something neither of us saw.'

'I will go and look.' Burrows went off through the trees towards the spot where the accident happened. Although Miles was curious himself, he did not want to follow and see his poor dead horse, lying there with a hole in his head and his lovely trusting eyes staring up at him. It had been one of the hardest things he had done, shooting that lovely beast. Caesar had carried him in many a battle and brought him out unscathed each time. If he had been riding him instead of his second horse on the day he was wounded, it might not have happened and he would now be whole in wind and limb. He felt the tears near the surface again and turned away so that Verity should not see. It was strange he had not minded Helen knowing how he felt, but not Verity. Helen, who appeared the harder of the two women, was, in truth, the softer. He feared his father had sent her away for good. And he loved her. There was no denying it now. He loved her.

He rubbed his face and turned back to Verity. 'Come, let us go back. I will send some men to fetch Caesar's body on a cart.'

She took his arm and they went back to where the crowds were still enjoying themselves. So a horse had died, that was nothing to be miserable about. Today the weather had been fine and they had enjoyed a day out, a welcome break from their daily work, or lack of it. Some of them had won money gambling on the horses, some had lost, some had won prizes and some made good bargains. Followed by his father, Miles helped Verity onto the dais and indicated to the bugler that it was time for everyone to gather for the prize giving. But his heart was heavy as lead.

Chapter Nine

On Tuesday morning the same black-clad man as before presented Helen with another sealed document. She wanted to tear it up, throw it on the fire, but she knew that would not help. She sat down hard in the chair by her desk before she could bring herself to open it. This time she was required to attend the Norwich Assizes in October on a charge of sedition. The words were flowery and long-winded, but their meaning was clear enough. She was accused of being a malicious, seditious person and greatly disaffected to our Lord the King and his administration of the government of his kingdom, unlawfully, maliciously and seditiously did intend to scandalise, traduce and vilify our said Lord the King and the regal power and office established by law, to stir up discontent and to alienate the affection and allegiance of his said Majesty's subjects in that she did on the twenty-fifth day of May in the year of our Lord eighteen hundred and sixteen cause to be published a newspaper article containing therein certain malicious, inflammatory matters concerning the militia, who were under the direction of a legal order to disperse a riot in the name of the King.

This was far more serious than defamation of character and, if she were found guilty, could well result in her execution, or certainly a long prison sentence. She sat down and let it flutter on her desk where it lay, a threat to her happiness, her livelihood, her very life. She could not move, could not take her eyes from it. What had she done to deserve such hatred?

She wished Miles were with her, but then remembered what had happened at the fair. The Earl had as good as told everyone Miles was to marry Miss Somerfield. And Miles had not denied it. She had no recourse to him now. She had never felt so miserable in all her life. It was her own fault. She knew when she allowed herself to get close to the Viscount it could only end in tears and that was exactly what was happening. Never until now had she wished for any other life than the one she had, but now she wished there was no *Warburton Record*, no printer's shop, no employees relying on her. She could have sold the business soon after she inherited it, but no, she was conceited enough to think she could make a success of it. Even knowing the trouble her father had had with the Earl had not dampened her self-confidence. How vain, how foolish she had been to think she could best him.

She picked the document up, folded it carefully and put it in the back of the drawer in her desk. She had until October to wind up the business and try to secure other employment for Tom and Edgar; she hoped to be able to retain Betty, supposing she was still free to do so. How much could she expect to get for the premises, the equipment and the good will? She would need it all to help her employees and pay for her defence, as well as a fine if she were let off with that. But she would not say anything to them for the moment. Tomorrow she would bring the *Warburton Record* out and with it her account of the Fair and the next installment of the progress of the Co-operative. Life had to go on, at least for the next four months.

Miles and James were talking quietly in the corner of the barn. Outside the men were working. The ground had been cleared of scrub and was being turned over with a plough borrowed from Home Farm. Potting sheds had been put up on several of the plots and the framework of the hothouse was up and one of the men who had been a glazier before enlisting was busy putting in the glass. The men were cheerful and optimistic. Miles should have felt satisfaction at that and he supposed he did, but knowing that Sobers had issued that second writ had made him depressed and apprehensive on Helen's behalf. She might come to the barn with the invoice for the glass and he hoped she would. He needed to see her and talk to her. She would be cast down by that second summons just when she thought it was all behind her and would need reassurance. Not that he could give her much, but he would do what he could. James had met him in the barn at his request.

'There are several counts upon which the Earl can bring a prosecution for seditious libel,' James was explaining. 'A written statement is seditious libel if it brings the King, the Government or Parliament into contempt; it is seditious if it attempts to change any matter established by law, or promotes hatred and ridicule of authority, and it is seditious if it causes hostility between British subjects.'

'I think the last two will be Miss Wayland's

downfall,' Miles said. 'She did ridicule my father and she did cause hostility between British subjects.' He gave a grim chuckle. 'Especially between me and my father. You will help her, won't you?'

'I will do my best, but the signs are not good. I had best make some enquiries, find out who the prosecution witnesses are and what they are expected to say.'

'I can probably help you there. My father is bound to talk to me about it, expecting me to agree with him.'

'He might want to call you. You were on the common and saw what happened.'

'He won't risk me telling the truth.'

'Did Miss Wayland write the truth?'

'Indeed she did. My father insists he simply told the lieutenant to prevent Hardacre from speaking and causing dissent. He will deny he told him to use any means and certainly did not intend him to use force. Unfortunately there is no way of proving otherwise.'

'The lieutenant?'

'He would not dare contradict my father, even if it means the blame is settled on him. He will undoubtedly say the crowd was hostile and threatening and he had no choice.'

'We have a mountain to climb, Miles.'

'I know, but the hearing is not until October, so you have four months to come up with something.'

'It would be better if you could persuade your father to withdraw the suit.'

'I have tried. He will not budge. I know he is autocratic and used to having his own way and hates to be opposed, but there is more to it than that. It stems from something in the past, something between him and Henry Wayland.' He gave a grunt of a laugh. 'Talk about the sins of the father—' He stopped speaking because Helen had just come into the barn and his heart went out to her, she looked so woebegone.

She seemed to hesitate when she saw him, as if unsure whether to come further in or turn and go away again. He hurried forwards to take her hand. 'Helen, I am glad you have come.'

'I only came to see how the men were getting on for the next entry in the journal for tomorrow's paper.'

'How are you?' he asked, studying her face. She was looking strained, her brow was furrowed and her hazel eyes were dark with anxiety. Her usual self-confidence had been sapped almost to breaking point and that was not a bit like the spirited Helen Wayland he knew.

'Do you really want to know?'

'Yes, or I would not have asked.'

'Then since you ask, I could not be more miserable. Your father is determined to continue his campaign against me. I have been served another summons.'

'I know,' he said quietly. 'And I am truly sorry.'

'I am accused of sedition. I do not know what I have done to deserve such animosity.'

He chuckled more to cheer her up than anything. 'My dear, you really should not have called the militia barbarians, you know. They serve the King.'

'They did act like barbarians. If you had not intervened, they would have killed someone. As it was, you were injured yourself, but I do not suppose you will stand up in court and say so.'

'I most certainly will, if James thinks my evidence will do any good.'

'You would stand up against your father?' she queried.

'Yes. I have told you before I am my own man. Why won't you believe it?'

She looked into his face and was almost undone. Her determination to hold him at arm's length and treat him with polite disdain faded to nothing when she saw the gentle concern in his face. For some reason she could not fathom, he cared what became of her. She might have been comforted by it if he had not been as good as betrothed to Miss Somerfield.

'James will help you.' He turned to James. 'You will, won't you?'

James gave a heavy sigh. 'I shall try. It would help if we knew what happened between the Earl and your father in the past.'

'I don't know what happened—if anything did,' she said.

He turned to Miles. 'Can you find out?'

'I can try, though my father will not speak of it. I wish there were some way to make him talk.'

'You could try throttling him,' Helen said, a little of her spirit returning.

The two men laughed and Miles said, 'Sometimes I am tempted to do just that, but I would not want to be accused of attempted murder. And I must think of my mother.'

'I must be off,' James said. 'I will delve a little at my end. Mr Sobers has been the Cavenham lawyer for a long time; he might know something. Good day to you, Miss Wayland.' He bowed and was gone, leaving Miles and Helen facing each other.

'How are you, my lord?' Helen asked, looking

at the graze on his forehead. 'Have you recovered from your fall?'

'Yes, I thank you. You were right to warn me. It was not an accident. Someone had tied a wire to a tree, just about the height of Caesar's chest. Whoever it was must have been hiding on the other side of the track, holding the other end. When he saw me coming, he pulled it taut. Poor Caesar ran straight into it. That's what makes me so furious; he wanted to kill or at least maim me and all he did was mortally injure a defenceless animal.' His face was screwed up in bitterness and anguish.

She put a hand on his arm. 'You were very fond of Caesar, were you not?'

'He was my friend. He carried me safely all through Spain and Portugal and I swear he saved my life on more than one occasion with his fleetness. And I could not even save his. Shooting him was the hardest thing I ever did.'

'I know,' she said softly. 'It was my fault.'

'How can it possibly be your fault? It was that blackguard Blakestone, though I doubt we will be able to prove it.'

'But if it had not been for me, you would not have earned his hatred. You intervened when he was threatening me.'

'I also intervened on the common and that had

nothing to do with you. I would have done what I did even if you had not been there. Besides, Blake-stone is nursing a grudge against me about what happened in Portugal.' He paused. 'We have got ourselves in something of a coil, have we not?'

'I have. You can go on being Viscount Caven-ham, doing whatever you like doing best, good works, riding to hounds, getting married and having a family, while I have to sell up my busi-ness to pay for my defence and help my employees over the time they are looking for new employ-ment, not to mention paying a fine. That is, if I am not hanged.' There was defeat in every line of her face. He longed to take her face in his hands and smooth away the furrowed brow, turn up the turned-down mouth, make her smile again and see those hazel eyes full of life and humour once more, but he dare not. His emotions were in too much confusion. If he touched her, he would kiss her again and that would not be fair to her. Better to hold himself a little aloof. But how difficult that was.

'It is not like you to be so downpin,' he said, falsely cheerful. 'Trust James, he will get you off the charge.'

'The Earl will only find something else to tor-ment me with. Anyone would think I was setting my cap at you, getting ideas above my station. Well, you can tell your father from me, there is nothing further from the truth. All I want is to be allowed to get on with my life, a life I have chosen.' She stopped, breathless and mortified to think she had spoken so rashly. No one had suggested she was setting her cap at him. It was all in her head. 'I will continue to act as bookkeeper to the Co-operative and, while the *Warburton Record* continues, I will write up its progress. Good day, my lord.' She gave him a curtsy and turned on her heel.

He watched her go with a heavy heart. Their respective fathers had a lot to answer for. He left the barn, spoke to Jack Byers and Edward Matthews, the glazier, and went over to his mare. She was a docile creature with none of the fire of Caesar, but she was reliable. He mounted up and went home, determined to have it out with his father.

He caught up with Helen on the road just as it started to pour with rain again. Dismounting, he grabbed his cape from the back of his saddle and took it over to her, wrapping it about both of them before drawing her into the shelter of a wayside tree, where he held her close so that the cape could cover them both. Neither spoke. The rain, bouncing off the leaves onto the cloak, was loud in their ears, but even so she was sure the loud beating of her heart could be heard above it. It seemed that whenever she determined to be strong and cut herself off from him, to turn her back on the love she had for him, something happened to throw them together again. And each time was more tortuous and more exquisitely sweet than the last. Perhaps she should bring forward the selling of her business and go somewhere else to live, then perhaps she might get over him. Oh, why did she have to fall in love so disastrously?

She stirred in his arms, but his grip on her tightened, not to hurt her, simply to tell her to stay where she was. 'One day,' he murmured quietly, 'the sun will shine again.' He was not talking about the weather, or not altogether. 'Have patience.'

'I have been thinking,' she said. 'There will be no sunshine and no peace while I remain in Warburton. I shall put the business up for sale and hope whoever buys it will give employment to Tom and Edgar.'

'Then what? Where will you go?'

'I do not know. Anywhere. It doesn't matter as long as it is where your father cannot find me.'

'Then he will have won.'

'Yes, he will have won. I have no more fight

left in me.' She did not tell him that it was not the fight with the Earl which had defeated her, but her fight with her inner self not to long for his son to love her. Miles Cavenham was destined to marry Miss Somerfield, someone of his own kind, and one day he would inherit Ravens Park. She did not want to be anywhere near when that happened. It would break her heart. She looked up into his dear face and had to fight back the tears. 'Do you think he will drop the charges if I do that?'

'Is that what you want?'

'Yes.'

'Oh, my dearest girl, I grieve for you.'

'Don't. I brought this on myself. I must cure it myself.'

'Helen, I…' He stopped. What had he been going to say? That he would do anything to make her happy again, fall out with his father, give evidence on her behalf, forgo his inheritance? A man would need to be hopelessly in love to say all those things. Was he? He looked down at her upturned face, saw the tears standing on her lashes, the pallor of her cheeks and her slightly open mouth and knew he was. It did not even surprise him. He had been blind not to realise it before. Could he let her go? He could not think straight, and he needed to think. He wanted to kiss her, to tell her not to worry, he would make everything right, but he knew he could not make everything right. Only his father and the court could do that. 'If you are sure, I will tell my father what you intend and try to persuade him that the feud is over and he can drop the charges, though I will have to consult Mr Mottram to see if that is possible.'

It wasn't what she wanted to hear. She wanted him to kiss her and tell her he loved her, but of course that was a daydream and she could not afford daydreams. 'Thank you,' she said.

'But you do not have to move away from War-burton, do you? Not if the charge is dropped and you stop publishing the *Record*. You could stay…'

'And do what?'

'Whatever you like. We are both working on the Co-operative project and I should be sad if we could not continue to do that.'

She would miss doing that, but it would not fill the great void parting from him would leave in her heart and mind. 'No, my lord, I could not stay.' She could not stay anywhere where she might come across him, where she might have to see him out with his wife and family, attend the same church, use the same shops. She would never get over him like that. 'I need to make a fresh start where no one knows me.'

'Oh, that it has come to this. If I can help you, by giving evidence or asking James to help you with the sale of your business, anything at all, I beg you to call on me.'

'Thank you.' One thing she was sure of, she would not ask him for help. The spattering of rain on the leaves of the tree was easing. She lifted the corner of the cloak and peered up at the sky. 'I believe the rain has stopped. We can go on our way.'

They emerged from under the tree to where the mare was patiently cropping the grass. He rolled up the cape and fastened it back on his saddle. Then he picked up the reins to lead the horse. 'I will see you safely home.'

'My lord, there is no need.'

'There is every need. I would never forgive myself if anything happened to you.'

She looked at him sharply and decided not to comment. 'As you wish.'

They walked in silence, dodging the water-filled potholes, the only sound the soughing of the wind and the rhythmic clop of the mare's feet. Overhead the lowering clouds skimmed across the sky, making it seem like twilight. The very earth was echoing their mood. It was far too muddy to take the path round the fields and so they continued over the crossroads. A cart overtook them and then a carriage came in the opposite direction. They both looked up as it passed, splashing their feet and legs as it rolled through a large puddle. It was the Earl's carriage and inside the Earl himself stared out at them.

As they reached the outskirts of the town, she stopped and turned to him. Already the gossips were talking about them being seen so often together and that wasn't fair to him. Or to her either. 'Do not come any further with me, my lord. I will go on alone from here.'

He took her hand and raised it to his lips. 'I will speak to my father and Mr Mottram for you and let you know what they say, then we will talk again. This is not the end.'

He watched as she made her way towards the market square and her shop. He had never known her so downpin and his heart, already aching for her, ached still more. He mounted up and rode home. One other thing he intended to do was ask James to hasten the buying of Ravensbrook Manor.

His father was sitting in the library with the door open, waiting for him, as he knew he would be. 'Miles, in here, if you please.'

'I must go and change, Father. My clothes are all muddied. I will be with you in ten minutes.' He went on up the stairs to his own room. He did not ring for his valet because he did not want to be fussed over. Instead he stripped off his riding clothes and dressed in pantaloons and tailcoat. Then he put a brush through his wet hair, which sprang into curls, decided it would have to do and went down to confront his father.

'You wanted to speak to me, sir?'

'Yes. Shut the door. I do not want your mother to hear and be upset.' And after Miles had obeyed, went on, 'You have been out escorting that woman again. I have already told you I want her out of your life—why don't you listen to me? She is nothing but a troublemaker, you cannot deny it.'

'I am not going to argue with you, Father, because nothing will stop me seeing Helen, whatever you say. She has been sadly misused. There are dozens of publications, hundreds, which carry comments far worse than calling the militia barbarians. And no one sues them. It is personal and I want to know why. It is something to do with that vendetta against Henry Wayland, is it not?'

'His vendetta against me, you mean.'

'Whichever it was, why do you have to punish his daughter? If it had been anyone else who had written that piece about the hunt, you would have laughed it off. You would not have bothered to pursue it, nor gone even further and accused the writer of sedition. Good God! Almost everyone at some time or other has a grumble about the government and they are not all dragged into court. It must have been something very bad for you to bear a grudge for so long. Miss Wayland does not deserve that. Whatever her father did, it is nothing to do with her.'

'You have no idea what her father did.'

'No, but I wish you would tell me.'

'It has nothing to do with you, except that your insistence on seeing her is making matters worse.'

'She has told me she is planning to sell her business and move away from Warburton.'

'Thank heavens for that. Every time I see her, I am reminded…'

'Of what?'

'Miles, I will not be quizzed on the matter, pray desist.'

Miles would have pressed on, but remembered that his errand was to have the charges dropped and antagonising his father would not achieve that. 'In view of the fact that Miss Wayland is giving up her business and leaving the area, she requested me to ask you if you would drop the sedition charge against her. She will not trouble you again.'

The Earl appeared to be considering this. 'It is true I was not looking forward to going to court again, especially if Phillips is hearing the case, but I shall have to consult Sobers. It is a serious allegation and it may be out of my control.' He paused. 'If I do, there is one proviso.'

'Which is?'

'You do not see Miss Wayland again. Sobers will contact her by letter.'

'But she is doing the books for the Co-operative and I go there from time to time.'   .

'Let Mottram deal with it, since he now owns the land. It is time you started taking an interest in the estate and put your mind to courting Miss Somerfield. She was upset that you paid her so little attention at the Fair…'

'My horse had just been mortally wounded…'

'I know that. I told her that was what it was and that you would be on top form at her ball on Friday. Everyone has great expectations…'

'No, Father, I cannot.'

'You can and you will. Or there will be no deal for Miss Wayland. Is that clear?'

Miles was shocked to the core. 'That's blackmail.'

The Earl shrugged. 'Call it what you like, but those are my terms.'

Miles turned on his heel and returned to his own room where he flung himself on the bed and stared up at the ceiling. His immediate reaction was to defy his father, go to Helen and tell her how much he loved her. But if he did that, his father would make good his threat and she would be brought to court where her chances of being found not guilty were so slim as not to be considered. He could pay a fine for her, if it was only a fine, but if she was sent to prison or even sentenced to death, he would not be able to help her then. He got up and began pacing the room, back and forth, back and forth until he was dizzy.

He went to the window and gazed out across the park. It was his home and his inheritance and he loved it. When he had been out in the Peninsula fighting the French, all he wanted was to come back to it. He could give it all up for Helen, but he knew with certainty that Helen's sense of honour would make her refuse him, even if she loved him as he loved her and he could not even be sure of that. Why would she? He was his father's son, as she had reminded him on several occasions. And there was his mother to consider; the scandal would surely kill her. He could not do it. His hand brushed his face; he had not wept since he was in leading strings, but he was weeping now. The tears were streaming down his face.

He scrubbed at his face with his handkerchief and turned back into the room as he heard the first dinner gong and Louis, his valet, came in to help him change.

'Edgar, go and fetch Tom in here, will you, please?' Helen said. 'I have something to say to you both.'

She waited until the two men were standing in front of her, then locked the door to keep customers away while she broke the news to them. They stood waiting patiently, both looking puzzled.

'I have decided to sell the business and move away from Warburton,' she said.

They looked at each other in shock and then back to her. 'But why?' Tom asked. 'I know we hen't been doin' so well lately, but that'll pass over now that court case is over and done with and you were acquitted.'

'I am afraid that wasn't the end of it,' she said. 'I have been served another summons, this time for seditious libel and I do not think I can get out of this one.' She gave them a rueful smile. 'It seems it is not permissible to call the militia barbarians.'

Edgar opened his mouth to speak, but she held up her hand to stop him. 'I intend to sell the business as a going concern to someone who will carry on with it and continue to employ you.'

'Mr Wayland must be turning in his grave,' Tom said. 'He was that proud of you and I heard him say more'n once you would make a go of it. And here you are giving up.'

'I have no choice,' she said wearily. She could not explain that the summons was only part of her decision—the other part was to do with Miles Cavenham. How could she stay in Warburton, loving him as she did? It was better to have a clean break.

'Where will you go?' Edgar asked.

'I do not know. I have not made up my mind.'

'Will you start up another paper?'

'I do not think so. I would rather do something less contentious.'

''Twas you made the *Record* contentious,' Edgar said. 'Writing what you did.'

She sighed. 'I know.'

'It was the way you were trained,' Tom said. He had worked for her father from the beginning, whereas Edgar had arrived when her father had become too ill to carry on and she needed help.

'Mr Wayland was always one to stir up people's consciences.'

'I know,' she said again. 'But now I have to find something else to do. I have four months to find a buyer and decide where to go. Until then we will carry on as usual. If either of you find other employment in the meantime, don't wait on me. Take it with my blessing. I will give you both good characters.'

'Thank you, miss,' Edgar said, though Tom was shaking his head in disbelief.

She smiled and laid a hand on his arm. 'It is for the best, Tom, believe me.'

'What about Betty? This is the only home she's known 'cep' the orphanage.'

'I am hoping I will be able to afford to keep Betty. I shall need a maid whatever I decide to do. I have told her that, so that she is not so cast down by my news. Now I will leave you to get the paper out. I have business in Norwich.'

Leaving them to mull it over and discuss it, she went upstairs to put on a bonnet and coat before crossing the street to the Three Cups to take the stage to the city.

Norwich had once been the second most important city after London and it was still a thriving place in spite of the economic difficulties of the country. It was said to have an inn for every day of the year and a church for every Sunday. How true that was, Helen had no way of knowing, but it certainly had its fair share of those buildings. Down by the river, where goods were being brought in and taken out by wherry, there were tanneries and breweries whose stink permeated even the inside of the coach as it rattled through the city towards its centre and the Maid's Head, where it would set down its passengers. Helen knew the city well; it was where she had shopped when Warburton and Lynn did not have what she needed. But she was not shopping today, she was going in search of Mr Mottram's office, which was situated in one of the old Tudor houses on Elm Hill.

She found it easily enough and pushed open the door to find herself in a lobby. There was a clerk sitting at a desk and it was to him she addressed her query. Her name was Miss Wayland, she told him, and would he ask Mr Mottram if he could spare her a few minutes of his time? He seemed doubtful if she could be seen without an appointment, but as she showed no sign of taking his word on that, he disappeared and came back a few minutes later to ask her to follow him.

They climbed some narrow stairs and he ushered her into an untidy office. There were books and piles of papers everywhere, on the large desk, on a side table, on shelves, even on the floor. But there was no James Mottram. She gingerly moved some books from a chair onto the floor and perched herself on it to wait, glancing round at the muddle and wondering how any man could do any work in the midst of it.

He hurried in and held out his hand to her, which she rose to take. 'Miss Wayland, how do you do? I am sorry I kept you waiting, I was in conference with Mr Sobers. Do sit down.'

She sat again and he went behind the desk to his own chair. 'What can I do for you? I assume it has nothing to do with the Co-operative?'

'No, nothing. It is a personal matter. I have decided to sell the *Warburton Record* and would like your help in finding a suitable buyer. I want one who will carry on the business and employ Tom and Edgar.'

'Goodness me, this is a surprise,' he said. 'I was just talking to Mr Sobers about your case. He knows nothing about a disagreement between your father and the Earl of Warburton, I am afraid.'

'I am not surprised.'

'Why have you decided to sell the paper?'

'Because I want to leave Warburton and make

my home somewhere else. I have decided that there can never be peace between me and the Earl and I am tired of fighting him. I have told Miles—Viscount Cavenham—that is what I mean to do and he is going to ask the Earl if he will drop the charges against me, if I do that.'

'And if he will not?'

'Then I will use the proceeds of the sale in my defence. You cannot defend me for nothing; as it is such a serious charge I am sure my previous benefactors will not continue to finance me.'

'They have not said that.'

'No, but I wish to be independent. I have never been a beggar, Mr Mottram, and am determined I never shall be.'

'I see. You are taking a gamble, Miss Wayland.'

'I have no choice. I must leave Warburton.'

'Where will you go? What will you do?'

'I have been mulling that over and have decided, if there is enough money to finance it, I should like to open a bookshop.'

He smiled. 'Bookshops often get into trouble when they sell material deemed to be seditious. Are you sure you would not be jumping out of the frying pan into the fire?'

'I do not intend to sell seditious material.'

'I must point out, Miss Wayland, you did not

realise you were selling seditious material when you accused the militia of being barbarians. It could happen again. Surely it would be better to open a haberdashery shop and sell ribbons and lace?'

'I know nothing of ribbons and lace, Mr Mottram, but I do know about print. I am interested in helping people to knowledge and enjoyment of books, especially those who have little learning. The library I set up in my shop in Warburton has been a great success. All manner of people have told me how they have benefited.'

'Yes, but you have not charged people to borrow books, have you? If they had to buy them, it might be a different story.'

'Then I shall lend some of them out at a penny a week. Do not include my books in the sale. I am going to need them.'

'And where will you locate this shop?'

'Here in Norwich, I think. It has a large population and a good proportion of those must like to read. I shall look for premises as soon as I know how much money I have to spare.'

'When are you planning to move?'

'The sooner the better.'

'And have you discussed this with Viscount Cavenham?'

'It is nothing to do with Viscount Cavenham,' she told him sharply, though she was aware of a tell-tale flush staining her cheeks. 'But, yes, I did tell him.'

'And what did he say?'

'He agreed with me. May I leave the sale in your hands, Mr Mottram? It goes without saying that I need the best possible price.'

'Very well. I shall need your ledgers for prospective buyers to inspect. They will want to know they are taking on a viable business.'

'I will see that you have them.'

'And as for the court case—am I still to act in your defence?'

'Yes, if it comes to court. I am hoping the Earl will realise he has nothing to gain by pursuing it when I am no longer in Warburton to incense him.'

'I think you are being wise,' he said slowly. 'A new start, in a new place. Best thing all round, especially if it gets you off that indictment.'

She thanked him and left. As she had an hour or two to wait for a return coach, she spent the time wandering about the streets of Norwich looking at the shops. Away from the river, in the area surrounding the cathedral, there were some smart premises selling a variety of merchandise and they seemed to be doing good business. Yes, this was where she would come and here she might learn to mend a broken heart.

Miles, from the room next to James's office, watched her go with an ache in his heart as heavy as a cannon ball. It restricted his breathing He had heard every word and longed to dash in and tell her he would love her and protect her for ever, that whatever happened in the future, she would not be alone. But he was constrained by his promise to his father, a promise extracted under extreme duress, a promise he would never have made if the consequences of not giving it had not been so dire for Helen, and if his mother had not been so unwell. Helen had gone and he would not speak to her again and, if he found himself near her, he must turn away.

James was back with them. 'Did you hear that?'

'Yes.'

'I'll do what I can for her, but it will not be easy selling that paper. It is only a small regional affair and I doubt it's making much of a profit. I shall be surprised if the proceeds do more than cover a fine, if that. As for defence costs, she expects them to come out of them, too.'

'She is a foolish child,' Sobers said. He did not

know about Miles paying for the defence and Miles did not want him to know. 'Her father was even more foolish to leave the business to her. It was bound to end in failure.'

'It ended because of those lawsuits, not her lack of business sense,' Miles said. 'So what about it? Can you get the charge dropped?'

'It's not so easy,' Sobers said. 'The defamation was a civil action, sedition is a Crown prosecution, but if his lordship and others he has recruited fail to turn up as witnesses, it might be dismissed. I will be surprised if the Earl consents to that.'

'I think he will,' Miles said grimly. 'He indicated to me he would, so long as Miss Wayland leaves Warburton.'

'That is a significant change of heart,' Sobers said. 'How did you manage it?'

'I simply pointed out that whatever grudge he had against Henry Wayland, it was unfair to hold it against his daughter.' He paused. 'Have you any idea what that grudge was?'

'I would not tell you, if I did. There is such a thing as confidentiality, you know. You had better ask the Earl.'

Miles knew from experience his father would not tell him. 'So, I can rely on you to do what you can to cancel that trial, can I?' Miles asked, preparing to leave.

'I will do what I can, when I have written instructions from the Earl to do so. To date, I have had nothing.'

Miles bowed to Sobers and went downstairs accompanied by James, who saw him to the door. 'I hope to God my father does not renege on his promise,' Miles said. 'It is the only hope Helen has.'

James looked at him with his head on one side. 'And what have you promised your revered father in exchange?'

'None of your business, my friend.'

'No, but I can guess. You have got yourself in something of a coil, have you not? And all because of a pretty face.'

Helen was more than a pretty face, but he had no intention of arguing with his friend about it. James would never understand, any more than his father and mother understood. He hardly understood it himself. He clamped his hat back on his head and limped out into the street. He had left his curricle at the Maid's Head and if his guess was correct, Helen would take the stage back to Warburton from there. He might catch a glimpse of her.

She was nowhere to be seen and he took charge of the curricle and set off for home. Helen was gone from his life and he might as well get used to the idea.

Helen tried to put her mind to her business. If it was to be sold as a going concern, she must make it as profitable as she could. She laid out notices and advertisements, wrote obituaries and kept up the journal for the Co-operative, reported on events taking place in the Assembly rooms, copied news from London that told of riots and disturbances everywhere, particularly in Norfolk. The poor were getting desperate and resorting to violence and arson. Armed with agricultural implements—axes, saws, spades—they were destroying threshing machines, which they saw as taking their livelihoods from them, stealing bread and chickens because they were hungry, demanding money of the wealthier farmers, though they, too, were suffering. Many of them had been arrested and executed, others sent to the hulks for transportation, many more sent to prison. Something would have to be done if the country was not to descend into anarchy.

She had not seen Miles since she told him she would leave Warburton. And she missed him. She missed him so much she did not know how she could bear it. Until now she had not realised how much she depended on him, how much she valued his advice, how much she was able to confide in him. But it was not only that; she missed his dear face, missed being held in his arms, wished she could feel again his lips on hers and the awakening of desire he had aroused in her. But it was gone, all gone. She did not even know if he had spoken to his father on her behalf or if he had been successful. He had not even come to tell her. And that hurt more than anything.

She went one day to the barn, ostensibly to write up the progress being made, but hoping desperately he would be there. Everything was coming on apace. The glasshouses were glazed and stoves put in to heat them, ready for delicate seedlings. Outside the plots, outlined by narrow grass paths, had been turned over and were being raked and the stones picked off them. There were piles of bricks in the barn ready to start on the walls of the new dwellings. She looked at the lines of white paint and remembered the day Miles had put them there, the day they had gone to Ravensbrook Manor and he had kissed her. That had caused all sorts of tumult inside her, comforting, achingly sensual, demanding and yet tender. Whatever was going on in the world outside had not impinged on that moment. But it had since then. The world and society had taken over and robbed her of happiness.

She left the barn, spoke to some of the men and set off back to Warburton. Today the weather was fine; the sun had even tried to get through. She walked swiftly, her head down. At the crossroads she paused. Here she and Miles had turned off for Ravensbrook Manor, near here they had sheltered from the rain, close together under one cape. Her memories tormented her.

She heard the clop of a horse and looked down the lane to see Miles riding towards her. She stood and waited, her heart beating a tattoo in her chest. He saw her, reined in and sat there, a hundred yards away, looking at her, then he wheeled his horse about and cantered away.

'Miles,' she called. 'Miles…' But her voice was carried away on the wind.

Chapter Ten

All of Gayton Hall's windows were ablaze with light. Lanterns were strung all the way down the drive and round the carriage sweep before the front door. Some had even been hung in the shrubbery that skirted the lawn. The road leading to the gates was lined with spectators come to see the grand people arriving, trying to identify them, commenting on their horses and carriages, their clothes and jewellery as they rolled up to the entrance and stepped down into the light streaming from the front door, where footmen in livery stood ready to open the carriage doors and let down the steps.

'His lordship ain't stintin',' Helen heard one of the bystanders say. 'Them candles alone must have cost a pretty penny.'

'Well, it's a grand occasion, i'n't it?' a woman's voice said. 'An' they've got money to burn.'

Helen had told Tom and Edgar she ought to be there to report who attended and what they were wearing, even if she could not go inside to describe the scene in the ballroom. She had even begun to compose the article in her head. 'Two of Norfolk's foremost families to be united,' would be the headline. And underneath she would write: 'On Friday last, Lord and Lady Somerfield of Gaynor Hall hosted a glittering assembly at their country estate in honour of their daughter Verity's come out. Among the prominent guests were the Earl and Countess of Warburton and their son, Miles, Viscount Cavenham…' What she was really doing was tormenting herself with the hope that she might catch a glimpse of Miles. Why had he turned his back on her at the cross-roads? He could not pretend he had not seen her; she knew he had. And he had cut her dead? It was the most hurtful thing he could have done and she could not get over it. Why? she asked herself over and over again. Why? Had he got to the bottom of the mystery about the feud and decided his father was in the right of it? But surely he could have had the courtesy to tell her so?

One after the other the carriages rolled up and disgorged their occupants, but there was no sign of the Cavenham coach. There were murmurings that the Viscount was keeping his prospective bride waiting. 'Good for him,' someone said.

'Not polite,' said another.

At last it could be seen making its way towards them and the crowd surged forwards to see as much as they could. Helen was almost knocked over in the crush, but forced her way to the front and was on the drive when the carriage rolled to a stop.

The Earl emerged first, clad in a lilac-coloured coat, pink waistcoat embroidered all over with mauve-and-yellow flowers outlined in gold thread, and white breeches. He held out his hand for his wife. She had covered her pallor with powder and had her hair piled high and powdered within an inch if its life. Not for her the flimsy muslin of the young ladies; her gown of dark blue silk had a full skirt and the waist was where nature intended it should be. She wore a necklace of rubies and diamonds with matching drops dangling from her ears.

Miles was the last to descend. He was dressed in a black cutaway coat, black breeches with white silk stockings and silver-buckled dancing pumps. His white muslin cravat was elegantly tied and his wayward curls brushed into submission. He stood on the drive and looked about him at the crowds;

then he saw Helen. She stood perfectly still and drank in the sight of him, both elated at seeing him and at the same time cast down to know this finery was not for her. They gazed at each other for a full minute. Behind her the crowds were noisy, behind him the sound of an orchestra could be heard. But they were in a world of their own, a world of silence, a world of memories and lost hopes, a world of despair. The Countess touched his arm and he turned to follow his parents into the house and the door was shut. Helen, blinded by tears, turned and groped her way through the crowd and down the road towards Warburton, unaware that she was being followed by a skinny little man in rags.

Miles and his parents made their way into the house where they were greeted by Lord and Lady Somerfield and Verity, who was dressed in a gown of pure white silk as behoved a young lady at her coming out. Its only splash of colour was a rose-pink sash tied just below the bust with two ends floating to almost floor level. She wore a slim tiara of rosebuds on her dark hair, which had been taken up to the top of her head from where it fell in corkscrew ringlets. Her mother was in dark red and her father in a plum-coloured velvet coat, white-brocade waistcoat and white breeches.

'There you are at last,' Lord Somerfield boomed. 'We had almost given you up. Thought something must be wrong at home, her ladyship ill or something.'

'Her ladyship, as you see, is well,' the Earl said. 'You must blame Miles. He has had that valet of his dancing round him for hours. He was so anxious that his appearance should be just right for tonight. You must forgive him, Miss Somerfield.'

She preened. 'Of course I forgive you, Miles. And you are not very late. Shall we go into the ballroom?' She tucked her hand under Miles's arm and led him forwards, followed by both sets of parents looking pleased with themselves.

Miles was in a kind of nightmare from which he was afraid there would be no awakening. He had dawdled over his *toilette*, fussed over by an excited Louis, who kept babbling about how Miss Somerfield would be bowled over by him, until he wanted to yell at the man to keep his tongue between his teeth. He had kept finding fault and rejecting muslin cravats one after the other, only to delay the time when he would have to go downstairs and climb into the carriage, wishing he did not have to go, but knowing all the time he had no choice, not if he wanted Helen to be free. To make sure Helen was free he had to shackle himself. If he could not have Helen, it did not matter whom he married—Verity Somerfield would do as well as anyone. But then to see Helen on the road like that had almost undone him. It had taken the greatest effort not to speed over to her and damn everyone else.

The ballroom was full to suffocating. It seemed to Miles that anyone who was anyone in Norfolk and Cambridge society and beyond was there, each trying to outdo the other in the magnificence of their turnout. Both men and women were dressed in a rainbow of colours, glittering with jewellery, and all had come to see him betroth himself to Verity. Flowers and drapery adorned every nook where they could be placed and at the end of the room was a dais on which a full orchestra played. Everyone turned towards them as they entered, looking them up and down as if appraising their attire and the way they comported themselves. As they seemed to be smiling, those who had been dancing continued to dance and those sitting on the sidelines watching went on with their conversations. Miles did not doubt they were talking about him and the announcement they thought was to come. And strangely, as he led Verity forwards, his limp seemed more pronounced than ever.

The Earl and Lord Somerfield escorted the ladies to prominent seats and then disappeared. Miles stood behind Verity's chair until the dance ended and a new one was announced. It was a stately country dance and he felt safe attempting it. He bent over to speak to Verity. 'Shall we join this, Miss Somerfield?'

She rose and he took her onto the floor. He bowed, she curtsied. 'You are looking particularly delightful tonight,' he told her as they promenaded between two rows of dancers. Politeness dictated he must compliment her, but he was reliving the dance he had had with Helen at the Assembly Rooms. He had been almost sure at that time that their difficulties could be resolved and there might be a happy outcome. She had won her court case and he had taken her to look at Ravenscourt Manor, in the hope that one day they might make it their home. Instead he had been forced to submit to his father's blackmail for her sake.

'Thank you, my lord,' he heard Verity say. 'It is such an important occasion, I am feeling quite nervous.'

He pulled himself out of his reverie. 'Oh, I am

sure there is no need. These are all your friends, are they not? They have come to wish you well in your life, a life which has all before it.'

'Yes, you have made me feel much easier.' She smiled at him as they turned at the end of the row and joined hands to execute the next steps. 'Do you not feel a little nervous yourself?'

'No, do you think I should?'

'I meant because of your limp. You must find it a handicap.'

'It may look ungainly,' he said, wondering why she had introduced the subject. Had she been schooled by her father to do so? It reminded him that his father had said Lord Somerfield required assurance that it would not interfere with his ability to sire children. It would serve them all right if he said he could not. 'But it does not prevent me from doing what I want and need to do, Miss Somerfield.'

If she understood the implication of what he was saying, she gave no indication of it. 'But you must feel self-conscious about it?'

'No. Do you?' It was a blunt question, but he did not like being quizzed over it.

'My lord, it is not I who has the disability,' she said. 'But Papa says I am not to mind it. It was got in the service of king and country.'

'Indeed it was.' He was growing more and more impatient with her. It was a strange conversation for a young lady who hoped she was going to receive a proposal. If they had been a loving couple, they would be exchanging compliments and displaying their affection for each other in a dozen different ways. Instead she was talking about his limp. 'I am lucky—there are many worse off than me.'

'I have not met such a one.'

'Perhaps because you are young and have been shielded from unpleasant sights by your parents.'

'I expect so.'

'Does it worry you? I mean my limp.'

'I don't know. You see, I do not know what it looks like.'

'What it looks like,' he repeated. 'Do you mean my leg?'

She blushed to the roots of her hair. 'I did not mean... Oh, dear. I am confused. It is just that Papa said...'

'What did your papa say?'

'That he had been assured it was not disfiguring.'

He was annoyed. 'Miss Somerfield, I am not sure we should be having this conversation at this time and in the middle of a dance, but since you have introduced the subject, we will continue it elsewhere.' He drew her away from the dance floor to the side of the room where they were half hidden by a huge display of flowers. 'Now,' he said firmly. 'You want to know what is wrong with me. I will tell you. Part of a shell pierced my thigh. It had to be dug out by the sawbones…'

She shuddered. 'Don't…'

'But you wanted to know and I am telling you. The muscle was damaged, which is why I limp and why one leg is scarred and much thinner than the other. If you wish to inspect it, I am sure that can be arranged.'

She gave a little cry and fled. He smiled grimly and left the ballroom by one of the long windows that looked out onto the terrace, where he began pacing up and down. He really should not have spoken to her like that, but if it put her off him, so much the better. The trouble was, it was not her but their respective fathers who were calling the tune. Suddenly it dawned on him that this was a business arrangement: the Somerfield wealth in exchange for a title for the daughter. His earlier suspicions had been confirmed—his father had pockets to let. Was that another reason why the Earl had been so keen to be rid of Helen? Because there could be no financial gain to be made from his son forming an alliance with a woman with no fortune?

Miles was perplexed. When he had left for the Peninsula, the estate had been in good heart, so what had happened in the six years he had been with his regiment? It did not make any difference to his reluctance to offer for Miss Somerfield. He could not give her the love she deserved, not while his heart was in bondage to Helen Wayland. Marrying Verity Somerfield would be doing her a great disservice.

'Miles, what the devil do you think you are at?' his father's voice demanded. He had approached from further along the terrace and Miles, immersed in his dilemma, had not heard him coming. 'Miss Somerfield is in tears and has had to be taken to her room to be comforted and everyone is talking about the abrupt way you left the ballroom. A lovers' tiff, they are saying, all agog to learn what it was about.'

'They will not learn it from me.'

'I should think not! But I will. What has put her in such a taking?'

'She quizzed me about my leg and so I told her how it had come about and offered to show her the scar.'

'Good God! How could you? She is not one

of your camp followers, she is a gently nurtured young lady of tender years. It was unforgivable of you.'

'I know and I am sorry for it, but I cannot marry someone who is revolted by the very mention of my lameness. It is part of me. It has to be accepted along with the rest of me.'

'Ralph is furious and so is Lady S~ for your mother…'

'I am sorry, sir. I wo~ Mama. Perhaps we

'Not until you ha Somerfield and d~ time act like a pr~

'I cannot.'

'You know the

'Yes, I know ~

'Do not think by Miss Wayl~ impossible all~ comely enou~ and self-will~ nothing and~ are to main~ tained whe~ are lusting

'I am n~

'That is the way it looks to me,' his father went on. 'Why do you think I have agreed to drop the charges against her on condition she takes herself off? You will soon forget her. And Verity Somerfield has all the attributes to make a wife for someone of your standing.'

'Pretty and empty-headed.'

'What's wrong with that? You can mould her to ᴏur ways.'

ᴍiles sighed. 'Have you told Sobers you are ᴅing the charge against Helen?'

ᴇt. Do you take me for a fool? When you ᴇ your duty and are betrothed to Miss then I will inform him I have no wish matter. Not before.'

ᴛ like the sound of that. His father and he was not sure he trusted ᴇ it has been taken out of your ᴀtion, it is not a civil matter.'

ᴀ I am sure something can ᴀve that to me. Now, are ᴜse or not?'

ᴇ with Miss Somer-

ᴛ again for appear-

ᴇ. I need to think

ᴇ a fool, and

you will pay for it as I paid for it. And it will have repercussions, make no mistake.'

'What do you mean? What happened in the past? It is something to do with Miss Wayland's father, is it not? Or was it her mother?' he added suddenly.

'None of your business. Forget I spoke. I don't want your mother upset by anyone, especially by you delving into things long forgotten.'

'But they are not forgotten, are they? Whatever it was has resulted in ill feeling and resentment towards a young lady who had nothing to do with whatever it was.'

'Rubbish. The boot is on the other foot. I do not want to hear another word about it.'

Miles was even more mystified, but his father had obviously regretted saying what he had and would not enlighten him. He turned to go back indoors.

They did not go into the house by the ballroom window but entered by a side door and made their way into the library, where Lord Somerfield waited. 'Well?' he demanded.

'Miles is full of remorse,' the Earl said.

'Sir, I can speak for myself,' Miles put in. Then, addressing Lord Somerfield, 'Where is Miss Somerfield, my lord? I must make amends for my brutish behaviour. She required to know about my disability and I am afraid I was more plain-spoken than I should have been.'

'I will have her fetched.' His lordship went to the door and instructed a footman standing in the hall to send for Miss Verity.

She arrived accompanied by her mother and curtsied to them all. Miles noted the evidence of tears disguised with fresh powder. She was little more than a child, unschooled in the ways of the world, and he wondered if she really wanted him to make an offer. Or was she, too, being coerced?

'Viscount Cavenham has something to say to you,' her father told her. 'We will leave you together.'

'Let Mama stay,' she said, reaching out for her mother's hand.

Her mother stood determinedly by her side. Miles attempted a reassuring smile. 'Of course, your mama must stay with you. I would not compromise your reputation for the world.' He knew, as they all did, that once she had been alone with him, especially under the present circumstances, it was as good as a commitment and he could not bring himself to that. Not yet. Perhaps not ever if he could only think of a way of sidestepping his father's blackmail.

The Earl and Lord Somerfield left the room, but not before the Earl had given Miles a meaningful look. As soon as they had gone, Miles turned to Verity. 'Miss Somerfield, I beg your forgiveness for being so outspoken. All I can say in my defence is that you seemed to want to know about my injury. If I was mistaken in that, I beg your pardon.'

'I only wished to know if it hindered you.'

'To some extent it does.' He paused. 'I think we have exhausted that topic for tonight; as you are so obviously tired and distressed, perhaps you should retire.'

'She will not,' her ladyship put in sharply. 'You have shamed my daughter in front of everyone and not to reappear will make matters worse. I require you to return to the ballroom together and at least put on some semblance of being in accord.'

'I will do that, of course,' Miles said, offering Verity his arm. 'Come, Miss Somerfield. Let us take another turn about the ballroom. I believe I can hear a waltz being played.'

They left the room together, followed by Lady Somerfield. Everyone turned as they entered the room. He bent to Verity's ear. 'Smile, my dear, or you will have the tabbies gossiping and saying we have had a falling out.'

She put on a brave face as he turned and put his hand about her waist for the dance. Acutely aware of the watchers, he did his best to appear relaxed, but he could not help remembering waltzing with Helen at the Assembly Rooms. They had danced so well together, fitting together so comfortably, his height matched by hers so that her head was just below his chin. He recalled the flowery scent of her hair, the clarity of her hazel eyes looking up at him in a kind of challenge. His limp had not mattered. Tonight was different; tonight he felt ill at ease and awkward. Verity's head only came up to his chest and she would have had to raise her head to see his face, but she was not even doing that.

'You dance very well,' he said, trying to make her smile.

'Thank you, my lord.'

'I think,' he said slowly, 'we will draw a veil over what happened tonight. I suggest you stand up with some of the other young men who will be a better match for you.'

She lifted her head at that. 'No proposal, my lord?'

'No, not tonight. You are too upset.'

'Thank you.' She let out a huge sigh of relief

and he realised she did not want the marriage any more than he did. 'But Papa will not be pleased.'

He felt like saying, 'Your papa can go to hell', but instead smiled and added, 'Miss Somerfield, his lordship will understand. You are not ready. Tonight is your come out. There will be other occasions to enjoy, new people to meet. You must be sure you are making the right choice.' And how he hoped and prayed that choice would not be him. It would be better for her to reject him than for him to mortify her by not making an offer. 'Spread your wings a little first. There is time.'

She brightened visibly, making the matrons surveying them from the sidelines smile in satisfaction; the quarrel, whatever it was about, must be over. 'You are very understanding, my lord.'

It was not understanding, he admitted to himself, but a fervent wish to haul himself out of the pit into which he had unwittingly tumbled. He stumbled on a turn, but righted himself swiftly and would have gone on, but she said suddenly, 'Do you think we might join Mama?'

Relieved, he offered her his arm and returned her to where their respective mothers waited. Other young men asked her to dance and he watched her go off with them and wished fervently that she would attach herself to one of them.

The evening was being brought to a close by fireworks. If any of the guests were disappointed that there was no announcement, their comments were made under their breath as they trooped out into the garden to see the display. Standing between Miss Somerfield and her mother, Miles watched in a kind of daze. He had averted disaster for tonight, but the problem had not gone away.

Helen, resigned to her fate, was sitting at the table in her upstairs drawing room attempting to take stock of her assets ready for the sale. She was alone in the house; Tom and Edgar had gone home before she left for Gayton Hall and Betty had asked for an evening off to visit a friend in the next village and planned to stay with her for the night. How much could she realistically expect to make on the sale? The building had been kept in good repair; though the printing press was old, it had been well looked after and could serve the business for several years before it needed replacing. The furniture was serviceable rather than fashionable and the desks in the shop worn and ink-stained, but there was years of usefulness still in them. Would anyone take it as a going concern? Would the Earl allow whoever it was to work in peace?

Thinking of the Earl inevitably led to thoughts of Miles and that last glimpse of him, standing in a pool of light at the Somerfield door. The ball would be in full swing and he would be dancing with Miss Somerfield. Had he already offered for her? Were the celebrations of the betrothal already in hand? She heard distant explosions and went to the window to look out towards Gayton. She could not see the village or the hall, they were too far away, but the night sky was lit up with fireworks, signifying the end of the evening. What had happened? Was there general rejoicing? Why could she not stop herself thinking about it? She went into the kitchen to make herself a cup of chocolate, which she took to her bedroom to drink once she had made herself ready for bed. It might help her sleep, but she did not hold out much hope of it.

She had undressed and was sitting on her bed, sipping the hot drink, when she caught sight of her mother's trinket box on the bedside table. Whatever had to be sold, she did not want to part with those. They were not valuable in any case, except to her. She picked up the green necklace. The last time she had worn that had been at the dance at the Assembly Rooms when she had danced with Miles. That had been a wonderful evening;

her court case was behind her with a not-guilty verdict, she was feeling and looking her best and Miles had held her in his arms, not for the first time or the last. There was the night the window had been broken and the day they went to Ravensbrook Manor and he had kissed her. Why had he done it if he had no feelings for her? Why had he suddenly turned away from her at the crossroads? Why was she tormenting herself with questions like that? He was not for her, could never be for her, Verity Somerfield or no Verity Somerfield.

She was startled by the sound of a roar and crash coming from downstairs. Someone had broken in. She sat there listening, expecting to hear footsteps on the stairs, but none came and she told herself not to be so fearful. Putting down the necklace and picking up the poker, she advanced towards the door and opened it. She was immediately engulfed in smoke. Through it she could see the stairs were in flames. Her immediate reaction was to shut the door again. The stairs were her only way of escape and they were on fire. Already smoke was curling in under the door, making her cough. She went to the window. Below her the flames were thrusting out through the broken window below her. The crash she had heard must have been the glass blowing out. The downstairs rooms were already well alight. The room behind her was filling with smoke and she could not get the window open. She was coughing badly now and her breathing was ragged. She crossed the room to retrieve the poker she had dropped in order to break the window but, overcome by smoke, she never reached it.

The Cavenham carriage was carrying the Earl and Countess and Miles home from the ball. The Earl had already let his son know how angry he was with him and would have gone on berating him all the way home, if the Countess had not begged him to desist. 'It is not the end of the world, Gilbert,' she told him. 'Miss Somerfield was content to leave things as they are for the present; to be sure, no one was in a mood for celebration. Miles will call at Gayton Hall tomorrow and all will be well.'

Miles had fallen silent, his chin on his chest, trying but failing to see a way out of his predicament. It was not yet dawn, but the sky seemed to be lighter than usual. Perhaps they would have a few sunny days at last. They would need them if what was left of the corn in the fields were to ripen and the men make a success of the Cooperative. They were good men, working with a will and Helen's optimistic reports were attracting attention, not only in Warburton but in the surrounding area. The *Bury and Norwich Post* had repeated them for its readers. When the business was sold, the reports would cease, unless whoever took on the business of the *Record* decided to continue them. He wished she did not need to go. He wished he could keep her by him and protect her, but the only way that could be done was by turning his back on her. Coming upon her at the crossroads, he had deliberately left her standing in the road, looking lost and bewildered. How he hated himself for that. Earlier tonight he had seen her with the crowd of curiosity-fuelled spectators at the approach to Gayton Hall and still he could not go to her.

'Miles, there is a building on fire,' the Countess said. 'Look.'

He was facing his mother and had his back to the direction in which they were going and had to lean forwards and screw his head round to see. 'My God! It's the *Warburton Record*.' He thumped on the roof to tell their driver to stop. 'Helen…'

The Earl was sitting forward, too, gazing in horror at the burning building. A fire crew with an engine were doing their best to douse the flames, but their efforts were having little effect.

Around them a crowd had gathered to watch the conflagration. The carriage stopped and both men tumbled out. The whole shop was in flames. 'Miss Wayland?' Miles asked one onlooker.

'No one's seen her. We think she must be in there.'

'Get her out,' the Earl yelled. 'For God's sake, someone get her out.'

Miles was already halfway to the shop. 'Ti'n't no use,' one of the fireman said, trying to prevent him entering the building. 'No one i'n't alive in there.'

Miles brushed him off, stood under the hose to soak himself in water and then disappeared inside the building, making for the stairs. They were well alight. Undeterred, he flung himself at them, coughing from the smoke. 'Helen!' he shouted. 'Helen!'

There was no answer. He reached the landing and pushed open the drawing-room door. The room was full of smoke and a few flames were already licking round the woodwork. He crawled on hands and knees, feeling about him in the dense smoke for Helen. She was not there. He went to the next room, knowing if he did not find her soon, it would be too late, the stairs and the whole house would be gone. He almost fell over her, lying on the floor. He did not even stop to establish whether she was alive or dead, but picked her up in his arms and made for the stairs. There was no escape that way. He turned back into the drawing room. Opening the door had allowed the flames to take hold and they were spreading inexorably across the floor and licking round the furniture. Taking his burden to the window, he smashed the glass with his elbow, pushing it in again and again until all the glass was gone. Below him some men had brought a blanket and were holding it out by the corners. Carefully he lowered Helen over the ledge and dropped her into it. She was caught and rolled in the blanket to douse her burning nightclothes.

'Now you,' someone shouted. He looked down. It seemed a long way and there was no other blanket. Behind him the fire crackled and the smoke became thicker. It was jump or be consumed. Before he could do so, he saw their coachman whipping up the horses to drive the coach under the window. He jumped onto the roof as it passed, grabbing hold of the edge to stop himself falling off.

The carriage stopped safely away from the conflagration and he slid to the ground amid the cheers of the onlookers. Ignoring them, he dashed off to where Helen lay on the ground, still wrapped in the blanket. His father was bending over her. There were tears in his eyes, as he turned his face up to Miles. 'To think it has come to this,' he said in a voice strangled by emotion.

Miles squatted down and pushed Helen's singed hair from her brow. Her eyelids flickered and he felt the pulse in her neck. She was alive, though how badly burned he did not know. Apart from singed eyebrows and hair, her face had not been touched. The extent of the burns on her body and limbs he could not know. 'Thank God.'

The Countess, who had left the coach soon after her husband and son, came over to them. 'She must be seen by a doctor.'

'Yes,' Miles said. 'We will take her to Ravens Park and send for Dr Graham.'

Surprisingly neither of his parents demurred at this and Miles picked Helen up and took her to the coach, propping her in the corner until he was in beside her and could lay her across his lap. The Earl and Countess took the opposite seats and they left the firemen to do what they could to stop the fire spreading to adjacent buildings. The *Warburton Record* would be left to burn itself out. No one spoke. Miles looked across at his father, whose eyes were on Helen's face. The hatred had gone and he looked worried to death. Miles found himself mentally echoing his father's words, 'To think it has come to this.'

Helen came round to find herself lying in a strange bed and the Countess sitting beside it, watching over her. 'What happened? Where am I?' she croaked, and found that talking hurt her throat. She seemed to be hurting everywhere, particularly her hands and arms. She looked down at herself. She was wearing a white linen nightrail which was certainly not her own and her hands and arms were bandaged. A nurse was sitting in a chair by the window. The room was large and beautifully furnished, certainly not a hospital ward.

'Oh, you are awake. Thank the good Lord,' the Countess said fervently.

'Where am I?'

'You are safe, here at Ravens Park.'

'Ravens Park?' she queried and struggled to sit up, only to find it brought on a fit of coughing that hurt her chest. She sank back again. 'How came I here? How long have I been here?'

'Two days. We brought you here in our coach. I am afraid there was a fire. Do you remember?'

'Fire?' She had a vague, terrifying memory of

smoke and flames and searing heat and being trapped. 'What happened?'

'We do not know how it started, but I am afraid your home has been completely destroyed.'

'Destroyed?' she echoed, thinking she must have misheard. 'All gone?'

'Yes, and you would have been gone, too, if we had not been passing in our coach—Miles went in to rescue you.'

'He did? Then I must thank him. Where is he? Was he burned? Oh, tell me he wasn't burned.'

The door opened and Miles peeped round it. 'I heard voices. May I come in?'

The Countess hesitated, but then smiled. 'It seems you are half in already. Come and see, Miss Wayland is awake and smiling.'

'Thank God.'

In seconds he was beside the bed and stood looking down at her. She swept her gaze over his face. He looked pale and there were dark rings round his eyes as if he had not slept. He had a bandage round his head and more on both hands. 'You were burned, too?'

'Only my hands and a small patch on my forehead. And like you, I have lost my eyebrows.' He smiled as he spoke. 'But we will both recover them, never fear.'

'How did you manage to rescue me? The stairs were alight. I was trapped.'

'I found you on the floor of your bedroom and dropped you out of the window into a blanket being held to catch you.'

'I'll never forget the sight of Miles at that window with the flames all round him,' the Countess said. 'It was terrifying. I thought he would die, that you both would die…'

'How did you get out?' Helen asked him.

'Greaves, our coachman, drove the coach under the window,' the Countess told her. 'Miles jumped onto its roof.'

'You were very brave,' Helen said.

'Not I,' he said. 'I did not relish having to jump from that height, but Greaves was quick-witted enough to see how he could help. It was an exceptional piece of driving, considering he had to get close and the horses were terrified of the fire. But he did it and I jumped and hung on until he could stop safely.'

'Thank God,' Helen said fervently. 'If you had lost your life trying to save mine, I do not know what I would have done.'

'But we are both alive and will recover, so think no more of it.'

'You are both very kind, but whatever were

you thinking of to bring me to Ravens Park? The Earl…'

'He was there when the decision was made to bring you here,' the Countess told her. 'I think he is sorry for what has happened and anxious you should be looked after.'

Helen could hardly believe that, but could not question it because there was a knock at the door and a maid entered the room and bobbed a curtsy. 'If you please, my lady, Lady Somerfield and Miss Somerfield are downstairs.'

The Countess rose. 'Tell the ladies we will be down directly, Janet.'

'I must go,' Miles said to Helen. 'We will talk some more later.' He nodded at the nurse, who rose and came to stand beside the bed. 'Look after her,' he said. 'She is very precious.' Then he followed his mother from the room.

Helen watched the door close on him and sank back into a bed more comfortable than any she had ever known, but she was restless. He had called her precious—she wondered how he could do that, when he was, in all probability, betrothed to someone else? And that someone was downstairs waiting for him. He was simply being kind to her because of what had happened. It had no more significance than that and she was being foolish to torment herself with that when there were far more important things to occupy her mind. What was she going to do? She had been in a mess before, but now it was infinitely worse. Her home and business had gone. How had that come about? She had gone round the downstairs rooms as she always did when she shut up shop and came upstairs for the evening. The fires had been doused and no candles or lamps had been left burning. It was true there were books and a great deal of paper, but it would have needed something to ignite it.

Surely to God no one had got in and set the fire deliberately? But why? And did they not know she was sleeping upstairs? But if someone had done it, they had effectively ruined her as surely as that summons for sedition. Without the building and its contents, there could be no sale and without a sale, she could not look for anywhere else to live. She had no money, no clothes, nothing. She did not even have the wherewithal to start again. Nor, she thought grimly, to pay a fine if that was the punishment in store for her. Her thoughts went round and round until she was dizzy, but she could see no way out of the coil she was in.

Why was she here instead of in the Warburton infirmary? Why had the Earl agreed to it? Had he had a change of heart? If he had, it was too late, much, much too late. She turned her face away from the nurse who was busy with her dressings and let the tears flow. 'Now, now,' the woman said sharply. 'It is nothing to cry over. You are alive, that is the main thing, and you are being well cared for here. Not many of the Earl's standing would take in a penniless stranger and treat them like royalty. You should be grateful, not weeping.'

'You would weep if you had lost everything,' Helen said. 'And the Earl of Warburton is no stranger.'

Miles was seated in the drawing room, making small talk with Lady Somerfield and her daughter, though Verity had very little to say. She seemed subdued, as if she would rather be anywhere but where she was. He tried smiling at her, but she did not respond.

'I hear you have given house room to that newspaper woman,' Lady Somerfield was saying. 'I must say, it is very noble of you, Dorothea.'

'We could not abandon her once Miles had rescued her, could we?' the Countess said. 'She had been burned and had nowhere to go. It was the Christian thing to do.'

'To think Miles risked his life and went into the

inferno to save her does not bear thinking about,' her ladyship continued. 'I am sure no one could have blamed him if he had said the flames were too great.'

'That would have been cowardly,' Miles put in. 'No one, least of all me, could stand by and let another human being burn to death if they had the means to save them. I am only thankful I was there to do it.'

'You were very brave,' Verity put in, looking at his bandages. 'Were you badly burned?'

'No, not badly at all. I am assured the injuries will heal. And some of them are cuts caused by breaking the window with my elbows. Luckily, my sleeves cover those.'

'But you will be scarred?'

He sighed. They were back to that, were they? Why could the silly girl not accept that not everyone was perfect and imperfections were part of a man's character? Love did not see them in any case; love was blind. But they were not talking of love, had never even mentioned it. 'I cannot tell. It will only be my hands, not my face. This…' he pointed to the bandage round his head '…is simply there to attract sympathy. There is nothing behind it.'

She seemed relieved. 'But your face is red and your eyebrows are singed.'

'Are they? Have no fear, my looks will be back to normal in a day or two.'

'We are assured there is no permanent damage,' the Countess put in. 'Miles will be able to call on you as promised in a few days.'

'How long is Miss Wayland staying?'

'She will stay as long as necessary,' Miles put in quickly. 'She is destitute and we cannot turn her out of doors until proper arrangements have been made for her.'

'I do hope it will not be long,' Lady Somerfield said. 'Having her here is bound to attract gossip and that will mortify Verity. She is upset enough as it is.'

Miles turned to Verity. 'Are you upset, Miss Somerfield?'

She looked from him to her mother and back again. 'I do not think it is quite proper to have an unmarried lady—'

'Not a lady,' her mother interrupted.

'An unmarried woman of business, a trades-person,' Verity went on, 'staying here when… when…' She could not go on. Miles suspected she had forgotten the drilling her mother had given her before they came.

'Having her here was not Miles's doing, but mine,' the Countess put in. 'Miles has had some business dealings with her in the past, that is all.'

'And do these business dealings involve you spending time in her bedchamber?' Lady Somerfield demanded. 'The maid who admitted us told us that was where you were when we arrived.'

'Miss Wayland had only a few minutes before regained consciousness,' Miles said, hardly able to disguise his anger. 'I went to see how she fared. My mother and a nurse were also in the room.'

'And how does she fare?'

'She is going to recover, but she was more badly burned than I. Her clothes were on fire.'

Verity shuddered. 'How dreadful. No clothes and everyone looking at her. I could not have borne it.'

'She was not conscious of it,' Miles said. The more he saw of Miss Somerfield, the more he realised how empty-headed she was. It was not her fault, but the way she had been raised. 'And we were all too busy putting out the flames and wrapping her in a blanket to worry about her lack of covering.'

'But you saw her without her clothes...'

'So I did. Let us hope fervently that you will never be put in such an embarrassing situation.'

The irony of his words was lost on her. 'No, indeed,' she said.

'I think we have said enough about Miss Wayland,' the Countess put in. 'Would you like a second cup of tea, Constance. Or another cake?'

'No, thank you.' Her ladyship rose to go. 'Come, Verity, we must not outstay our welcome. Unlike some. We shall expect you at Gayton Hall in a few days, my lord, and perhaps by then your visitor will have departed.'

The Countess rang for a footman to show their guests to the door and when they had gone, sat back in her chair with a heavy sigh. 'Do you know, Miles,' she said, 'I do not particularly like Lady Somerfield. She does not have an ounce of human sympathy in her body.'

He had been on his feet to bid farewell to their callers, but now he sat down facing her. 'It is Verity I feel sorry for. She does not want to marry me and is trying to find excuses not to do so and all she can come up with is how scarred I am.'

'And you do not want to marry her, do you?'

'No, Mama, I do not.'

'You cannot marry Miss Wayland, you know.'

'Miss Wayland has nothing to do with how I feel about Verity Somerfield. She is too immature and silly. If we married, I should soon lose patience with her. It would not be fair to her.'

'I do not see how you can get out of it now. Everyone knows you have been courting her and to withdraw suddenly will create a scandal. And it would definitely anger her father and yours.'

'I do not consider a couple of reciprocated calls and a dance or two courting, Mama.'

'You may not, but others will think differently.'

'I am hoping Miss Somerfield finds enough strength to stand up to her father and reject me. I am quite prepared to act the disappointed suitor if it saves her face.'

'How are you to bring that about?'

'I do not know. I might be able to if I could see her alone, but her mother sticks to her like treacle and she looks to her ladyship for the answer to every query as if she could not think for herself.'

The Countess smiled. 'Most likely she cannot.' She paused. 'I wish I could do something for you, but your father is determined. I tried to reason with him, but he says he expects you to obey him.'

'He has made that very clear to me. Perhaps when we call at Gayton Hall you could draw her ladyship away for a few moments to leave me to talk to Verity.'

'She will think you are going to propose.'

'I cannot think of any other way, can you?'

'No.'

He was at an impasse. Two autocratic husbands, two acquiescing wives and an obedient daughter who could not see beyond the superficiality of a wedding and becoming Lady Cavenham, were almost impossible to overcome. But overcome them he must, or leave Ravensbrook and Warburton altogether. With Helen? Oh, how he would like that, but the subsequent gossip would kill his mother and there was still the not-so-little problem of that trial hanging over Helen's head. Besides, Helen herself would not let him do it.

The fact that his father was distraught when he saw that fire and his words said over the unconscious Helen—'To think that it has come to this'—had him wondering if the old man had had a change of heart. He knew Helen was being nursed under his roof and, though he had not been to see her, had raised no objection to her being there. If he could get to the bottom of that, he might find some answers. He excused himself and went in search of his father.

Chapter Eleven

The Earl was in the stables talking to Greaves, whom he had amply rewarded for his quick thinking and bravery by promoting him to head groom, giving him a fat purse and a cottage on the estate. He turned when Miles entered the stables looking for him.

'There you are,' he greeted him. 'I was just talking to Greaves about replacing Caesar. That mare of yours is too docile by far, you want a horse with some spirit. I heard about a well-bred stallion for sale in Swaffham and thought I might buy it for you. How about going to look at it?'

Since the fire the Earl had changed, become less bombastic, more tolerant. It was as if the flames had cauterised whatever it was that had made him like he was. Perhaps the gift of a horse was meant as a peace offering. It gave Miles hope, though he was well aware that, proud and stubborn as his father was, it would take a huge effort for him to climb down. The trip to Swaffham might afford the opportunity to talk to him without the risk of him walking away if he did not like the way the conversation was going. 'Yes, I could do that. When were you thinking of going?'

'In an hour.'

'Then I shall be ready.'

He went indoors and climbed the stairs to the sick room. Helen was sitting in a chair by the window wrapped in blankets while the nurse changed the sheets on the bed. He fetched a chair and joined her. She turned to look at him. He looked tired, his eyes heavy beneath his singed eyebrows. 'Have your visitors gone?'

'Yes, they did not stay long.'

'Am I to congratulate you on your betrothal?'

'No. There are important matters to resolve before I can think of marrying anyone.'

'Oh.' She did not know quite what to make of that. What important matters? The dowry, perhaps, marriage settlements, repairing and refurbishing the Manor?

'How are you, Helen?' He spoke softly so that the nurse could not hear him.

'Better, I think, though my burns are still a little painful.'

'I expect they will be for a while yet. I wish we had arrived on the scene sooner; I might have prevented some of it.'

'But you did arrive and saved my life. I cannot thank you enough for that.'

'Think nothing of it, I do not. I am glad I was there because if anything had happened to you because I failed to do what I could, I should not have been able to live with myself. Can you tell me how it happened? Did you turn a lamp over or something like that?'

'No, it started downstairs after I had locked up for the night. I went round as I always do to make sure all the lamps and candles were out and the fires doused. I am sure I left nothing burning. I cannot think how it started and it took hold so quickly. If you had not come I should have burned to death.' The thought of what might have happened made her shudder.

'Thank the good Lord you did not. You are here and safe. Do you think someone could have started the fire deliberately?'

'I did wonder about that, but why would they? And if they did, did they mean to kill me or simply damage the building beyond repair?'

'I think probably the latter. With all the paper and your books down there, the shop would have burned like a furnace once it was alight. Whoever it was would not have been able to control it.' He paused. 'Did you see or hear anyone?'

'No. Only the fire crackling and the windows blowing out.' She gave a cracked laugh. 'And I had only just replaced them, too.'

'I intend to get to the bottom of it,' he said. 'If it was deliberate, it will not go unpunished. I have asked the men on the Co-operative to keep their eyes and ears open. Did you have any fire insurance?'

'A little, but it was so dear I could only afford enough for the fire engine to come and douse the fire, not to rebuild or replace the press. It was old anyway. How badly is the building damaged?'

'I went to look. The walls are standing, but the interior and the roof have gone. It is in a dangerous state and will have to be pulled down.'

'Then I have lost everything. Oh, Miles, what am I to do?'

He reached out and laid a hand on her arm above the bandages, longing to do more to reassure her that she had nothing to worry about, that he would look after her for the rest of her life, but it was too soon. He had first to solve the problem of Verity Somerfield to everyone's satisfaction 'Not quite everything,' he said. 'I found this.' He reached into his pocket and withdrew the necklace she had been holding when the fire started. Its green stones glittered against the bandages on his hands as he held it up to her, though the silver setting was blackened. 'I saw it shining among the ashes. It is the one you wore at the Assembly dance, is it not?'

'Yes. Oh, I am so glad you rescued it. It belonged to my mother. I was not aware of its existence until I went through the trinket box after Papa's death.'

'I believe it might be valuable.'

'Do you think so? I thought it was paste, though it is very pretty.'

'Shall I have it valued for you?'

'Yes, please, but I doubt it will help me out of my predicament, do you?'

'No, but you are not to worry about it. You do nothing for the moment except recover and then we will decide what is to be done.'

'We?' she echoed.

He smiled. 'You did not think I would let you bear it alone, did you?'

'But I am a burden to you. And it is not fitting…'

'You are not a burden and as for it not being fitting, that is nonsense. And where else would you go? Now I am going to Swaffham to buy a horse to replace Caesar.' He stood up and bent over her to kiss her forehead. 'Do not worry. All will be well.'

She watched him leave the room and then sank back in her chair, touching the spot where his lips had pressed. Why had he done that? Why was he kind to her when it would be better if he were indifferent, then she might not be so torn apart by loving him? He was nothing like his father, he cared about people, cared about her, but not enough to love her. It was all very well to tell her not to worry, but how could she help it? The nurse came to help her back into bed and she lay back against the pillows in despair.

Fancy Miles thinking that necklace might be valuable. She was sure he was mistaken; her parents had never been wealthy and when her father had been taken to court by the Earl, he would surely have remembered if there was something he could sell to pay the fine. On the other hand, if it was something her mother treasured, he would have been reluctant to do that. If her mother had treasured it, she had never worn it. If Miles was right and it was worth a little money, selling it might mean the difference between managing her life and penury. It might fetch enough to buy her some clothes. Without clothes she could not even leave the sick room.

'Here, miss, drink this,' the nurse said. 'It will ease the pain and help you to sleep.' A small glass was put to her lips and she drank obediently, though it tasted bitter. Her last thought before she drifted off was of Miles. Why did she have to go and fall so hopelessly in love with the son of her implacable foe, a man about to become engaged to someone else? As soon as she was strong enough to leave, she would take herself off, away from the source of her misery. But where? Everything was going round and round in her head, her thoughts too muddled to make sense.

Miles joined his father in the coach and they set off for Swaffham, about fifteen miles distant. They were silent for a time, while Miles cogitated how to begin asking his questions. 'Miss Wayland is recovering slowly,' he said.

'Good.'

'It looks likely that the fire was started deliberately.'

'Who would want to do that?' The Earl twisted round to face his son. 'I may have wanted her out of town and no longer tormenting me, but if you think—'

'No, Father, I do not think that at all. You are not the only adversary she has. She has ruffled quite a few feathers in her time at the *Record*. I have put some men onto making enquiries.'

'I doubt you will find a culprit now.'

'Perhaps not, but in view of the fact that she is ruined, you will withdraw that court summons, won't you? You no longer have anything to gain by it.'

'Oh, but I have. I want you married to Verity Somerfield.'

'Verity Somerfield does not want to marry me.'

'She will do as her father bids her.'

'I hope not. I hope she will have the courage to stand up to him. We should not suit and both of us would be made miserable. Is that what you want?'

'Oh, come, it is not as bad as that. You do not have to live in each other's pockets, you know. You will have your own interests to occupy you, though I hope they do not include mixing with the lower orders as you do now, and she will have her wifely duties. I am persuaded she knows what is expected of her. What more do you want?'

'I want a strong affection between us, a meeting of minds, interests in common. I want to love and respect the woman I marry.'

'Pshaw, that is sentimental nonsense.'

'You may think so, but for me it is essential.'

'You are besotted by Miss Wayland, I know that, but it cannot be, Miles.'

'Sir, I am of age, I do not have to ask your permission to marry, nor who my bride should be. Miss Wayland is all I hope for in a wife—gentle, forbearing, intelligent and hard working, besides being very beautiful. She cares for those around her and helps those in need…'

'I know all that. Her mother was the same…'

'How well did you know her mother?'

'I knew her when she was Eleanor Brent and lived at Ravensbrook Manor.'

'And? I am persuaded there is more to it than that. Did you love her?'

'I was betrothed to her.'

'Betrothed?' Miles repeated in astonishment.

'Yes. Is that so extraordinary? We were both from good families who had been friends and neighbours for years. There was a grand ball. Everyone was there, including a whole tribe of her Brent relations. She looked magnificent in a blue-green gown and emeralds at her throat…' His voice faded and his eyes clouded, as he remembered.

'What happened? Why didn't you marry her?'

'One night the Manor went up in flames. The fire engine was sent from Warburton and everyone from miles around ran to hand buckets of water to try to put it out, but by then it had taken hold and nothing could be saved. Lord and Lady Brent were in the part of the house where the fire started and could not be rescued, but we pulled Eleanor out alive.'

'We?' Miles queried.

'Henry Wayland and I. Eleanor was taken to Ravens Park to recover. She was suffering from the smoke, but not badly burned. Henry Wayland called every day to ask how she was.'

'Was he a printer then?'

'No. He was a curate.'

'A what?' Miles was astounded.

'A curate, a man of the cloth. He hardly had a penny to his name. His visits were allowed because everyone thought it was part of his parish duty to visit the sick, but they went on even after she had recovered. Fool that I am, I allowed it. One day Eleanor disappeared, took herself off and then it was discovered Henry Wayland was missing, too. There was a terrible scandal. The Brent relations cut Eleanor out of their lives and Wayland was defrocked. I found out they had married and gone to live in London.'

What he had been told was a revelation, but it explained a great deal and for the first time Miles felt real sympathy for his father. It perhaps explained why he had become ill-tempered and autocratic and why his poor mother had suffered and was still suffering. 'I am sorry, Father, I did not know any of this. How much of it does my mother know?'

'I cannot be sure. I did not meet her until a little time after the fire, but she may have heard the rumours. Nothing was ever said between us. We married and you were born and all might have been well if Henry Wayland had not come back to Warburton years later and set up his newspaper.'

'I had joined my regiment by then.'

'Yes. Why on earth they decided to return I cannot imagine, unless it were done to rub my nose in my humiliation.'

'So that is how the feud came about,' Miles said. 'It is hardly surprising, but is it reason enough to hate Helen?'

'She is the image of her mother. Every time I see her I am reminded. Even that might have been bearable if she had not taken over where Wayland left off and waged a campaign against me.'

'And that was why you wanted her out of our lives.'

'Can you blame me?'

'Perhaps not, but Helen is not her mother, Father.'

'She has enough of her mother in her to have inherited some of her bad blood.'

'Nonsense! All she has inherited are these.' He pulled the necklace from his pocket. 'I found them in the ruins of the shop after the fire. Helen thinks they are paste, but I am not so sure.'

'They are not paste,' his father said. 'They are real emeralds. What are you doing with them?'

'Helen asked me to have them valued.'

'Does she want you to sell them?'

'I do not know. I shall have to ask her. I imagine she will be reluctant, but if they are all she has, she might be forced to part with them.'

'You will not get the best price in Swaffham, you know. Better take them to London. They should make enough to start her up in a new business venture somewhere away from Warburton.'

'Only if you stop that court case.'

'We are back to that, are we? You know the conditions.'

'Those have surely gone by the board since the fire and Helen came to Ravens Park to recover.'

'I am tired of your quizzing, Miles, leave it be.' The Earl leaned back in his seat and deliberately shut his eyes. 'I will speak to Sobers; more than that I will not promise.'

It was a small step and Miles could not be sure his father meant it, but he could go no further until he knew what Helen wanted. If the stones were real, then she would not be as destitute as they had thought, but then she might assert her independence and leave Warburton as she had planned and he did not want that. More than ever he was determined to make her his wife. If only she would have him. He could not even be sure of that.

His father was right about the necklace, he discovered, when his first call on reaching Swaffham was to consult a reputable jeweller. The stones were particularly fine and he was offered several thousand pounds for them. He thanked the jeweller, put the necklace back in his pocket and rejoined the Earl, waiting outside in the coach.

'You were right,' he said, getting back in the vehicle and directing the driver to take them to the horse dealer. 'They are worth a small fortune.'

'I knew that. I bought them. They were my betrothal gift. Now, can we concentrate on looking at this horse?'

* * *

The animal, called Pewter on account of its dark-grey coat, proved to be a good buy, sound in wind and limb and with a spirited temperament that would repay firm handling. Miles had brought his saddle and, after mounting and trotting the animal up and down for some minutes, decided he would have it, but insisted on paying for it himself. Leaving his father enjoying a meal in the George, he set off for home. He wanted, more than anything, to see Helen, though what he would say to her, he did not know. Knowing the reason for the enmity between their fathers did not solve his problems. Helen had loved her parents and would be distressed to be told the tale and he did not think he would tell her. But would it be a good start to a marriage to keep it from her, especially if she found out from another source? She would hate him for that and turn him down. She might turn him down in any case.

He rode at a canter and then a gallop to test out the horse's stride, then set it to walk while he gave himself up to thinking how he could resolve the impasse he was in. First he had to settle things with Verity Somerfield without hurting her and without subjecting her to her father's ire. How to do that occupied several miles and he came to no firm conclusion. Then he had to tell Helen how he felt about her, that life without her by his side would be barren and empty and if she did not agree to marry him he would be the most miserable being alive. Hardest of all, he had yet to persuade his father to accept the situation and withdraw that writ. Then, somehow or other, the lawyers must get to work and make sure the case was dropped. It was going to take all his ingenuity to bring it all to a successful conclusion. Failure did not bear thinking about.

Apart from her hands, Helen had not been badly burned and she knew she could not stay under the Earl's roof a minute longer than she had to. But she had no clothes, not a stitch to her name, no home, no money, no means of earning a living. Whoever had started that fire had well and truly ruined her—not only ruined her, but made her beholden to the Earl of Warburton. And being so close to the man she loved when nothing could come of that love was sheer torture.

She had been looking towards the window, watching the wind swaying the tops of the trees, which was all she could see from the bed, but turned when the door opened, half-expecting Miles and preparing herself to tell him she must leave. But it was the Countess who came into the room, carrying a bundle of clothes, which she laid on the foot of the bed. 'How are you today, Miss Wayland?'

'I am feeling much stronger, my lady.'

'Good. Would you like to dress? I have found some clothes I think will fit you and Nurse will help you into them.'

'Thank you. You have been very kind to me, but I cannot stay here. It is not fitting.'

'You are right, my dear, which is why I wrote to your Brent relations. Your cousin, Lord Brent, has come to fetch you.'

'Lord Brent? How can that be? There were a few Brent relations at my mother's funeral, but they never wanted anything to do with us.'

'But you are his kin and, under the circumstances, he is prepared to look after you. I gather he has a large family and room enough for one more. He has come all the way from Cambridge to take you back with him, so shall we see if these clothes fit you?' She nodded at the nurse who was standing nearby. 'I will be down in the drawing room when you are ready.'

The clothes were cast-offs of the Countess's, but the materials were of better quality than Helen had ever had. The undergarments were of the finest cotton and the gown striped silk in two shades of blue. The neckline was edged with a ruff of pleats, which was repeated round the hem of the skirt. It fitted well enough, but because Helen was taller than the Countess the skirt revealed a little more of her ankles than was altogether proper. She was given white stockings and a pair of black pumps. Dressing took a little time because of her bandaged hands, but at last she was ready, her hair brushed and a shawl draped over her shoulders.

She was unsteady on her feet, but the nurse took her arm to help her downstairs. In the drawing room she came face to face with a cousin she had seen only once at her mother's funeral. In his forties, he was a tall man, elegantly dressed in a brown double-breasted tailcoat, which had a very high collar from which a starched muslin cravat erupted. His mustard-coloured pantaloons were fastened under the instep of his shoes by straps. He put down the teacup he was drinking from and rose to bow to her. 'Cousin Helen.'

'How do you do, my lord.' Helen was helped to a seat and the nurse withdrew.

'I am sorry to find you in this predicament,' her cousin went on. 'I trust you are recovering?'

'Yes, thank you.'

'I hear you have lost everything.'

'Yes. Even these clothes are borrowed.'

'Oh, you may have them,' the Countess put in. 'I do not want them back.'

'I never did hold with that newspaper business,' he said.

'I was not equipped to do anything else, my lord, and I had to earn a living.'

'Quite. Now that is all behind you and best forgotten. I will give you a home. My wife will be glad of some help with the children in return for your keep. I trust you will agree to that?'

She had to be thankful, but she did not view the prospect of living with this cousin who obviously looked down his nose at her with any degree of enthusiasm. But she had no choice. The Countess was as anxious to be rid of her as she was to go. 'Yes, but until my hands are healed, I will not be much use.'

'I understand that, but I am assured they are on the mend and the children's nurse will help you until you can begin your duties.'

'Thank you.'

'Then we will go now, if you are ready. I had to postpone a meeting to come here and there are other matters at home needing my urgent attention.'

'I am ready,' she said, wondering what Miles

would say when he returned and discovered she had gone. Would he be a tiny bit sorry? Would he miss her as she would undoubtedly miss him? Her heart was in pieces as she followed her haughty cousin out to his carriage.

They were silent for the first few miles. Helen, pretending to look out of the window, was thinking about all she had left behind: her home, her friends, her business, Tom, Edgar, Betty and the men of the Co-operative. She would miss them all, but most of all she would miss Miles. Without him there was a great void in her life that could never be filled. And what lay ahead? She did not know. She risked a glance at the man who sat opposite her. He was staring straight ahead, both hands on the top of the cane he held between his knees.

'My lord, I remember you coming to my mother's funeral, but as we were never introduced I am not sure what our relationship is.'

'I am your second cousin, William. My father was your mother's first cousin. He was at the funeral, too, but he passed on last year and I inherited the title. Did your mother never speak of us?'

'No. Could you tell me about her? I know so little of her early life.'

'I never met her and only know what I was told by my father just before we attended her funeral. As far as I can tell her childhood was uneventful. She lived with her parents at Ravensbrook Manor and grew up to be a beautiful young woman. When Gilbert Cavenham offered for her and she accepted, both families were pleased. A grand wedding was planned, half the arrangements were made.'

'Gilbert Cavenham?' she queried in astonishment. 'You mean she was engaged to the Earl of Warburton?'

'Yes. He wasn't an Earl then, nor even a Viscount, but he was Lord Cavenham's heir.'

'What happened?'

'There was a fire…'

'At Ravensbrook Manor. Yes, I know. Was my mother there at the time?'

'Yes. She was rescued and taken to Ravens Park to recuperate.'

'Then what?'

'She ran off with the curate.'

'The curate?'

'Yes, Henry Wayland was a curate. Did you not know that?'

She was astonished. 'No, I did not. My parents rarely talked about the past. I knew nothing of what had happened. But I do know they were devoted to each other and to me when I was born. I could not have had more loving parents.'

'That came at a cost. There was a terrible scandal. Gilbert Cavenham was in a dreadful state and vowing revenge. Henry Wayland was forbidden by the church to practise as a cleric for the rest of his life and your mother was disowned by her family. My father, as the closest living male relative, inherited the title, but he was disinclined to rebuild the Manor and live there on account of the scandal and moved to Cambridge, which is where I now live.'

'I did not know any of this. You have taken my breath away.'

It took her several minutes to absorb what he had said, during which neither spoke. Miles was several years older than her, so the Earl must have found his new bride very quickly and her own parents delayed having her until some time later. Her father was probably trying to establish himself as a printer before they started a family. 'Viscount Cavenham said there was a feud between my father and his, but I did not believe him,' she said, at last. 'I thought it was simply my father's determination to stand up for the poor and downtrodden and that the Earl did not like being criticised.'

'There was more to it than that.'

'Yes, I can see that now. But I cannot believe my mother would do anything wicked. There must have been something behind it all.'

'She said she had fallen in love and could not help herself. Love! Bah! It is the cause of half the world's ills; people have no self-control and no sense of propriety. From what Countess Warburton has told me, you were in the way of following in her footsteps…'

'Whatever do you mean?'

'Setting your cap at the Viscount when he is about to become betrothed to another young lady.'

'I did not set my cap at him. We worked together on a project to help the poor and unemployed; there was nothing more to it.' She hoped she sounded convincing. She had not deliberately set out to love Miles and he did not know of it in any case, so there was no need for anyone else to know what was in her heart. It must stay hidden.

'Now you are away from there, it will silence the gossip.'

'I was not aware there was any gossip.'

'Of course there was. How could there not be, when the man rescued you from the fire and carried you half-naked to his coach and brought you to his home? Some of the older inhabitants have long memories and they will recall the scandal of your mother and the curate.'

'Then I am glad you came for me. I would not compromise the Viscount's reputation for worlds.'

'I am glad to hear it.'

'Did you know the Earl has had me arraigned for seditious libel?' she said, abruptly changing the subject. 'The case comes up in October.'

'Yes, I did know. We shall, with the Earl's co-operation, try to get the case dropped, but there are conditions.'

She sighed. 'I expect there are.'

'First, you will not return to Warburton, but remain under my roof at my behest. Secondly, you will not speak or write anything against the Earl of Warburton. Thirdly, you must not communicate with Viscount Cavenham under any pretext, and fourthly, if we cannot get the case against you dropped, you are to attend the hearing and throw yourself on the mercy of the court and blame your father for the way he brought you up. You are to plead that you did not understand what you were doing and you will promise never to do anything like it again. You will tell the judge and jury you have given up the newspaper.'

'I have had to do that,' she said tartly. 'It went up in flames.'

'And the other conditions? If you are to reside under my roof, I need those assurances.'

It hurt her pride to agree, but what choice did she have? 'You have them,' she said and turned again to look out of the window so that he did not see her tears. Her heart was aching for Miles, but he was not for her, had never been for her, and she had to make the best of a bad situation. To think that all this upset came about because her mother had fallen in love with the wrong man. If it had not happened, Mama would be Countess Warburton now and more than likely still be alive because the Earl could afford the best doctors and nurses, which her father could not.

She gave a twitch of a smile; she might have had the Earl for a father. And Miles would be her brother. She stopped herself thinking of that. It had not happened. Her mother had given it all up for love. Fancy her father being a curate. He had never once breathed a word about that. Had he felt guilty about what he had done? Had he felt in the least sorry for Gilbert Cavenham? Had her mother? Did Miles know the tale? She did not think so. And after all he had done for her, he would think her terribly ungrateful to dash off and never see him again. Oh, how was she going to endure it?

Miles had to pass Ravensbrook Manor on his way home and decided to have another look round. What he hoped to discover he did not know—evidence of how the fire started, perhaps. It seemed strange that history should repeat itself like that, but fires were a common occurrence when lamps and candles were carried about and often left unattended, and fires were banked up to cook and keep houses warm. Sparks from spitting coal could ignite rugs and carpets. He should not read anything into it.

As he suspected, he learned nothing new. The house was just as derelict, just as overgrown, just as dark. Whoever was squatting in the back parlour was still doing so. The remains of a recent meal lay on a plate before the hearth and the kettle was still warm. There was also a large can of oil, which he supposed the man used to fuel a lamp, but strangely there was no lamp, simply a burned-out candle. There was no sign of the interloper; he had obviously heard him coming and made himself scarce. Miles was curious and did a quick search of the house and outbuildings, but found no one. Returning to his horse, he gave the stallion his head and covered the last mile home at a gallop.

He was eager to talk to Helen, only to be told by his mother that she had gone.

'Gone?' he queried in dismay. 'Gone where? You mean she took herself off. She can't have done—she had no clothes, nowhere to go.'

'Her cousin came and fetched her,' the Countess said, almost cringing from his blazing eyes. 'He offered to give her a home. It is best for everyone.'

He was especially annoyed that it had been done secretly while he was absent. His parents had colluded to have him out of the way when it happened and even his normal deference to his mother and her frailty deserted him. 'Best for you, perhaps, and my father, who is determined to see me married to Verity Somerfield. Well, it will not happen. I am going to find Helen. I mean to marry her, if she will have me, and nothing on earth will divert me from that and do not tell me she is a nobody because I have discovered she is as well born as I am.'

'I know that. It was Lord Brent who came to fetch her.'

'How did he know she was here? Someone must have told him.'

'I did. I wrote to him.'

'You?' He could believe it of his father, but not his mother.

'Miles, please calm down. Miss Wayland was destitute, she has lost everything. Where better to be under such circumstances but in the bosom of her family? She could not stay here, it was causing gossip and...'

'Lady Somerfield was laying down the law. We are not beholden to the Somerfields, Mama.'

'Your father...'

'Why are you so afraid of him? He has never beaten you, has he?'

'No, of course not. But he is impossible to live with when he is angry, you know that. And he has told me Lord Somerfield is prepared to inject some capital into Ravens Park when you marry Verity. He assured me it was vital to the future of the estate.'

'I am sorry for that, Mama, but it makes no difference. Verity Somerfield does not want me and I do not want her and there's an end of it.'

'Then you had better make that clear to her, though what your father will say I dread to think.'

'I think he already knows it. Where is he?'

'Did he not come home with you?'

'No, I left him in Swaffham and rode the new horse home. He ought to have arrived almost as soon as I did, considering I stopped on the way. He must have been detained in Swaffham. Perhaps he met someone he knew.'

'Perhaps. What are you going to do now?'

'It is too late to go calling, but tomorrow morning, I am going to ride over to Gayton Hall to settle things once and for all. And then I am going calling on Lord Brent.'

'Do you know where he lives?'

'No, but you are going to tell me.' This statement brooked no denial.

But none of that happened, because Greaves came home long after dark with the horses pulling a flat cart on which lay the covered body of the Earl of Warburton.

The whole household was put in a spin, with servants running hither and thither, not knowing what to do. The Countess swooned clean away and had to be administered to, the body had to be lifted from the cart and taken to a bedchamber and Dr Graham sent for to confirm the death, though it was obvious there was no life in the man. Only then was Miles able to set aside his own real grief to question the groom.

'Tell me exactly what happened.' He had gone out to the stables where Greaves was seeing to the horses. They were lathered and in distress and needed soothing.

'It were an accident. I couldn't stop it. When his lordship came out of the George to come home, he suddenly decided he would drive the carriage himself and got up beside me. I did not want him to, on account of he was—' He stopped suddenly.

'On account of he was a little foxed, you mean.'

'Yes, my lord.'

'Go on.'

'He were goin' along all right, but a little too fast for my likin', but he took no notice when I suggested he oughta ease up a bit. We were going round a bend when a dog fox ran across the road in front of the horses and they got all of a flurry and his lordship couldn't hold them. They ran the coach into the ditch. His lordship were flung off the driving seat and hit his head against a tree. I reckon he died there and then. I was thrown off and dazed for a while, but when I came to, I could see the coach was smashed beyond repair. The horses were struggling to rise, so I got them free and was thinking of putting his lordship's body on one and riding the other, when another coach stopped to see what was happening. I do not know the name of the man and did not think to ask, but he said it would be more fitting to send his lord-ship home on a cart, so he arranged for one to come from a nearby farm. When it came I hitched our horses to it so the farmer could take his own horses back. He said he needed them to work on the farm tomorrow. So that's how I came home.'

'Thank you, Greaves.'

'It weren't my fault, my lord. I did tell his lord-ship, but he would not listen and it would ha' been more dangerous to wrestle the reins out of his hands. Any case, I daren't do that, the mood he was in.'

'I understand. No one is blaming you. See to the horses, will you, and then arrange for that cart to be returned to its owner.'

He went back indoors to see his mother. She would need comforting and there was a funeral to arrange and heaven knew how many people who must be informed. He was going to be busy for the next few days. It was only when he sat down with his tearful mother to talk about it that he realised he was now the second Earl of War-burton. It was an awesome responsibility, come much sooner than he had ever anticipated. For the moment, duty must come before love.

Chapter Twelve

It was her cousin, William, who told Helen that Miles had succeeded to the title on the death of his father. She could hardly take it in. The Earl had been hale and hearty the last time she had seen him, and, for all his antagonism, she had never wished him dead. She wondered how Miles was managing. And the Countess. What a blow it must have been to them. Miles was now Earl of Warburton and that seemed to end whatever slim hope she might have had that she might see him again.

'I must write and offer my condolences to the Countess,' she told her cousin.

'You may do that,' he agreed.

Although only a quarter the size of Ravens Park, Larkspur House was a substantial four-storey mansion set in a small estate in a village on the western outskirts of Cambridge. As soon as she arrived it had been made very clear to her that she was going to be treated as the poor relation. She was given a room on the top floor and a doctor was sent for who subjected her to a careful examination of her burns. 'Take the bandages off and let her wear mittens,' he had told Lady Brent. 'Her hands are all but healed and the scars will fade in time. There is no need for her to stay in bed.'

A mantua maker had been fetched to provide her with a simple wardrobe befitting her lowly station. As soon as she was suitably clothed and provided with some cotton mittens to cover her hands, she had been introduced to her charges. There were three of them: Harold, a boy of seven, and twin girls, Sophy and Chloe, who were five. Her task was to begin their education, although Harold would soon be sent away to school. They did not treat her with any deference, but she was fond of children and set out to win their trust. This was her life, she could have no other, and must make the best of it, but when she found her bed at night, she was overcome by desolation. She was lonely and she missed her own home and independence, but most of all she missed Miles.

She would lie in bed, wondering what he was doing and, until she learned of the Earl's death, had tortured herself with wondering whether he and Miss Somerfield had become officially betrothed. She supposed that now he was in mourning that would be postponed. It did not make her feel any better.

Lord Somerfield, along with many of the Earl's male friends, his tenant farmers, Dr Graham, Mr Sobers, James Mottram and as many of the estate workers as could be spared, attended the funeral while the ladies, including Lady Somerfield and Verity, waited at the house for the menfolk to return. All were in unrelieved black, a colour which, on the Countess, heightened her pale complexion. She looked almost ghostly.

'I am glad to learn that Miss Wayland has left,' Lady Somerfield said, when everything that could be said about the tragedy had been said and they were, for a moment, lost for something to say.

'Yes, her cousin, Lord Brent, came from Cambridge and fetched her,' the Countess told her. 'He has offered her a home.'

'Good. Of course, with the Viscount—oh, I meant the Earl—in mourning, we cannot make an announcement. It will have to wait.'

'Mama,' Verity put in, 'the Earl has not offered for me and may not do so now.'

'What nonsense are you talking?' her mother said crossly. 'Of course he will.'

'If he does, I am not sure I wish to be a Countess. The idea frightens me.'

'I am losing all patience with you, child,' Lady Somerfield went on. 'What has got into you? You are not likely to get a better offer.'

'Papa is rich enough to buy me any husband he chooses,' her daughter went on. 'But I should like to have some say in the matter.'

'Oh, give me patience,' her ladyship said. 'What do you say, Dorothea?'

'I should not like to think either of them was made unhappy by a marriage they do not want,' the Countess said, choosing her words carefully. 'There is nothing worse than being locked in a loveless marriage.'

'You have changed your tune,' Lady Somerfield said sharply.

'The circumstances have changed. My husband is dead and Miles must take over the estate. I have no idea what his plans are for that. It is too soon to say.'

Miles had arrived back from the funeral and was on the point of entering the drawing room when he heard his name mentioned and so he stopped outside to listen, and what he heard made him smile. Dear Mama, she was doing her best for him. He entered the room and made his bow to the ladies.

'It is over?' his mother queried.

'It is over. He has been laid to rest. There was a goodly crowd there and many villagers watching in the road. The carriages are following and will be here directly. Shall I order the refreshments to be brought in?'

'Yes, please.'

The room was suddenly full of people and the servants were passing between them with trays of drinks and food and Miles's time was spent receiving condolences and hearing tales of his father and fielding questions about his intentions. When most of the mourners had gone except the Somerfields and the immediate family, Mr Sobers read the will, which contained nothing surprising. Miles spoke to the lawyer alone afterwards.

'I want that case against Miss Wayland dropped,' he told him, after Sobers had offered his condolences and at the same time his felicitations on his succession to the earldom. 'I do not care how you do it.'

'I am not sure it can be done. Sedition is a serious matter and the Crown is prosecuting.'

'You know it was never sedition. No one would

have paid the least attention to it if my father had not taken offence. Now he has gone to his Maker I cannot think there is anything to be gained by proceeding. The premises of the newspaper have gone up in flames and I doubt there are copies of the offending article in existence. People use them to light their fires, you know. Miss Wayland has lost everything. There will be no more reports, seditious or otherwise. I think I can guarantee that. If it takes a purse, then so be it. I will pay.'

He was well aware that Sobers was looking at him critically and would have liked to question why he was so anxious on Miss Wayland's behalf, but he was the Earl now and could call the tune.

'Very well. I will see what I can do.'

Relieved to have put that matter in hand, Miles could at last turn his attention to the little group of Lord Somerfield, his wife and daughter.

'My lord,' he began, determined not to be side-tracked, 'the death of my father has changed the arrangements that were made between you.'

'I realise they will have to be postponed for the mourning period.'

'Not postponed, cancelled,' he said firmly, look-ing at Verity for her reaction. If anything, she looked relieved, which gave him the impetus to carry on. 'I was never party to them.'

'You mean you are reneging?' His lordship was clearly angry.

'I cannot renege on something I never agreed to in the first place. Miss Verity is a delightful young lady and will undoubtedly attract many suitors more worthy than me. I would not, for the world, hurt her feelings, but I am sure she will be relieved rather than disappointed.' He turned to her with a smile. 'I am right, am I not, Miss Somerfield? Do not be afraid to say.'

The young lady looked from her father to her mother and back again, then she took a deep breath as if gathering her courage. 'Yes,' she murmured. 'I do not think we should suit.'

'Well, of all the ungrateful…' His lordship stopped, lost for words.

'Leave it,' his wife told him. 'If that is how Verity feels about it, then we must accept it.' She turned to Miles. 'My lord, I hope you will allow, for appearances' sake, that it was Verity who turned you down.'

He bowed, trying very hard to remain sombre, though his heart was singing. 'Of course. She just did.'

There was nothing more to be said and they took their leave. Miles went to find his mother.

The most important of his many obstacles had been overcome. He could go to see Helen.

He was in the stables seeing to the harnessing of the horses the following morning, when Byers arrived and detained him. 'I come to pay the men's respects, my lord,' he began. 'And we was wondering if it made any difference to the Co-operative.'

'None at all, Jack, none at all.'

'Good, 'cos we've put a deal of work into it.'

'I know. Long may it continue.'

'An' I was sent to ask how Miss Wayland be,' he said. 'We miss her at the barn and there's the accounts…'

'Yes, I know, Jack. Miss Wayland is recovering, but she has gone to live with her cousin. I am afraid the accounts will have to wait. Do you need money for anything?'

'We hev made a start on the barn,' the man said. 'We need materials for that.'

'Order what you need. Have the accounts sent to me. We will sort everything out later.'

Byers grinned. 'You was behind it all along, my lord, weren't you?'

'Yes, but there is no need to spread it abroad. Is

there anything else?' He was impatient to be on his way.

'You asked us to try an' find out who set fire to the *Warburton Record*.'

'I did. What have you discovered?'

'One o' Blakestone's minions admitted throwin' the brick through the window, but he swears he knows nothing about the fire.'

'Do you believe him?'

'Yes, he'd ha' said if he did. I made sure o' that.'

'I hope you did not hurt him.'

Byers grinned. 'Only a little. He is a coward. What do you want done about him?'

'Nothing for the moment. I am more concerned about the fire.'

'I reckon it was that there fire raiser what's bin goin' round setting fire to things. Did no one tell you that Ravensbrook Manor burned ag'in last night? Strange, in't it, seeing it ha' bin standin' empty for years. There's those that think it's haunted. Flickering lights have been seen there at night.'

'I had no idea about the fire, but rest assured— there are no ghosts, Jack. There was a tramp squatting there. Did he get out?'

'Dunno. Nobody said nothin' about no tramp. Oh, my Lord! He may still be in there.'

Miles left the hitching of the horses to Greaves, saddled Pewter and set off for Ravensbrook Manor at a gallop.

As soon as he came within sight of it, he could see it had been totally destroyed. The roof had gone and two walls had collapsed. The ivy growing on the remaining walls was blackened and still smoking. All the remaining windows had gone. He dismounted beside what had been the kitchen and made his way over the rubble to the back parlour. Everywhere was blackened, some of it still smouldering. His fears were realised when he saw the badly burned body, lying face down. Carefully he turned him over. His face was burned, but he might be just recognisable to anyone who had known him. It was the idiot.

He was looking round to find something to put him on when Byers and Greaves arrived, scrunching their way over cinders and broken glass to join him.

'That's Jimmy Little,' Greaves said, looking down at the dead man.

'Jimmy Little?'

'He was the boot boy at the Manor. Years and years ago it was when Lord Brent lived here. He was a bit simple in the attic even before the fire, but after that he went off his head altogether. He loved Lady Brent, doted on her. When the house went up in flames he danced about, dashing backwards and forwards getting in everyone's way, screaming his head off. He had no family and no one knew what to do with him. He were put in an asylum. Where he went after that, I cannot say. Someone must know. What do you reckon we ought to do?'

'Send for the undertaker and the parson to arrange a funeral,' Miles said. 'Do you think you can find something to put him on, a door or something like that?'

It had taken several hours for everything to be arranged and all the time Miles had been fretting to go to Helen, but it was the following morning before he finally left for Cambridgeshire, deciding to ride Pewter and not take the carriage. It would be quicker across country and he was in a hurry...

Helen was trying her best to settle down in her new life, but she was finding it very difficult. She was neither servant nor family and, apart from the children and their nurse, hardly spoke to anyone. She had her meals with the children and, after they were in bed, spent her time in her room, reading. There were books in the house and she found one or two to read, but she could not concentrate. Again and again her thoughts turned to Miles. She had had no reply to her letter of condolence and did not expect one, but she could not help wondering what was happening in Warburton and Ravensbrook. William did not approve of ladies reading newspapers, let alone producing them, and so she had no access to news. It was a kind of imprisonment and it irked her, but until she could think of something else to do, she had to put up with it.

The weather did not help. It was so wet, windy and cold that Lady Brent refused to allow the children out of doors, which was not good for them. Harold was particularly difficult to contain. He quarrelled with his sisters and dashed about the upper regions of the house, making a din, which did not please his parents and she was told to keep him in check. It was only high spirits, which could only be released by going out of doors. But at last the rain stopped and a weak sun tried its best to break through the clouds. Helen decided it was time to take the children out and sought permission to take them for a walk.

'Yes, do that,' their mother said. 'I am tired of their noise. You can hear them all over the house.'

And so they ventured out. The air was fresh and Helen breathed deeply, filling her lungs. It was so good to be out. The trees dripped water, there were puddles everywhere and the grass was lush and wet, but they picked their way, while Helen pointed out the names of the trees and the bedraggled wayside flowers. They walked as far as the little girls could manage and turned for home.

'Miss Wayland has taken the children out,' Lady Brent told Miles after she had offered her condolences on his loss and felicitations on his inheritance and he had stated his wish to speak to Helen.

'How long will she be?'

'I do not know. It is the first fine day we have had for some time and no doubt the children will want to make the most of it.'

'May I wait?'

'My lord, with all respect to you, I do not think anything can be gained by seeing her. She is settling in and her past life has been put behind her, which is as it should be. You will only re-awaken things best left alone.'

'I think, my lady, that is for me to decide. I have news for her regarding several matters that were left in abeyance when she came here. It is important that I speak to her.'

'Then you must make an appointment to come when my husband is here. He will want to be present. She is, after all, his responsibility.'

He was furious. How dared she try to prevent him seeing Helen? He bowed his way out, but if she thought he would give up, she was wrong. He rode down the drive until he was out of sight of the house behind the bushes that lined the carriageway, dismounted and prepared to wait.

He saw her coming towards him on a footpath that emerged from a small stand of trees on the other side of the drive, clasping the hands of two little girls, and his heart gave a great leap of joy. He stepped forwards, smiling. 'Helen.'

She gasped with shock and then delight, and that was followed by despondency, all in the space of a few seconds. 'My lord, what are you doing here?'

'Waiting to see you. That dragon up at the house was determined to deny me.'

'If you mean Cousin Caroline, no doubt she had my interests at heart.'

'I will not be denied, Helen. There are important matters we must discuss.' He looked down at the girls, who were staring at him with curiosity. 'We cannot talk here. Can you meet me somewhere?'

She gave a cracked laugh. 'That sounds like an assignation and what my cousins would say about that, I dread to think. I was obliged to promise I would not communicate with you.'

'You have not communicated with me. I have come to you.'

'I doubt they would take that into account. I should send you away.'

'Are you happy here?'

'I am content.'

'I do not believe you. Please say you will meet me, or I shall camp on the doorstep and make a nuisance of myself. Lady Brent suggested I should make an appointment when her husband could be present when I spoke to you. I am not having that. What I have to say is for your ears only.'

'I cannot think what you can have to say to me, my lord, though I should like to know how the Co-operative is coming along.'

'I will tell you that along with everything else when I see you. There is a coaching inn in the village. I shall take a room there and later this evening I shall take a stroll along the river bank towards the bridge. Meet me there, please.'

'Very well. I shall try to come after the children have gone to bed. Eight o' clock.'

Harold came bursting through the trees. 'I have just seen a badger,' he said. 'Come and see.'

She turned to Miles. 'I must go.'

He watched her being pulled along by the exuberant boy until she was out of sight, then mounted and rode to the inn to contain himself in patience until the evening.

'Who was that man?' Harold demanded.

'What man?' Helen was not paying attention. Miles had come. Miles wanted to talk to her. Matters to be discussed, he had said. Perhaps he had some questions about how she had kept the books for the Co-operative. Or perhaps he had come to tell her he was sorry, but the necklace was worth nothing. Why could he not have said that to Lady Brent? Why all the cloak-and-dagger nonsense? Unless he was afraid of Miss Somerfield finding out he had visited her. But then he would not have ridden up to the house. She would be on tenterhooks until she knew and though she realised the meeting could only lead to more heartache, she could not wait for the evening to come.

'The man you were talking to,' Harold answered her. 'Servants are not supposed to have followers.'

So he thought she was a servant, the same as the nurse and everyone else who was paid to administer to his needs. It was not surprising, but someone must have put the idea of followers into his head; she doubted he knew what it meant. 'That, Harold, was a gentleman. Could you not tell by his dress and that fine horse?'

'What is his name, then?'

'He is the Earl of Warburton. I knew him before I came here.'

'What did he want?'

'I do not know. I expect he was just visiting your mama and papa.'

She had known that would not be the end of the interrogation because he would be bound to tell his mother of the encounter, which he took great delight in doing when the children were taken down to see her before dinner, which they did every afternoon. She spent an hour or so with them, questioning them about their day and what they had learned. It was soon out that Helen had been talking to a gentleman in the drive.

'I assume the gentleman was the Earl of Warburton,' her ladyship said when the children had been sent upstairs again.

'Yes, Cousin Caroline. I met him as he was leaving. We spoke briefly to each other in passing.'

'He said he had some matters to discuss with you.'

'If he did, he must have changed his mind. We exchanged polite greetings and he went on his way and I on mine.'

'Good. We cannot have you upset by what has happened in the past. You have the children to consider…'

'Yes, Cousin, I realise that.'

'You had better go and have your supper.'

Later that evening, she checked the children were all asleep and the nurse was dozing by the nursery fire and, wrapping herself in a cloak, crept down the back stairs and out of a side door. She was not at all sure she was doing the right thing, but the prospect of seeing and talking to Miles was too great to resist.

At this time of year it should have been broad daylight at this time, but for most of the year it had been so gloomy that lamps were needed indoors even during daylight. But tonight, for some reason, the general murk had lifted and a fitful moon and a few stars lit her way. The village was little more than a hamlet, which stood where the road crossed the river. It had a coaching inn, a church, a few cottages and one or two small agricultural businesses. She made her way along the high street to the bridge.

He was there, leaning against the parapet, looking down into the water. Suddenly shy, her footsteps slowed and she almost stopped. He must have heard her because he turned towards her, a smile lighting up his face. 'Helen, at last.'

He stepped forwards and took both her hands in his own and raised them one by one to his lips. He did not stop at kissing them once but turned them over and pressed his lips to the palms over and over again. She looked up at him and saw something in his eyes that made her heart leap, but almost instantly remembered Miss Somerfield. 'My lord...'

'Don't you dare "my lord" me, Helen Wayland. I am Miles. I will always be Miles to you.' He put a finger under her chin and tilted it upwards, searching her face. 'I have missed you more than I can say. Without you my life is empty. I cannot live without you...'

'Don't say that.'

'Why not? It is true. I have been hoping and praying you might feel the same.'

She did, but how could she admit that? 'My lord,

it is not fitting that you should say things like that to me, when you are as good as engaged to Miss Somerfield.'

'I am not engaged to Miss Somerfield, never have been, never contemplated it except under duress.'

'Duress. Whatever do you mean?'

'My late father promised to drop the case against you if I offered for Verity. He had made a bargain with her father, apparently, and for your sake I fell in with it, but all the time I knew I had to get us both out of the bumblebath we were in and come to you. Miss Somerfield did not want to marry me any more than I wanted to marry her and that issue has been resolved. I am free of it. And you are free of that court case, or you will be when Sobers has done his work.'

'Oh.' Why was she crying? Why were there tears rolling down her face?

'It is nothing to cry about, sweetheart.' He mopped her face with his handkerchief. 'I feel a little too exposed here. Let us find somewhere private because I want to kiss you.'

Bewildered, she let him lead her off the bridge and round the back of the inn. There were stables there for several horses, cart sheds and storage sheds. He took her into one of these. He shut the door and turned to face her. 'Now, Helen Wayland, before I kiss you, will you answer one vital question?'

'What is that?'

'Will you make me the happiest man alive and agree to marry me? You see, I love you dearly and have done almost since the first moment I set eyes on you and my dearest wish is to make you my wife.'

She was in a dream—this could not be true. She was not standing in Miles's arms in a poky little shed half-filled with bales of hay, listening to a declaration of love that sent her wild with joy. He was waiting for an answer. 'Miles…'

'Do you love me?'

'Yes, but I thought it was hopeless.'

'Nothing is hopeless if you want it enough and I want this very, very much. So are you going to say yes?'

'Yes, oh, yes.'

'Thank goodness for that.' He did kiss her then, long and hard over and over again until they were both breathless. When they had calmed down, he drew her to sit beside him on one of the bales of hay. 'I am in mourning and will have to observe the proprieties. Do you think you can bear to stay here for another three months?'

'Yes, if I know I shall be with you at the end of it. Oh, I can't believe this is happening. I thought I had lost you and it was breaking my heart.'

He drew her close and kissed her again. 'Is it mended now?'

'Oh, yes.'

'I will come courting in the approved manner; once that has been established, your family will perhaps be kinder to you.'

'I found out why they cut my mother off. My Cousin William told me. She was engaged to marry your father and ran off with my father after that terrible fire. She told her family that she had fallen in love and could not help herself.'

'I can understand that, can't you?' he said softly.

'Yes.'

'My father told me the story himself the day he died. It explains a lot of things, doesn't it?'

'Yes. Your father's enmity towards my father, though it was not my fault.'

'No, but I am told you are exactly like your mother and he was reminded of it whenever he saw you and when you criticised him, it must have seemed like the last straw. I can feel some sympathy for him now.'

'Yes, so can I, but it does not alter the way I feel about the treatment of the labourers and old soldiers. We will still carry on with helping them, won't we?'

'Of course. And we will find work for Tom and Edgar. They might consider carrying on with the *Warburton Record* in new premises. We can discuss it with them later.'

They were silent for a few moments, then he said, 'Jack Byers found out that it was one of Blakestone's men who threw the brick through your window. Blakestone himself has been arrested in Lynn for attempted murder and causing the death of a valuable horse. He will trouble us no more.' He paused to stroke her hair from her forehead and kiss the end of her nose. 'But he did not set the fire. It was that poor idiot we saw on the common and later in town. It was he who was squatting in the Manor. I learned from Greaves, who has been in the service of my family since before I was born, that he was once the boot boy at the Manor. Lady Brent, your grandmother, was soft-hearted and used to visit the poorhouse and take presents for the children. She took a shine to Jimmy, who had no family, and took him to live and work at the Manor. It was the first home he had ever known and as far as he was concerned Lady Brent was an angel from heaven. That fire and the death of her ladyship destroyed whatever wits he had. He had an obsession with fire. They put him in an asylum, but he set fire to that. Luckily it was quickly doused and no one was hurt, but Jimmy was a danger to himself and to others, so he was put into a room on his own. He couldn't be allowed anywhere near a naked flame, so he was never allowed a fire or a light after it got dark. He must have escaped and returned to what he thought was his home.'

'But why did he set fire to my home? I never harmed him.'

'No, but in his muddled brain he thought you were your mother and he had heard about her going off with your father. He wanted to punish you. I am only guessing, of course. No one can really know what was going on in his head. Yesterday Ravensbrook Manor burned again and he was inside. No one knew he was there, so no efforts were made to rescue him. I did not know about it until this morning. We found his body in the ruins.'

'Oh, how sad that is.'

'Yes.' He paused to hug her to his side and stroke her hair before kissing her again. 'But I do have some good news. Your necklace is valuable. It was given to your mother by my father along with a matching ring as a betrothal gift.'

'Oh. I never saw a ring.'

'No. I found it in the safe among my father's things. She must have left it behind. Your father would not have wanted her to wear it. Do you wish me to sell the necklace on your behalf?'

She was thoughtful for a moment. 'Yes, please. I do not want reminders of an unhappy past and I shall need to buy wedding clothes befitting the bride of an Earl.' She laughed suddenly and it was such a happy sound he joined in and they began kissing gain, until he was afraid his self-control would desert him.

'I am going to take you back to the house,' he said, standing up and dusting the straw from his riding breeches before holding out his hand to help her up. 'Can you creep back in again?'

'Yes.'

'Tomorrow, I shall call and speak to your cousin. We will do this thing properly and, though we cannot publicly announce an engagement just yet, it will be known in the family and you can begin your preparations so that we can be married in three months' time.'

'Oh, Miles, I cannot believe this is happening. Do you really love me? Have you really asked me to be your wife?'

'Yes, to both questions. And you have made me

the happiest man alive by agreeing.' He kissed her again, more gently this time, though it held the promise of much more to come. And then he took her hand and led her from the building and home to Larkspur House and it seemed the moon and stars had never been brighter. The miserable summer had gone and tomorrow the sun would shine, she was sure of it.

Epilogue

Her cousins' attitude towards her changed completely when they realised that the Earl of Warburton had every intention of marrying her. She was brought into the bosom of the family and made a great fuss of, taken out and about and introduced to all their friends. Betty was sent for to maid her and three months went by in a dream, sometimes unbearably slowly, sometimes so swiftly she was sure everything could not be ready in time. Miles himself was busy bringing the estate back to what it was, but whenever he could he called at Larkspur and it would have been difficult to keep their hands off each other if they had not been closely chaperoned. The dowager Countess came sometimes and expressed her delight at the match. It was she who brought the news that Verity Somerfield had become engaged to a young man she had met at her coming-out ball.

At last the big day came and Helen went to her wedding with a full heart, secure in the knowledge that this match was made in heaven and would last into eternity and beyond. Dressed in a gown of palest lemon silk, she went down the aisle on the arm of her cousin William, who was to give her away. Behind her, Harold and the two little girls followed, awestruck by the occasion. Helen was only vaguely aware that the church was packed because she was looking straight ahead to where Miles waited, magnificent in his dress uniform. He smiled down at her as she joined him and she responded before facing the parson, who stood ready to conduct the service.

They made their responses in strong voices and, when it was over, went back to Larkspur House for the wedding breakfast and everyone's congratulations. Soon it would be time to go on their wedding trip to the Lakes and after that back to Ravens Park and her new life as the Countess of Warburton. The idea that she was a Countess made Helen smile. Miles met her eyes from across the room where he was talking to Sobers, who had just told him there would be no court case, and he grinned back at her. He would be glad when the formalities were done with and he could be alone with his beloved bride. They had been patient long enough.

* * * * *

Author's Note

Seditious Libel

In the eighteenth and early nineteenth century, the libel laws were used to repress rebellion against the government, but their implementation was inconsistent. Writers and producers of newspapers and radical literature were under constant threat of prosecution and, when taken to court, were often faced with a hostile judge and jury. A defendant's counsel could raise points of law, but could not summarise the case on behalf of the defendant until 1836. On the other hand, the Home Office lacked the means to prosecute everyone who published seditious matter and the writers often took their chances and got away with it. The prosecutions dwindled because defendants frequently managed to obtain an acquittal by exploiting the language in which the arraignment was made, and the legal authorities gave up trying for all but the most serious cases.

The year without a summer

The year of 1816 was known as 'the year without a summer', not only in England, but all over the world, particularly in Northern Europe and North America. The year before there had been a huge explosion in the Mount Tamboura volcano on the Dutch East Indies, which had been rumbling since 1812. Thirty-eight cubic miles of dust and ash was sent up into the atmosphere, the ash column rising thousands of feet. The debris, including vast quantities of sulphur, took a year to circulate, its sheer volume obliterating the sun. The result was a cold, wet and miserable 1816. It rained off and on from May to September and, without sunlight, temperatures dropped dramatically. In the English countryside crops rotted in the fields before they could be harvested and those that were gathered rotted in storage because of the damp. Farm labourers were put out of work and added to the unemployed soldiers returning from the war with Napoleon.